SARAH BENNETT has been reading for as long as she can remember. Raised in a family of bookworms, her love affair with books of all genres

Ever After: getting

Born and r

her own Offic

wherever he lays his hat, best family is the one you create from friends as well as relatives.

When not reading or writing, Sarah is a devotee of afternoon naps and sailing the high seas, but only on vessels large enough to accommodate a casino and a choice of restaurants.

You can connect with her via twitter @Sarahlou_writes or on Facebook www.facebook.com/SarahBennettAuthor

Also by Sarah Bennett

The Butterfly Cove Series

Sunrise at Butterfly Cove
Wedding Bells at Butterfly Cove
Christmas at Butterfly Cove

The Lavender Bay Series

Spring at Lavender Bay
Summer at Lavender Bay
Snowflakes at Lavender Bay

Christmas at Butterfly Cove

SARAH BENNETT

ONE PLACE. MANY STORIES

HQ
An imprint of HarperCollins*Publishers* Ltd
1 London Bridge Street
London SE1 9GF

This paperback edition 2020

First published in Great Britain by
HQ, an imprint of HarperCollins*Publishers* Ltd 2018

ISBN: 9780008389253

MIX
Paper from
responsible sources
FSC
www.fsc.org   FSC® C007454

This book is produced from independently certified FSC™ paper
to ensure responsible forest management.

For more information visit: www.harpercollins.co.uk/green

Printed by CPI Group (UK) Ltd, Croydon CR0 4YY

Chapter One

Nee Thorpe stared at the brown oblong of modelling clay sitting on the workbench in exactly the same spot she'd dropped it two hours earlier. The tactile material had always been her favourite medium to work with, but these days the earthy scent of damp clay did little more than bring bile to the back of her throat. After a month staying with her sister, Mia, and her new husband, Daniel, she'd run out of excuses as to why she wasn't working on anything. Daniel had recently opened a set of bespoke artist studios in the old barns adjacent to his wife's guesthouse in the idyllic coastal village of Orcombe Sands – known to the local population by the far prettier nickname of Butterfly Cove. They were still taking regular bookings, even this late in the season, with sun-worshippers giving way to the hardier walkers who wanted to make the most of the outdoors before winter set in and kept them closer to home.

Perched on the edge of the cove, at the head of a private beach, Butterfly House had provided a welcome haven for Nee's tattered spirits. It had also become the new hub of their family. Her middle sister, Kiki, had relocated to the village in the spring, finally escaping her disastrous marriage. With her two small children in tow, she'd not only made a new start, including running

1

the latest family enterprise – a beautiful little teashop and gallery in what had recently been a scruffy-looking garage block – she'd also found a new love in the shape of Daniel's best friend, Aaron Spenser. Nee swallowed. She should be thrilled Kiki had found happiness with someone who would finally treat her in the way she deserved, and in truth she *was*. She would just have preferred it if Aaron hadn't been the elder brother of the man whose heart she'd broken, smashing her own to pieces in the process.

Desperate for a distraction, anything to avoid the lump threatening to choke her every time her eyes strayed to the formless block of clay on the worktable, Nee rinsed her still-clean hands at the sink then pulled the studio door shut behind her. Soft music drifted from the open door of the space next door, accompanied by a deep baritone hum which was enough for her to identify the occupant. Bryn was a broad-shouldered, softly spoken car mechanic who also produced the most delicate, ethereal watercolours she'd ever seen. He was staying for a week and appeared to be relishing the calm serenity of the cove. Not wishing to disturb him, or to be caught up in an awkward discussion of what she was working on, or *wasn't working on* as the case may be, she tiptoed past his door then hurried down the corridor to escape onto the gravel driveway which separated the barns and the house.

A quick glance towards the teashop put paid to her hopes of drowning her sorrows in a cup of tea, and she checked her watch. If she was quick, she might still catch up with Mia and Kiki in the kitchen. Tuesday was turnaround day at the guest house, and in addition to running the teashop, Kiki helped out changing the beds and cleaning the rooms.

Opening the back door, she paused to toe off her shoes and caught their familiar voices deep in discussion over arrangements for Aaron's upcoming birthday. Circumstances had led to her middle sister and her two children sharing a nearby cottage with Daniel's best friend. After a shaky start, the two had finally admitted to feelings that were obvious to everyone around them, and they were a picture of domestic bliss. The kids adored Aaron, and it sounded as though they wanted to throw him a surprise party.

'It's such a sweet idea, especially when you think they came up with it themselves. I just wish things weren't so awkward, with . . . you know.'

Awkward. Nee stopped short at the word, her call of greeting frozen on her lips. Heart dropping with a knowing premonition, she waited anxiously for Mia's response.

'I know.' Mia sounded sympathetic and resigned in equal measures. 'But we can't keep ignoring the situation.'

Kiki sighed. 'You're right, but I don't want them thinking I've manufactured a situation to force them to face each other. But how can we possibly have a party for Aaron without Luke there?'

Nee sagged against the cool plaster wall, shivering from more than the cool air gusting through the open door behind her. The soft, familiar voices of her sisters continued their discussion, but she couldn't make out the words over the pounding of her heartbeat in her ears. Tightness filled her lungs and the walls of the cloakroom seemed to constrict around her. She had to get out. Had to get away. Reaching blindly for a jacket, she spun on her heel and fled across the grass. A bitter voice whispered in her ear. *That's right. Run away, just like you always do.*

Nee huddled deeper into the padded jacket she'd borrowed from the row of pegs beside the back door at Butterfly House. The sleeves hung past the tips of her fingers, and the material smelled faintly of the kind of citrusy scent that spoke of aftershave rather than perfume. She hadn't stopped long enough to examine her choice, just grabbed for the first one her hand reached as she flew out of the kitchen and into the beautiful, sprawling garden behind the guesthouse. Her headlong flight carried her down the flagstone path to the short flight of steps leading to the beach. Only once her shoes sank into the soft, pale sand did she slow her frantic pace.

3

The thick fleece collar blocked the worst of the wind howling in across the open water, and she narrowed her eyes against the sting of sand whipped up by its fury. The approaching storm transformed Butterfly Cove from a seaside idyll into a wild, desolate space. The normally gentle waters churned and roiled as though a monstrous beast twisted below the surface. Gone was the peaceful blue blanket she'd grown accustomed to over the summer, replaced by a murky, green-grey morass. Dark clouds scudded across the sky, and the first icy drops of rain hit her raw cheeks. It had to be rain because, after the past few weeks, Nee was sure there wasn't a tear left inside her.

The rain fell harder – fat, cold drops that soon plastered her short blonde hair flat against her skull. Her face began to ache, a combination of the harsh bite of the wind and the desperate clench of her jaw. Everything was such a bloody mess, and she had no one to blame but herself. Luke had committed no sin, unless falling in love with her could be considered a sin. A bubble of hysteria formed a tight knot at the top of her chest. He would probably consider it more of a curse. And who would blame him when she'd done the unthinkable and left him alone in their marriage bed without a word.

Her decision to leave had made sense at the time. They'd acted impetuously; wouldn't be the first couple to confuse a heady rush of lust with something deeper. Better to make a quick break, go out on a high before the humdrum reality of life crept in and shattered their perfect fantasy. The hurt would fade, leaving behind fond memories of a foolish summer of love. All perfectly sensible and rational conclusions, and every one a complete and utter lie. The moment she'd seen him staring at her across the platform, the one hope she'd clung to, that Luke had moved on without her, had been destroyed. She'd put her own ambition before his heart, and ruined both their lives in the process.

'One cannot make true art without first suffering, my dear.' The only voice she hated more than her own guilt intruded on her thoughts, and Nee raised her hands to her temples. She squeezed her fists into the sides of her head, as though applying the right amount of pressure could force him back into the skittering darkness of her deepest subconscious. It didn't help. The moment she let her guard down, he was there.

Staring out across the tossing waves, Nee could almost sense him reaching out across the miles to drag her back across the ocean. 'I won't come back. You can't have me!' She shouted her defiance. The wind swooped to snatch her words away, stealing her strength with it. Dropping to her knees on the wet sand, she lowered her head and acknowledged the truth. Devin Rees had stolen the most important thing from her, leaving nothing but an empty shell behind.

Even if Luke could be persuaded to give her another chance, what could she offer him? She stared down at her shaking hands. Short nails edge with raw skin. Stubby fingers bereft of any traces of dark clay. An artist who couldn't create – was there a more pathetic kind of creature? Putting pen to paper to help her niece make the place cards for Mia's wedding had been an exercise in torture.

Staying in Butterfly Cove, watching week in and week out as her former peers descended on Daniel's studios to paint, carve, sculpt and hammer beauty from nothing had become an exercise in self-flagellation. The thought of sitting in the sweet, cosy warmth of Kiki's new teashop, gorging on slabs of cake which were masterpieces in their own right, as the visiting artists added new pieces to the planned gallery collection, might just break her.

There was nothing here for her. Mia and Kiki tried their best to help her, but she kept them at arm's length. She didn't want their sympathy, feared even more turning it into something harder, colder, if they discovered the reason she'd left Luke. They would continue to love her, of that much she was certain, but Kiki's loyalties were already divided between her sister and the brother of the man she loved. The conversation she'd overheard earlier had made it crystal-clear. It hurt Nee to be the cause of any distress to her middle sister, who'd borne the brunt of so much already. But it hurt even more to watch her unfolding joy and contentment in the arms of the man who reminded Nee of everything she'd lost.

No. Not lost. Thrown away. Lying to herself had caused this ugly mess. There could be nothing but truth from now on. Nee would not become a millstone for her sisters to bear. They'd been happy before she'd shown up, would be happier once she left again, regardless of how much they would protest otherwise.

And, most important of all, she owed it to Luke.

She'd usurped his place here in Butterfly Cove and it was time to give it back. Never one to indulge a sulk for long, Nee gave herself a mental kick in the arse and forced her cramped body to stand. The lower half of her jeans were soaked, and her bones ached from the cold and rain soaking her skin. She folded down the collar of the coat, the once-cosy fleece now wet and clinging unpleasantly to her cheek. Shoving her frozen hands into the depths of her pockets, Nee trudged across the beach towards the beckoning warmth of the guest house.

A hot shower and a change of clothes did wonders for her outward appearance, though they couldn't help much with the growing coldness inside her. Telling herself she needed to leave was one thing, but where the hell could she go? Not back to London, that was for damn certain. She'd find herself making excuses to hang around the places Luke liked to go, the way she had in the intervening weeks between her return from New York and her fateful decision to attend Mia's wedding. Perhaps the answer lay in finding somewhere new . . .

Energised by the idea, she hurried down the remaining stairs and into the private sitting room Mia had created away from the guest spaces. The large wooden bookcase in the corner was stacked high with myriad different books, and she knew her brother-in-law had an old atlas somewhere around. She'd seen him poring over it with Kiki's little boy, Matty, the other weekend. Bursting into the room, she pulled up short. A white-faced Kiki clung hard to Mia's hand whilst their older sister frowned and nodded at something the person on the other end of the phone pressed to her ear was saying.

Kiki glanced up and Nee could see the tear tracks on her cheeks. 'It's Mum,' she whispered.

A wave of relief washed over Nee, followed swiftly by a sharp stab of guilt. Of the three of them, her relationship with Vivian was the most fractured, having never known the kindness and care she'd been capable of before her alcoholism had dug its claws deep. The two women sitting opposite her had, to all intents and purposes, raised her. Given her more than enough love to buffer their mother's neglect and their father's indifference. She crossed the room to sit cross-legged on the carpet in front of them, placing a hand on Mia's knee in silent support.

Kiki leaned towards her. 'She's taken a turn for the worse,' she whispered.

'What else did the doctor say, Dad?' They both turned towards Mia, who was staring off into the distance, uttering soothing noises as she listened to George's response. The curve of her shoulders increased, as though the words she heard had a physical weight to them. Nee patted her leg, wishing there was something she could do to help. Mia sat up straighter, spine going ramrod-straight. 'Okay. I need to sort a few things out and then I'll be up first thing.'

Nee closed her eyes. Mia to the rescue, just like always. She dug her fingers into the rich pile of the carpet beneath her. An image of the sitting room, all warm creams and soft browns with splashes of rich red, filled her mind's eye. She thought about the other rooms, the stylish bedrooms, the cosy warmth of the kitchen, each one a testament to the beautiful home Mia had built from the ashes of her past. Love and laughter infused every corner of the guesthouse. Just a few short weeks since their beautiful wedding, Mia and Daniel should be on their honeymoon, but they'd postponed it to throw all their energies into the guesthouse and studios. They had enough on their plates as it was without facing the prospect of spending time apart so soon.

Decision made, she opened her eyes. 'I'll go.'

Chapter Two

Luke Spenser tapped on the frame of the kitchen door to get his mother's attention. She glanced up with a quick smile, then finished sliding the roasting tray into the oven. 'Beef,' she said before moving to the sink to rinse her hands, turning her back to him in the process. 'It's your brother's favourite.'

A quick handful of steps carried him to her side, and he leaned down to brush a kiss against her cheek. 'Thanks, Mum.'

She looked at him through veiled lashes, and he wondered what was going on inside her head. Aaron had been tight-lipped about his visit home a couple of weeks' previously, other than to say it had gone better than he'd expected. It would take time to bridge the gap between the two of them, but at least they were both trying. And Luke couldn't ask for any more than that.

When Cathy had called, asking if he'd come down for an early birthday lunch for Aaron, he'd been happy to accept. Happier still when his dad had taken him to one side and told him it had been her suggestion. He squeezed her shoulders in a quick hug, noting the tension in her stiff frame. He kissed her cheek again. 'I thought I'd take Aaron down the road for a pint. It'll get us out from under your feet for a bit.'

He didn't miss the flicker of relief in her eyes. 'That'll be nice.

I don't suppose you'll get much time together now he's settling down with Kiki.' There was a hint of a question in her tone, and he wondered whether she knew he hadn't been back to Butterfly Cove since Mia and Daniel's wedding. The work to convert the garages into the teashop had been straightforward enough that no one had questioned his absence. Daniel had called him a couple of times to clarify a point with the designs he'd drawn up, and Aaron had brought an album full of photos from the grand opening last weekend.

'Things are really picking up at work, and now the last of the conversion works are finished, there's no need for me to visit Butterfly Cove so often.' He forced a laugh. 'Besides, although it's lovely down there in the summer, I'm not sure I fancy staying somewhere so exposed to the elements now the weather's on the change.'

Cathy reached for a tea towel and dried her hands before turning to face him. 'It sounds lovely, from what Aaron has told us. I hope to see it one day.'

'Give it time, okay?' He knew with things still so delicate between them, Aaron was unlikely to bring the old and new parts of his family together.

His mum tilted her head to one side and studied him carefully. 'Is that what you're doing, too? Giving things time?'

Damn it. Aaron must have told them about Nee. He crossed his arms over his chest. 'Don't. Okay?' His tone brooked no argument.

She opened her mouth, caught the glare he threw at her, and closed it again with a nod. She glanced at her watch, breaking the tension between them. 'I'm aiming for half two for lunch. No crème de menthe.'

Luke shook his head and laughed. 'You're never going to let that go, are you?' His parents had gone away for the weekend, leaving a twelve-year-old Luke in Aaron's care. With nearly five years between them, his brother had seemed impossibly grown-up. When Aaron snuck a couple of friends round for drinks,

Luke hadn't wanted to miss out. He'd raided the drinks cabinet, a bottle of the mint liqueur the first thing his hand closed around.

Aaron had nursed him through his first, and, to this day, worst hangover, and though shaky, he'd been able to face his parents when they returned on the Sunday evening. Aaron's hours on hands and knees, scrubbing at the bright-green stain on the peach bathroom carpet, had proven less successful. Despite Luke's protestations, his big brother had taken the blame. And Cathy had been all too happy to let him. She'd refused to leave them alone in the house for years afterwards, making it clear she couldn't trust Aaron to be responsible. The fact she could make a joke about it now was little short of a miracle.

Cathy placed her hand on his chest, smoothing a non-existent crease from the front of his navy T-shirt. 'Your dad and I are here, if you need us.'

He covered her hand with his and gave it a squeeze. 'I know, Mum. I'm fine, though. It's water under the bridge.' Releasing her fingers, he walked away before she could read the lie on his face. His thick, grey hoodie hung over the bottom of the banister, and he shrugged it on as he called up the stairs. 'Pub?'

'Pub!' Aaron's enthusiastic response was followed by the thunder of footsteps on the landing above. His brother jogged down the stairs, a wide grin on his face. 'You're not as thick as you look, are you, Spud?'

'Wanker.' Luke aimed a punch at his brother's arm. Aaron clutched his arm, staggering down the hall with an exaggerated cry of pain.

Their father appeared from the living room with a folded copy of *The Sunday Times* in his hand. He gave them both a playful swipe with the paper. 'Silly sods, the pair of you. Don't be late back, all right?'

Aaron pulled his jacket down from where he'd hung it neatly on a peg. The contrast between the care he took to do everything right and Luke's own casual disregard struck him anew.

Things might be thawing, but it would be a long time before Aaron would feel completely comfortable in what should be the safest of spaces. Luke shrugged off the tinge of melancholy. 'You coming with us, Dad?'

Brian shook his head. 'I've got a date with a vegetable peeler, and then I'm going to check out the apple trees, see if I can talk your mum into making a crumble for pudding.' There was a small cluster of fruit trees at the end of the garden, cookers, not eaters.

Luke's mouth watered at the thought of hot crumble and custard. It was another of Aaron's favourites and he knew then his dad's casual comment was to try and play down how much work Cathy was putting into the planned lunch. 'Sounds great. I'll see if they've got a couple of bottles of that Cabernet Mum likes. It'll go nicely with the beef.'

'Good lad.' Brian hooked his arm around Luke and drew him close for a quick hug. He did the same to Aaron, adding a kiss to his cheek. Their dad had always been demonstrative, no stiff-upper-lip backslapping or awkward handshakes, and both his sons had carried that naturalness and warmth into adulthood.

Luke had seen it in the same gentle interactions between his brother and Matty, his girlfriend's young son. For someone who'd been adamant about not wanting children of his own, Aaron had taken to Kiki's little ones with alacrity. It pleased Luke to see. His brother had a heart as big as a lion's and lived to care for others. At least one of them seemed capable of forging a successful relationship with a Thorpe sister.

Two of them, if he included Daniel. Recently, and sickeningly happily, married to the eldest of the three sisters, his brother's best friend was close enough to be considered blood. Which left Luke and Nee, and their marriage that wasn't. *Bollocks.*

Feeling the heavy weight of his brother's arm slung around his neck, Luke allowed Aaron to steer him off the street and onto the flagstone patio in front of the King's Arms. 'Penny for them,'

Aaron said, although he probably had a pretty good idea where his brother's thoughts had strayed to.

Luke couldn't get Nee out of his bloody head. Every time he closed his eyes, her pale, strained face swam into view. Too pale, too thin, like she hadn't been taking proper care of herself. He hated how much her miserable appearance bothered him, and his voice came out harsher than he intended. 'They're not worth a bloody penny.' He took a breath and softened his tone. 'Come on, I'm parched.'

They kept the chit-chat light as they waited for Tony, the convivial landlord, to pour their pints. They'd known the red-cheeked man since they'd had to be lifted onto the bar-stools to see, excited at the idea of a glass of pop and a packet of crisps. He added the cost of two bottles of red to their tab and promised to drop them at their table shortly. Given a choice, Luke would rather have stayed at the bar. Less chance of Aaron raising any awkward topics in front of others. Aaron ignored his suggestion, leaving him little choice other than to follow his brother to a small, round table perched in the corner beneath a collection of horse-brasses ubiquitous to every country pub he'd ever set foot in.

Hoping to head Aaron off at the pass, Luke searched for a neutral topic of conversation. 'How're the kids?'

A slow, easy smile spread over his brother's face, his mega-watt grin as Kiki called it. 'They're brilliant. Just amazing. They surprise me every day. Matty's settling in at school far better than we might have hoped, given all the upheaval he's been through.'

There was no mistaking the pride in his voice at the boy's progress and Luke grinned at him. 'Still stargazing?'

Aaron rolled his eyes. 'I think we've got the next Professor Brian Cox on our hands. Now the nights are drawing in, he's out there with his telescope every evening the skies are clear enough. We've been through every programme he can find on catch-up. I'm not sure he grasps the depth of some of the science, but you should see his eyes when the images of galaxies come up.'

Luke sipped his beer. 'Can you imagine Dad out there with him? They'd be partners-in-crime, for sure.' A shadow crossed Aaron's face and he could have kicked himself. He hadn't meant anything by it. Brian Spenser loved astronomy and had passed his interest down to both his sons. 'Sorry. I didn't think. I understand why you're taking things slowly in that direction.'

Aaron shifted on the bench beneath the window, throwing his arm along the back of the seat as he settled back to study him. 'What do you think about it all?'

'Mum? I don't know what you said to her, but it's definitely had an impact. You know she's making roast beef and Yorkshire puddings for lunch? *And* apple crumble.'

A faint blush edged his brother's cheekbones. 'She didn't need to go to so much trouble.'

Luke made a rude noise. ''Course she bloody did. Don't tell me you're letting her off the hook already! You want to milk this, mate, for as long as you can.'

Aaron shook his head, mouth twisting in amusement. 'You're incorrigible.'

He preened. 'It's a skill, don't be jealous.' They burst out laughing.

His brother took a deep draft of his beer, amusement fading. 'We're thinking about having them down for a weekend next month. Mia and Kiki have already set their hearts on some huge family Christmas, so we're thinking it would be a good idea to introduce them to the children beforehand.'

'Christmas? It's months away. Who the hell is thinking about Christmas?' Luke sputtered.

'It's exactly ten weeks today,' Aaron said in a way that told Luke he'd been subjected to more than one conversation on that point. 'It's the number-two topic of conversation between the ladies of Butterfly Cove.' The way he eyed Luke, it was obvious what subject was at the top of the gossip hit parade.

Luke stared into the depths of his beer, knowing the amber

14

liquid held no answers, but hoping Aaron would get the message and not press the point. Aaron cleared his throat, and Luke braced himself for the worst. What he heard instead shocked a laugh out of him. 'There's a surprise birthday party for me next weekend.'

'I thought the clue was in the word "surprise"?'

Aaron chuckled. 'Charlie told me about it. Made me promise to keep it a secret. I had to cross my heart and everything.' Luke could picture him doing exactly that. The little girl hung the moon and stars for his brother. He had a sneaking suspicion it had something to do with Aaron being able to indulge his love for Disney films.

'Well, I'm sure it'll be a hoot. Show me your shocked face – you can't spoil the surprise.'

Aaron gurned at him, contorting his face into evermore ludicrous expressions until Luke held a hand up in surrender. 'Stop, stop, for God's sake, before I do myself an injury.' He clutched a hand to his aching ribs, marvelling at his brother's ability to lift his mood.

'I don't know what you're laughing at,' Aaron sniffed. 'You'll have to pretend you don't know anything about it when Kiki calls to invite you.'

And, he was even better at blindsiding him. Knowing the way those bloody women schemed, they'd probably cooked up the idea of the party just to try and force him to go down there. 'I'm not coming to Butterfly Cove.'

'Luke . . .'

The ever-present simmer of anger in his gut boiled over. 'Leave it!' Damn. None of this was Aaron's fault, not Kiki's or Mia's either. There was only one person responsible for turning his life upside down.

Again.

He shoved a hand through his hair. 'Sorry.'

His brother hunched closer across the table. 'You have to speak to her sometime, bro. I don't know what happened to her in New York, but she's a mess.'

His temper spiked again. 'And how is that my problem?'

Aaron gripped his forearm. 'She's your wife, Luke. For better, for worse and all that.'

He'd heard enough. He loved Aaron, but if he didn't shut the hell up, Luke would say something unforgivable. He stood up, lifted his glass and drained the last third of his pint. 'We'd better get back.' He left the table without another word.

He was a couple of hundred yards up the road before Aaron caught up with him. Falling into step, he kept his eyes fixed on the road ahead of them. 'We heard your argument, Kiki and me. After the wedding.'

Luke stopped dead. 'What?'

Aaron faced him, one shoulder lifted in an apologetic shrug. 'Outside the barn. We didn't mean to. We were in the shadows at the side of the building.'

What the hell had they been doing lurking in the dark like that? It had been the night Aaron finally opened his heart to Kiki and . . . *oh*. The embarrassed flush on his brother's face spoke volumes. He raised an eyebrow at him and the redness darkened.

'Yeah, anyway. We weren't snooping, but we heard what Nee said, about leaving you being a mistake. She sounded pretty sincere to me. Can't you at least give her a chance to explain?'

A car approached, and they stepped onto the grass verge to let it pass. As soon as the road was clear again, Luke started walking. He didn't want to think about the wedding. Didn't want to think about how delicate and slight Nee had looked, the aching sorrow in her voice when she'd tried to talk to him. He heard Aaron's footsteps behind him. Without looking around, he held up a hand in warning. 'No more. The subject is closed.'

He couldn't give her a chance to explain, because then he'd have to admit to the true source of his anger – himself. For all his protestations, he didn't care why she'd left. He just wanted her back. And what kind of an idiot did that make him?

Chapter Three

It had taken all her powers of persuasion, but Nee had eventually convinced Mia and Kiki she was the best person to travel home to help their dad. She'd made sure not to give any hint leaving Butterfly Cove was anything more than a temporary arrangement. A bit of space away from everyone would hopefully give her time to think, and to come up with a plan for what she would do now her art was lost to her.

She had other reasons too. So many things had moved on whilst she was away, and running to catch up was exhausting. Her sisters had reached a compromise with their father over the past and were moving forwards. Nee had watched him at the wedding, especially with the little ones, and hadn't been able to stifle a bite of jealousy when he'd balanced a laughing Charlie on his feet and danced around the marquee with her. She rolled her shoulders to shrug off the unwelcome reminder. Nee had never been a jealous person, never doubted her own worth and importance to the people in her life who mattered, until . . .

The announcer called her station and she watched the people around her stand and sway their way between the seats towards the door. She remained seated. Her suitcase perched in the rack by the corridor door, hemmed in on all sides. What was it that made people so desperate to be first off? She'd never been on a train where people didn't start queueing five minutes before arrival. Nor on a flight where someone didn't pop their seatbelt open before the indicator light turned out. Once that first click sounded, a wave of others invariably rippled around the cabin. As if once one person had disobeyed the rules, it made it all right for them too. You could always spot the Brits in those situations by their guilty glances, as though they expected to be told off.

The platform came into view through the window beside her and Nee watched the people crammed by the door and counted silently in her head, *three, two, one* . . . The train jerked to a halt as the driver applied the brake, sending one unprepared passenger staggering into the person in front of him. A domino ripple of bumps, pushes and glares followed. She shook her head. *Every time.* As soon as the crowd thinned, she slipped from her seat to join the back of the group, pausing to haul her case down from the rack as she passed it.

A tall, dapper figure waited for her on the platform, and she couldn't help the small smile on her lips. Rain or shine, George Thorpe would be dressed in his usual uniform of pressed trousers, smart shirt and a jacket or buttoned-up cardigan. Today, he'd added a black woollen coat and a dark, felt trilby hat. He moved towards her, then stopped, an uncertain expression on his face. He removed his hat, turning the brim in his hand in a nervous gesture. 'Hello, Eirênê, how was your journey?'

She popped up the handle on her rolling suitcase and closed the gap between them. 'Fine, thanks.' They did an awkward little dance when he tried to take the case from her, and she hung on to it. 'Leave it, I can manage.'

George shrugged awkwardly. 'The car's not far.' He settled his hat upon his head, checking the brim was straight. *No jaunty angles allowed.*

The silly thought made her smile, and she made sure he saw it as she gestured in front of her. 'Lead on, MacDuff.' He started a little at her words, and she frowned. It was one of those things she'd always said, picked up unconsciously from somewhere long ago. A memory tickled the back of her mind, of a smiling, happier-looking George lining his three daughters up in a row. Nee could feel herself bursting with pride at being put at the front of the line. '*Lead on, Macduff!*' George had ordered, and they'd marched down the front path. Where they'd been going was lost to her now, but the long-discarded memory reminded her things hadn't always been doom and gloom.

Traffic was light, and they made quick progress through the town, the dark saloon purring through the streets. Gentle strains of classical music drifted from the speakers, negating the need for either of them to make much small talk. There was no denying the air of tension between them, though. Nee swallowed a sigh. Between her father's natural reticence and her own resentment towards him, the next few days were likely to be a struggle. One of them would have to make the first move, and somehow, she couldn't imagine it would be him. Time to break the ice.

'Matty's settling in well at school. Still a bit shy, Kiki says, but he's coming out of his shell nicely. There's even talk about him joining the local cubs. They've got a taster session coming up. The teashop opened last weekend, did you hear?'

George drew to a halt at a set of lights and half-turned in his seat. 'That was quick.'

She nodded. 'The conversion works didn't take long, and we all pitched in with the decorating.' She might not be able to find the inspiration to create something of her own, but she'd wielded a brush and roller easily enough. They'd found some pretty stencils at the local DIY store, and Nee had added bright, summer flowers and a spray of butterflies to one crisp, white wall. It was the closest she was likely to come to having anything of hers on display.

Breaking away from those thoughts before she slipped into another spiral of melancholy, she continued the conversation, although George had turned his attention back to the road. 'If the weather picks up next week, they might entice a few half-term visitors looking for a bite to eat. Mia's guests are going to be directed there and there's enough people using the studios to make it worth their while being open.'

'Ah. That makes sense, I suppose. I've rather lost track of dates now I'm not working.' His voice sounded a little wistful. George had left the job he loved at the local university, making way for Kiki's ex-husband to succeed him, in exchange for his agreement to a trouble-free divorce. It had been a remarkable sacrifice for a man who'd attached his entire self-worth and image to his career. His passion for ancient Greece and its history had trumped everything, including the needs of his wife and daughters.

'How are you coping with retirement, Dad?' she asked as he turned into the driveway and parked before the smartly painted garage door. He didn't immediately answer, choosing instead to exit the car. Nee sighed and followed him out. Perhaps she should have stuck to less difficult topics.

Waiting whilst her dad retrieved her case from the boot, she studied the familiar red-brick edifice of her childhood home. Ruthlessly weeded borders sat beneath the front windows, and there was not a hint of moss on the path dividing the tightly clipped lawn. With its neat net curtains and tidy paintwork, it presented a perfect façade to the outside world. How many other houses in this quiet street hid the kind of dark secrets that lay behind the innocuous-looking front door? Letting George manage the burden of her luggage this time, she squared her shoulders and followed him inside.

Braced for the floral-sweet scent of her mother's perfume, and an onslaught of memories, Nee smelled only lemon furniture polish and the rich gravy of some kind of stew. It was as though the house had already shed Vivian's presence. 'You made dinner?' George had never been one for that.

He placed her case at the foot of the stairs, then hung his hat and coat on one of the hooks by the door. 'I asked Wendy to make something nice for you. I thought you might be hungry.' He raised a finger to her cheek, stopping just short of touching her skin. 'You look tired, my dear.'

The unexpected tenderness of his tone and the concern shining in those dark-brown eyes that matched her own broke through the wall she'd tried so hard to maintain. Tears stung the backs of her eyes. 'I'm tired, Daddy. So bloody tired.'

'Come here.' George opened his arms and she stumbled into them, breathing in the familiar scent of his soap as she started to cry in earnest. It was like a dam had broken within her, and all the tension of the past few weeks came pouring out. Her throat hurt with the force of the ugly sobs racking her body.

Her father's hands settled on her back, patting her with the tentative gestures of a man unused to offering such comforts. Her heart gave a funny little flip. He was trying so hard to do right by them all. She hiccupped a few breaths, forcing herself to regain a bit of control. The wool of his cardigan clung damply to her cheek. Poor George – she was making a terrible mess of it. Easing back, she raised her arm to scrub her face.

'Use this.' George offered her a perfectly folded handkerchief. Her breath hitched in a little laugh and she mopped at her face. 'Sorry. I don't know what came over me. I'm supposed to be here to help you.'

He rubbed the top of her arm. 'Maybe I can do something to help you a little bit too. God knows, it's past time I acted like a father should.' She nodded, fearing any attempt to speak would set her tears off again. He checked his watch. 'It's still early. Why don't you go and lie down for an hour and then we can see about dinner?'

'Okay.' Nee reached for her bag, but he shook his head.

'Leave it. I'll put it outside your door in a minute.'

Obeying meekly wasn't a feature of Nee's skillset, but she didn't have the energy to protest that she could manage for herself. Right now, she wasn't sure that was entirely true. Letting George fuss over her wouldn't do any harm, might give him something else to focus on. And it spoke to a quiet, yearning part of her heart she hadn't realised existed, having grown up convincing herself she didn't need to lean on anyone.

She started to climb the stairs, stopping before her foot touched the first tread when she realised she still had her outdoor shoes on. Some things were too deeply ingrained, it seemed. Toeing off her shoes, she tucked them beneath the coat pegs then padded upstairs in her socks. Exhaustion dogged her heels and by the time she reached her old bedroom, she could do little more than shed her jeans before crawling under the floral quilt.

Heavy-eyed, she stared at the old band posters scattered between paintings of trees, animals and birds she'd applied directly to the pale-yellow paintwork. It was exactly as she'd left it six years previously, ready to take on the world and make her mark. Only things hadn't worked out quite how she'd planned. The world had left her scarred and scared, whilst she'd made barely a ripple.

She closed her eyes against the prickle of fresh tears. Twenty-four was too damn young to feel this old.

f overload had got to her, or it was just the sheer comfort of lying in a bed her body knew every inch of, Nee slept like the dead. Dark shadows had crept into the corners of her room, and when she checked her watch, more than two hours had passed. Feeling groggy, but much calmer for the rest, she donned her jeans, retrieved her case from the hallway and swapped her wrinkled top for a clean one. A quick splash of water on her face and cleaning her teeth chased any lingering drowsiness away. The smell of dinner drifted up the stairs, and her stomach rumbled in anticipation.

The door to her father's study stood wide. *Well, that's something that's changed in this house, at least.* George's study had always

22

been a private sanctorum, not to be entered by little girls with grubby fingers who might cause chaos in a space dedicated to order. Feeling every inch that little girl, Nee made sure her toes didn't cross the brass door plate which divided the pale-green hallway carpet from the navy of the study.

George bent over a large, leather-bound notebook, filling the lines with his neat script. Several textbooks lay open across the dark wood of his desk, each secured with a paperweight. The faint strains of Radio 4 drifted from a digital radio on the bookcase behind him. He glanced up in surprise at her light tap on the doorframe. 'Oh, hello, Eirênê, I didn't hear you come down. Feeling any better?'

She nodded. 'Much, but you shouldn't have left me so long. Aren't you hungry?'

Capping his fountain pen, George glanced at the small carriage clock on the corner of his desk. 'I didn't realise the time. Got caught up in . . .' He cast an embarrassed wave over the papers in front of him and she couldn't help but smile. He was never not going to get caught up in his books.

She braced a hand on the doorframe and leaned forwards, trying to read the titles on a small stack of books. 'What are you working on?'

He sat back in his chair. 'You can come in, you know.'

'Old habits,' she said, taking a couple of steps inside.

'You were always my little rule-breaker on everything but that.' A shadow crossed his face, but he forced a smile. 'To answer your question, I decided to try and write a children's version of some of my favourite Greek legends. The book I found for Matthew about the origins of the constellations was a bit dry for a seven-year-old. I'm hoping to have some new stories ready for my visit at Christmas.'

Her stomach twisted at the happy expectation in his tone. Christmas had been a tightrope of hope and disappointment growing up. One of the few times their mother roused herself

23

from her room and re-engaged with the family. Embracing the chance to be the perfect hostess, Vivian threw herself into the performance, decorating the house, planning meals and buying gifts. Nee and her sisters would receive new dresses to be worn, and for the next twelve months the mantelpiece would carry the image of a family that didn't exist for the rest of the year.

She could still feel the flutter of excitement, the shake in her hands as she forced herself to carefully unwrap the beautiful stack of presents under the tree, trying to do everything just right to keep Vivian happy. There would always be something, though. A little hiccup, an insignificant incident most people wouldn't think twice about. But Vivian would dwell upon it, pick it over until it overshadowed everything else. She would inevitably retire to bed, and their father would disappear into his study, leaving the three of them to watch television and try to play board games without someone there to teach them the rules.

It was only as she grew older that Nee became aware of the extent of her mother's drinking, and the excitement of opening presents was overtaken by waiting with trepidation for the first morning sherry to be poured. She'd begun to rebel against it at twelve, becoming the catalyst which would shatter the pretence. At fifteen, she'd refused flat-out to participate, not knowing it would turn out to be the last Christmas they would all be under the same roof. A year later, Kiki and Mia were both married and making their own homes, leaving Nee caught in the spiralling tragedy of her parents' unhappiness.

Angry. She'd been so angry with them both for as long as she could remember. Looking at George now, a grey shadow of his former self, face lined with the pain of all those years, she let it go. However bad things had been for her, how much worse must it have been for him, for him and Vivian both, to have spent thirty years tied to someone you loved, but couldn't make happy.

She hoped this year he would find some peace, and spending time at Butterfly Cove with everyone might be just the thing to bring it to him. Just a shame she wouldn't be there to witness it. She shook her head. Now was not the time to think about it, because then she'd start thinking about the reason why she wouldn't be there, why she couldn't be there. *Luke.* 'Come on, Dad, let's eat.'

Feeling stronger after the hearty stew and a decent night's sleep, Nee decided to seize the bull by the horns and visit her mother after breakfast the next morning. George had offered to accompany her, but she couldn't be sure of her reaction and didn't want to risk the fragile peace they'd begun to build. She'd left him with a cup of tea in his study to continue working on the stories for Matty.

Although her father had tried to prepare her for the changes in Vivian, her first sight of the birdlike figure lost in the harsh whiteness of the bed stole Nee's breath. Strands of wispy, almost-colourless hair straggled around her mother's face. The knotted hanks were so far from the gleaming coiffure of her memories that she knew little of the woman she'd known remained. Making her way quietly into the room, Nee noted the potted plants and bright accessories scattered around, and felt a quiet appreciation for the owners of the home for trying to minimise the institutional feel of the place.

The bed, though, was like those found in every kind of hospital. They'd positioned it where Vivian could look out of the window to the gardens below, although whether she had any awareness of the view remained to be seen. Memories flooded her mind of all the times she'd seen her mother supine on the couch beneath the window of her bedroom at home. The picture of delicate, ethereal beauty, almost professionally weak and wan. Helplessness had always been Vivian's stock-in-trade – a damsel in distress, unable to cope with the pressures of life. That façade had fooled many, but not Nee. She remembered too clearly the cynical glitter in her mother's eye as she twisted poor Kiki round her little finger.

A ghost of the anger she'd nurtured for so long against her parents began to stir in her stomach. If either one of them had faced up to the basic realities of life, then it wouldn't have been left to Mia to try and raise a baby sister when she'd been little more than a child herself. Kiki, too, had done her best for Nee, offering every ounce of love in that big heart of hers to ensure she never lacked for affection. She clasped a hand over her stomach to try and settle the beast stirring within. Sometimes it felt like she'd been angry for ever.

The tempest of emotions had served her well in the past, bringing a fire and passion to her earliest artwork that caught the attention of teachers and, later, college tutors. Feed the fire, they'd urged her, so she'd tapped the well and poured it forth into every line drawn, every handful of clay moulded. She developed a reputation for dark, brooding pieces and the juxtaposition with her sweet, elfin appearance had intrigued more than one patron. Whispers had rippled through the art world of a bold, bright new star-in-the-making and she'd been encouraged to dream big.

Her dreams had crystallised into the ultimate goal for a young sculptor – a chance to study under the tutelage of Devin Rees, the mercurial, undisputed master of their medium. Even applying for a place at the Reinhold Institute had seemed like the ultimate act of hubris, and when her submission had gone unanswered for months, Nee had shrugged it off. London was more than good enough for her, and she'd thrown herself wholeheartedly into the trendy art scene, determined to make her mark. She'd found a group of like-minded souls, and had been out celebrating a friend getting signed by an agent when a fallen angel with the devil's smile walked into her life.

She hadn't known it was possible to be so happy. Luke filled every dark and lonely place inside her with a passion so raw, so intense, it consumed her every waking moment. Finding out how much she'd missed out on as a child, he'd made it his mission to spoil her. A trip on the London Eye, a magical sunset safari tour

26

at the zoo, where they'd ridden the kiddies' train and eaten huge whippy ice-cream cones, lying back in the Planetarium as they travelled through space and time. So many cherished memories crammed into a couple of magical months.

He'd taken her to his favourite place – the beautiful garden created in the magnificent ruins of St Dunstan's in the East – and when he'd dropped to one knee in the shadowed corner beneath an elegant stone arch wrapped in vines, the only word on her lips had been yes. Drunk on champagne, love and the euphoria of becoming Mrs Luke Spenser, she'd believed herself satisfied with the path her life had taken.

Then the email with a plane ticket and an eight-hour deadline had arrived.

Chapter Four

Having moped around his flat for a couple of days, it had been on the tip of Luke's tongue to refuse Kiki's invitation when she called him about Aaron's 'surprise' party. She'd confessed the adults all knew Charlie had let the cat out of the bag, but the children were so excited about the prospect, they'd agreed to keep up the pretence. Much as he might have liked to see the growing bonds in his brother's new family, he hadn't wanted his presence to be a wet blanket.

Poised to decline, his words froze on his lips when Kiki said quietly, 'He misses you, Luke. We all miss you. Please come.'

Once he'd agreed to attend the party, there was no getting around the fact he would be coming face to face with Nee again. Aaron had been right; they needed to resolve things between them. For the sake of both their families. He had two choices – forgive her or let her go for good. Leaving him had been a mistake; she'd said as much during their brief, anguished exchange at the wedding. He'd already admitted to himself he still wanted her, had spent the last twelve months waiting for a call, an email, *anything* from her and then let his bloody pride get in the way. If she thought it was a mistake, that meant she wanted to try again, didn't it? *God, he hoped so.*

Feeling lighter and more hopeful than he had in weeks, not even the rain lashing the small platform at Orcombe Sands station could dampen his mood. Hunching down into his thick jacket to try and avoid letting the rain inside his collar, Luke shouldered his bag and splashed across the small gravel car park towards a familiar blue hatchback. Tugging open the back door to throw in his bag, he stopped short as a mournful howl greeted him from the small plastic crate on the seat. He ducked his head into the car and met Kiki's worried brown eyes as she stared at him over her shoulder. 'Who's your friend?'

'This is Tigger. He's Aaron's birthday present from the children.'

A tiny, pink-tipped nose poked out through the bars in the front of the crate, and Luke forgot the rain soaking his back as he started to laugh. 'You've bought him a dog?'

Kiki shook her head, a look of despair on her face. 'Don't. Just don't. I can't believe I let the kids talk me into it.' She cringed as another heart-wrenching noise split the air. 'He's been like that since I picked him up half an hour ago. I was supposed to collect him tomorrow, but the shelter's short-staffed so they asked if I could do it this afternoon because Saturday is always their busiest viewing day.'

'Poor fella, he's probably scared.' Luke dumped his bag on the far side of the back seat, then unhooked the catch securing the crate closed. Reaching inside, he scooped out the tiny brindle puppy and the soft, blue blanket he was huddled in. Unzipping his coat, he tucked the dog inside then jumped into the front passenger seat. A pink tongue peeked out to lick the underside of his chin as he secured the seatbelt around himself, and Luke was instantly smitten. He tried to lift the puppy out to get a better look at him, but it squirmed in closer to his body, so he decided to leave it where it was. At least the howling had stopped.

Kiki blinked at him. 'Are you some kind of dog-whisperer?'

He shoved the damp curls off his forehead and gave her a

wink. 'Just irresistible,' he said, making her laugh. 'So, what's the plan for tomorrow?'

She peered through the rain-soaked windscreen as though seeking out some blue sky. 'I'm opening the tearoom as usual, but closing early after lunch to get everything set up. If the weather stays like this, I won't get many customers, but there's usually a few of the guests who wander in for a bite to eat. Mia is winding down the guest house for the winter, so she's only got one couple staying, but the studios have a few guests. Leo's back down for a few days, so he's coming to the party too.'

Luke grinned. 'I bet he'll love that.' The artist was both a client and friend of his brother, and had taken something of a shine to Kiki when he'd first stayed at the studios for their grand opening weekend.

Kiki's tut didn't cover the slight colour rising in her cheeks. 'Behave yourself.' Flicking the wipers onto their highest setting, she negotiated her way across the car park, avoiding the biggest puddles under which potholes lurked.

'No chance.' He settled back into his seat with a smirk; winding Aaron up was his duty and teasing him about Leo fancying Kiki would be too good an opportunity to pass up.

The car bumped over the curb as they exited the car park, causing the puppy to whimper and squirm inside his jacket. Lowering the zip, Luke adjusted the blanket until the little dog rested across his lap. Black button eyes blinked up at him and a pair of typical French bulldog bat ears twitched. 'Oh God, he's adorable.'

Kiki flicked a glance across at him when she paused at the crossroads leading to Honeysuckle Cottage, the chocolate-box home she shared with Aaron. 'I know. The children were smitten the moment they laid eyes on him. Charlie cried when she realised we couldn't bring him home immediately.' She turned left into the lane, sticking to the centre of the quiet road to avoid more deep puddles. 'Thank goodness we passed the inspection from the shelter, or I'd have had a mutiny on my hands.'

They pulled into the short driveway and Kiki parked as close to the front door as possible. Even the miserable weather couldn't dim the beauty of the place. Luke lifted the puppy up to show him the pretty white cottage with a thatched roof. 'Hey, fella. What do you think of your new home?' Tigger yipped, a funny little high-pitched sound, and a trickle of warmth slid down Luke's wrist and into the sleeve of his coat. 'Gee, thanks,' he said as the tang of dog pee filled the air.

'Oh dear, I'm so sorry.' Kiki's apology might have been more convincing if she hadn't been laughing quite so hard. Luke tucked the uncontrite dog back into the blanket and, shielding him with one half of his coat, ducked out into the rain. Kiki dashed out to join him, but her key had barely scraped against the lock before the front door swung open to reveal two giggling, very excited children.

'Did you get him?' Matty barely spared Luke a glance as he fixed his sparkling eyes on his mother. Luke grinned and pulled aside the edge of his jacket to show the wriggling bundle.

'Yes. Shh, not so loud or you'll spoil the surprise.' Kiki pressed her finger to her lips and tried to herd the children further into the hall so she could close the door against the driving rain.

'Surprise?' Inevitably, the commotion had drawn Aaron from his study. Hands in the front pockets of his jeans, he stared in bemusement at the impromptu party before him. 'I guess you guys really missed Luke, huh?'

Caught red-handed, it was too late for Luke to tuck the puppy out of sight. The dog began to squirm in earnest and worried about dropping him, he sank to his knees and placed the blanket on the red-tiled floor. The puppy yapped and wriggled free of the soft material, his tiny claws skittering on the tile as he took a couple of cautious steps forward. Charlie made a grab for the pup, but Kiki held her back, whispering to the little girl to be gentle.

Aaron crouched down. 'Who's this then?' He extended his fingers towards the puppy and it gave them a tentative sniff, then a quick lick.

Matty hunkered down beside him, keeping his voice low to match Aaron's. 'This is Tigger. He belongs to you.'

Luke watched his brother glance from the boy next to him to Kiki. She raised her shoulder in an apologetic shrug. 'I asked the children what they wanted to give you for your birthday, and they were adamant.'

Matty put his hand on Aaron's knee. 'Remember when we were at the beach and that man let us play with his dog? You said you'd always wanted a dog when you were my age, but you weren't allowed one at home. You have a new home with us now, and we decided you should have whatever you want.'

Luke coughed around the big lump forming in his throat and he caught a suspicious glint in his brother's eyes. 'That's very kind of you both.' Aaron's voice came out so rough it sounded like he'd been gargling rocks.

Matty leaned in closer to his side. 'And we didn't want you to be lonely. When Charlie goes to school, you'll be all on your own during the day. Now you'll have Tigger to keep you company.'

Tigger yipped, like he was accepting the responsibility, and wiggled his bottom in the air. Moving slowly, Aaron scooped the puppy up in one big hand and lifted him close against his chest. 'Hello, Tigger. Hello, good boy.' He touched a finger to each of the dog's little ears then let Matty give him a pat. Mindful of her mother's soft warnings, Charlie edged closer, giggling when Tigger licked her hand with a tiny pink tongue.

They painted such a picture of domestic bliss, Luke felt like an intruder amongst them. Tightness spread across his chest, and he pushed to his feet. 'I'll grab my bag.' He held his hand out to Kiki for the car keys. 'Just the crate from the back, or is there anything else?'

She smiled up at him. 'There's a few things in the boot.'

Aaron shifted his weight, like he meant to get up. 'I'll give you a hand, Spud.'

He waved him down. 'No, stay put. No point in both of us getting soaked.'

By the time he'd hauled in his bag and about a ton of doggy essentials, the others had decamped to the kitchen. A zesty-chemical smell rose from a shiny patch on the floor tiles and Matty was busy spreading sheets of newspaper by the back door. Tigger had obviously made his mark again. Shrugging out of his wet jacket, Luke held it up to Kiki. 'Any chance of sticking this in the wash?'

'Of course.' She nodded to the sleeve of his sweatshirt, 'You might want to add that too.'

Luke examined the wet cuff ruefully. 'How can such a small dog have such a big bladder?' The soft patter of liquid on newspaper was the only response.

With the kids finally ushered upstairs by Kiki, Luke and Aaron finished tidying up the kitchen and settled at the table, each with a beer in hand. On the right side of a double helping of chicken stew and dumplings, Luke was drowsily full and grateful he'd changed his mind and decided to come for the weekend. He raised his bottle towards his brother. 'Happy Birthday, Bumble.'

Aaron clinked beers with him and grinned with a hint of smug satisfaction. 'It bloody well is at that.' A snuffling sound came from the big basket they'd corralled behind a temporary barrier made from a laundry rack with cardboard sellotaped around the bottom half of the rungs. 'I still can't believe they got me a dog.' He sounded pleased as punch about it.

An image of his big, strapping brother walking the tiny puppy on a lead came into Luke's head and he covered the laugh welling in his chest with a swig of beer. He was sure Aaron would take to looking after this new addition to his household as well as he had the rest of it. The affection he held for the children showed in every look, every small, reassuring touch he shared with them. And as for him and Kiki . . . Luke's heart fluttered at the prospect of once again sharing a love like that. 'It suits you.'

Aaron cocked an eyebrow in query so Luke stretched his arms out wide. 'This. Domestic bliss. A lovely woman, two point four kids and now a dog. You're a cliché, mate.'

His brother shook his head. 'Not sure about the point four. Two seems to suit us just fine, and it's two more than I ever expected to have. Besides, I don't even know if Kiki wants any more . . .'

Luke opened his mouth to point out that people, *adults*, normally had serious conversations about things like that before they took the plunge and settled down together, then shut it again with a snap. Considering he'd married a woman based on little more than a bone-deep knowledge she was meant to be his, he didn't have a leg to stand on when it came to commenting on the relationships of others. 'You've got plenty of time to sort things like that out. You're not *that* old.'

'Cheeky sod.' Aaron tapped his fingers against the glass bottle in front of him. 'Things happened pretty fast, you know.'

He laughed. 'I *know*.' He cocked his head at the gurgle of water passing through the pipes overhead. Sounded like bath time was over, but it would take Kiki some time yet to get the children settled down for the night. He had Aaron to himself for a few more minutes at least. Enough time to ask the one question pounding in the back of his head. 'So, how is she?'

His brother relaxed back in his chair, the expression on his face making it clear Luke's attempt at sounding casual had been a miserable failure. 'I don't know.' He held up a hand when Luke would have jumped in. 'Physically, she seems better. Lord knows, between Mia and Kiki, she can't turn around without being fed. Last time I saw her, she'd lost the worst of that gauntness from her frame.'

'Last time?' His brother and Kiki spent almost more time at Butterfly House than they did at home, so how long could it have been?

'Shit. Kiki didn't tell you?' Aaron looked stricken.

His gut clenched, and a sick, familiar dread crept up his spine. 'Tell me what?'

Aaron puffed out his cheeks. 'Nee's up with their dad. Vivian took a turn for the worse and, well, given how things were between you two at the wedding, Nee thought it would be best if she steered clear of the party tomorrow.' He frowned and rubbed the heel of his hand against his forehead. 'Sorry, Spud. It all happened rather suddenly. I know Kiki's hoping it will mend a few fences between George and Nee, and it certainly took the pressure off her and Mia feeling one of them had to go up there.'

Forcing himself to unclench his painful grip on his beer, Luke placed the bottle carefully on the table. Everything Aaron said made perfect sense – Nee would certainly have had no expectation of his attitude towards her having changed after their brief encounter at the wedding. She was also the most logical choice of the three sisters to make the journey, and yet he couldn't shake off the feeling she'd run away from him.

Again.

Well, that was something he would have to deal with in due course. He'd let her go without a fight once before. There was no way he was going to do it again. Right now, he needed to get the conversation back on track. He met this brother's worried gaze and shook his head. 'Forget about it. I'm sure everyone sighed in relief at not having to deal with the two of us together in the same small space. I also can't blame you for not wanting to even mention her name to me, given the way I bit your head off at Mum and Dad's the other week.'

Aaron reached across the table to give his forearm a quick squeeze. 'I shouldn't have stuck my nose in. I'm getting as bad as Madeline.' They both grinned. The older woman was a huge favourite of theirs, even if she did have a tendency to interfere. His brother's expression sobered. 'Kiki's still worried about her, though. As I mentioned before, it's obvious something happened in New York, but Nee won't talk about it, no matter how hard they try to persuade her to open up.'

Luke frowned. The pale, haunted woman he'd seen in

September had been a mere shadow of the bright, sparkling girl he'd fallen head over heels in love with. What could change a person in so short a time? 'I don't even know why she went there in the first place.'

'She got a placement at the Reinhold Institute.' Kiki's soft voice came from the doorway and they turned to face her. 'Sorry, I didn't mean to interrupt. Charlie wanted a drink.' She held up a yellow plastic beaker.

The name meant nothing to Luke, but the way Kiki said it, it sounded like a big deal. Making a note to Google it later, he took a sip of his beer as he tried to corral his racing thoughts. Even in the short time they'd been together, it had been clear to him Nee was ambitious about her art career, and with good reason from the feedback she'd been getting. If this place was as prestigious as it sounded, then of course she would have wanted to go.

Had she thought he would try and stop her? Luke's stomach churned at the idea. Had she understood so little about him she believed him to be some misogynist who expected his wife to put aside her own desires and needs for his? As if he would chain her, the freest of spirits, and try to make her less than the very best she could be!

He looked from Aaron to Kiki, flinching at the sympathy written clear in their expressions. He needed to get out of there and think. Standing abruptly, he grabbed the back of his chair before it could topple backwards. 'I'm off to bed.'

The soft murmur of their voices followed him down the hallway. He rolled his eyes, imagining them exclaiming 'Poor Luke' and other pointless expressions of pity. *Pity him?* No! Better pity Nee, because she had no idea what was coming.

She'd obviously thought the worst of him; it was damn well time he showed her his best. People had always underestimated him – mistaken the easy-going face he showed the world for shallowness or a lack of feeling. But they'd missed one vital detail in their casual dismissal of him. Once he set his mind to something, nothing would deter him. When Aaron had gone up to London, Luke had applied himself to his studies, ensuring he attained the grades needed to win his own placement at the same university. He'd had his fair share of fun during his degree course, but never so much to cause him to miss a class, or risk the prestigious placement he'd set his heart on.

His mother had done her best to infuse her own misplaced resentment of Aaron into her beloved boy, and he'd set his face against her. *Stubborn little sod*, his brother had always called him, and Luke took it as a badge of honour. Nee was his wife, and until the moment she stared him in the eye and told him it was over, he would fight with everything he had to reclaim her.

The following afternoon, Luke paused on the threshold of the teashop, and grinned. If there was one thing the Thorpe sisters knew how to do, it was throw a party. Balloons and streamers hung from the exposed beams, adding bright spots of decoration to the light, airy room. Another swirl of colour caught his eye, this time a beautiful swirling mural on the whitewashed wall. Butterflies and flowers danced around a bright ribbon, leading the eye naturally to the glass-fronted counter dominating the top end of the space. Clusters of white-pine furniture were dotted around the room – the tables draped in red-and-white-checked cloths and bright-red bows decorating the backs of the chairs.

Cheers and laughter rang around as the waiting guests yelled 'Surprise!' and Aaron did his best to look shocked as they swarmed towards him offering hugs, kisses and neatly wrapped presents. Inviting smells drifted from a buffet table near the counter, and he edged past his brother's shoulder to take a better look. He shook his head at the sight – finger sandwiches, fondant fancies, sausages on sticks. Even a rabbit-shaped jelly wobbled at one end of the table, surrounded by little jelly bunnies.

Turning back, he surveyed the room. Aaron's mega-watt smile was bright enough to illuminate half of Blackpool pier as he accepted the greetings and congratulations of their friends and family. Hopefully, things would continue to improve between him and Cathy and then everyone who mattered to Luke could be together again.

Well, almost everyone.

A sudden rush of annoyance dimmed his mood. Nee should be there. If he could put things behind them and act like a grown-up, why the hell couldn't she? He was the wronged party in all this. His stomach soured and he dropped his half-full plate on the edge of the buffet table, appetite gone. Footsteps came from behind him and Luke forced a smile to his face. This party was important to Aaron so he needed to stop sulking.

Daniel waved a cheese and pineapple stick at him in greeting. 'This is the best party ever, mate. There's a Black Forest gateau in the fridge for later, too.' His eyes glazed a bit as he mentioned the rich chocolate dessert.

Luke shook his head. 'Yeah, if you're five maybe.' He hadn't meant to sound like a miserable git, but damn it, he'd had it all laid out in his head how the weekend would proceed, and she'd put the kibosh on it by buggering off to her dad's. *So much for not sulking.*

His friend gave him an appraising look. 'What's crawled up your arse?'

Sighing, he shook his head. 'Nothing worth worrying about. Come on, let's party!'

And they did, Butterfly Cove-style. It wasn't just the buffet that was nostalgic; Mia and Kiki had lined up a host of old favourite games. A very competitive pass-the-parcel saw Richard expelled from the circle for holding on to the gift-wrapped box for too long. Musical chairs proved little short of carnage – Luke wouldn't be the only one to bear a few bruises come the morning. And the current game of statues looked to be going the same way. Insults and outrageous comments flew from those already disqualified as they tried to sabotage the handful of people remaining.

'Been skipping those gym sessions again, Spud?' Aaron cat-called him. *Git.*

Luke gritted his teeth against the urge to suck in his stomach and held still. Apparently not satisfied with his failure to distract him, Aaron crouched down to the puppy at his feet and gave him a little push in Luke's direction. From the corner of his eye, he watched Tigger scamper over to sniff at his shoe. *Don't you dare* . . . The puppy shuffled his rear end, and Luke's nerve broke. Scooping Tigger up before he could even think about cocking a leg, he carried the little dog out of the teashop and plonked him down on the ground. Aaron's laughter followed him out of the door and he span around, checked the kids weren't looking, then flipped his big brother a rude gesture before pulling the door closed behind him.

A cold wind whistled through his long-sleeved T-shirt. Shivering, he stepped out of the shade and into a patch of sunlight, enjoying the autumn warmth whilst the puppy scampered and sniffed from place to place. The door creaked behind him and he glanced round to see Madeline slipping out to join him. Even with her cheeks flushed from the games, her hair hung in an immaculate curtain against her cheeks. Hooking an arm through his, she smiled. 'They've broken out the Twister mat so I thought I'd hide out here with you.'

'I'm not hiding.' His automatic retort earned a small sniff of disbelief. 'Well, not much,' he conceded.

Mads tugged on his arm. 'If we go for a stroll, we'll both look less like we're hiding.'

Keeping to the sunny patches, they took a turn around the garden. Luke kept a weather eye on the puppy as he gambolled from bush to bush, tail wagging like he was in seventh heaven.

'So, have you spoken to her?' The foul mood that had settled over him blew away on the freshness of the breeze, and might have stayed away had Madeline only kept quiet.

Luke sighed. He could act the fool, pretend he didn't know

who she was talking about, but what would be the point? It would only postpone the inevitable. 'I planned to, this weekend.'

'Ah.' Madeline loosened her hold on his arm to adjust the length of twine holding some flopping stems to a stake. 'We should have cut these back last weekend, but they're too pretty.' Tightening the string did no good, and the wilting flowers continued to droop. Crouching down, she gathered a handful of them. 'There's a pair of secateurs in the shed. Get them for me, will you?'

Irritation itched beneath his skin. 'That's all you've got to say to me about the situation? One bloody syllable and now we're on to *Gardener's World*?'

Sitting back on her heels, Madeline raised a hand to shield her eyes from the sun as she stared up at him. 'There's a roll of green sacks in there too. Fetch them as well, there's a good boy.'

Luke stomped across the lawn towards the shed and yanked the door open with more force than was strictly necessary. Damn it, he needed to stop being so damn touchy over everything. He should be grateful if Madeline had nothing else to say on the matter of him and Nee. She'd stuck her nose in enough with his brother's relationship, and Daniel's before that. Luke didn't need her help, didn't need anyone else's help. He just needed to talk to Nee, clear the air and everything would be fine. He'd decided to forgive her, so there was nothing else to be said about it.

With a deep breath, he swallowed his temper and returned to Madeline's side with the tools, and a pair of flowery gardening gloves he'd found on the shelf. 'Thank you, darling. Hold these, will you?' She nodded towards the limp stems.

Crouching beside her, Luke did his best to keep the shiny toes of his brogues from sinking into the wet soil of the flowerbed. He grasped the flowers where she indicated, holding them taut whilst Madeline snipped them short. She moved on to the next cluster, and he trailed at her heels, doing a damn good impression of Tigger. 'I've decided to forgive her.'

'That's nice, dear.' Madeline deadheaded a few more blooms,

chucking the discards in the sack he held open for her. 'What exactly are you forgiving her for?'

He frowned. What kind of game was she playing now? 'For leaving me, of course.'

'Of course.' She moved to the other side of the bush, snipping as she went. 'I thought you said you hadn't spoken to her since the wedding.'

'I haven't.' Luke huffed out a breath. 'Look, Madeline, coy doesn't suit you. Just spit it out, will you?'

Straightening up, she dropped another handful of beheaded flowers into the sack, then met his gaze. 'If being coy doesn't suit me, then being a fool suits you even less. It's not much more than a month since you couldn't bear to be in the same space as Nee. You've not spoken to her since, and yet you're happy to forgive and forget?'

He ground his teeth. 'I love her.'

'And Richard loved me, but I still wanted to throttle him when he went behind my back and got a vasectomy. He did it for the best of reasons, and that just made it so much worse. I tried to swallow my resentment and anger with him, and it almost destroyed us.'

If a fly had chosen that moment to buzz over he'd probably have swallowed it, so low had his jaw dropped. There were few certainties he'd stake his life on: the sun rose in the East, Marmite was revolting, and Madeline and Richard had the happiest marriage in the world. To hear her speak of such things shook him to the core. 'You always seem so happy together.'

'And we are, darling, but things might have been different if I'd carried on trying to ignore the elephant in the corner.' Madeline rested a hand on his chest. 'Richard hurt me, whether he meant to or not. With the noblest of intentions or not, he *hurt* me. If I hadn't found someone to talk to about it, I don't know where we'd be. Certainly not as content as we are now.'

Her hand pressed hard over his heart for a couple of beats. 'Nee hurt you. Whatever her reasons. And if you don't acknowledge that, it'll fester away and eventually poison everything.' She lifted her hand, returned it to brush a few spots of dirt left behind by her gardening gloves, then smiled at him. 'You mean the world to me, and I want more than anything for you all to be happy.'

A scratchy feeling rose in his throat, and Luke had to swallow around it. 'I know, Mads.' He shut his eyes briefly against the feelings her words stirred up. 'I'm scared. Scared I won't be able to cope with the truth. When I saw her, I knew I'd do anything to get her back and it made me so angry – at myself, not her. It just kept going round and round in my head, so I decided to ignore it instead.' He laughed. 'I'm an idiot.'

Madeline patted his arm. 'We've all been fools for love, sweet boy. I'm always here and ready to listen, or I can recommend a service I've used in the past. I know Kiki benefited from their assistance recently.'

Had he agreed to talk to somebody then? He ran back through their conversation in his mind, but couldn't pin down when his position on it had shifted, only that it had. The lid was off the box now, and if he tried to shove it back on without facing his fears, he would be doing both himself and Nee a disservice. If he truly wanted to try and make things work with her, he needed to be on completely solid ground, and the only way to achieve that would be to do as Madeline suggested. He just wasn't sure if he could talk to *her* about the jumble of emotions inside him; nor did he feel comfortable with the idea of pouring his heart out to a total stranger.'

Whether his expression gave his hesitancy away, or whether she was just a bloody mind reader, Madeline offered him a sympathetic smile. 'Maybe you could find someone a bit closer to home. I'm only suggesting you think about it, that's all.' Stripping off one of her gloves, Madeline dug into the pocket of her neat slacks and produced a neatly folded tissue. 'Dry your eyes and let's go and eat a couple of obscenely large slices of that gateau.'

Luke blotted his cheeks, unaware he'd been crying until she mentioned it.

'Everything all right, Spud?' Luke spun round to see Aaron watching them from a few feet away, a frown of concern etched between his brows. He recognised that look, knew Aaron was in full big-brother mode, ready to step in and fix whatever the problem was. Tigger scampered out from beneath a bush to crouch at his master's feet, tail wagging. Keeping his eyes fixed on Luke, Aaron bent down to stroke the puppy's head.

The tightness in Luke's chest eased. He had his family and friends around him, and they would do everything within their power to help him and Nee. All he had to do was reach out to them, and make sure he did everything he could to help himself. Tucking the tissue away, he hooked his arm around Madeline's shoulders and pulled her into his side. 'Everything's fine, Bumble, thanks to a certain meddling old bag.'

A sharp elbow dug him in the ribs. 'That's Fairy Godmother to you, cheeky bugger.'

'Oof!' Luke staggered away clutching his side as though she'd delivered a much harder blow, almost bumping into his brother in the process.

Aaron hooked an arm around his neck, tugging him into a half-hug, half-headlock. 'You would tell me if there was something wrong, wouldn't you?'

'Yes, of course . . .' He cut off the instinctive response and swallowed. 'Actually, I could do with a chat later, if you have time?'

Shifting his hold, Aaron brushed a quick kiss on his cheek. 'Always got time for you, Spud. You know that.'

Yes. He did.

Chapter Five

When the end came, it was surprisingly quick. Nee had finally settled into a routine with her father only to be thrown into the bureaucratic nightmare brought on by Vivian's death. Even for someone with little in the way of personal assets, the world seemed determined to thwart them at every turn. George battled valiantly with solicitors, banks and all the other institutions who demanded a ridiculous amount of detail before they would accede to close accounts and update their records. Nee said a silent prayer of thanks for his meticulous record-keeping as she did her best to relieve him of as much of it as she could. An air of eerie acceptance had settled over her dad. True, he'd never been the most demonstrative of men, but his preternatural calm worried her more than if he'd broken down in tears.

Arrangements for the funeral had been made with a sympathetic undertaker, and the others would be heading up from Butterfly Cove in the morning for the service at the local crematorium the day after. Much as Nee wanted to be the one to shoulder the responsibility, in her heart it relieved her to know Mia would soon be there with her. Her doughty, capable sister would pick up whatever balls Nee dropped.

She sighed as the tinny, cheery music in her ear flipped back to the original track. She bet Mia wouldn't have spent so long on hold. 'Come on, come on,' she muttered into the phone.

'Thank you for calling Middleworth's. My name is Sonia, how may I assist you this morning?'

Stunned that for once her impatience had been rewarded, it took Nee a moment to shake off her wool-gathering. 'Hello. I was talking to one of your colleagues about cancelling an account?'

Keys clicked, the familiar sound of fingers skittering over a keyboard. 'I'm sorry to hear you are thinking of leaving us. Can you give me the account number in question?'

Nee ground her teeth. 'I've been through all this once already. Can you transfer me back to . . .?' She glanced down at the notepad in front of her. She'd been given the bloody runaround so often over the last few days, she'd taken to writing every single detail down. ' . . .Colin.'

'I'm sorry, he's on another call. Can you give me the account number in question, please?'

Fighting the urge to scream, she took a deep breath and reeled off the number, *again*. More clicking, then, 'Thank you, Mrs Thorpe, I have your details on the screen. Can you please confirm the first line of your address, and the postcode, please?'

Nee stared at the automated clock on the phone. Ten bloody minutes she'd been on the phone and they were back to this again. She clung to the final shreds of her temper and tried to keep her tone even. 'As I told your colleague, I'm not Mrs Thorpe, I'm her daughter—'

The rep cut across her. 'I'm sorry, I'm only authorised to speak to the account holder. Data protection, and all that.'

Her fake sympathy snapped something inside Nee. 'Well, unless you're a fucking clairvoyant, you're out of luck because we're cremating her tomorrow.' She regretted the words the moment she'd said them. It wasn't this poor girl's fault, it was the same damn 'computer says no' system every so-called customer services department seemed tied to. 'Sorry, I'm sorry, that was completely unnecessary of me. My mother died recently, and I've already been through all of this once with your colleague. I just want to close her account.'

'There are no notes on the system regarding your request. I can only go by the information in front of me.' The defensive tone from the operator made her feel lower than a snake's belly. 'Do you have probate on your mother's estate?' the woman continued.

Nee sighed. She'd banged her head against the probate brick wall several times already. 'No, we don't have it yet. It's only a store card, for goodness' sake. You must be able to see from your records that it hasn't been used in months. I'm just trying to spare my father the upset of receiving any more blank statements like the one that arrived in the post this morning.'

'I'm sorry, but our procedures require a copy of the probate certificate before we can terminate this account. We cannot act on a phone request, as we have no proof of your identity. I'm sure you understand.'

Because people randomly phoned and cancelled store cards belonging to strangers all the time, no doubt. All at once the fight left her, leaving her bone-tired. 'Can you at least mark the account so no more statements are sent out?'

The line went quiet for a moment. 'I'm sorry. Mrs Thorpe didn't authorise anyone to act on her behalf, but I have requested a copy of the account closure form to be sent out to the address listed. It details the steps to follow.'

It was the best she could hope for, apparently. 'Okay, thanks. Sorry again for being rude.'

'It's fine. Thank you for calling Middleworth's.' Nee stared at the phone, not quite knowing whether to laugh or cry, then placed it very gently back into its cradle. It was that, or smash the wretched thing against the wall.

The sharp ring of the front doorbell jarred her and she rose from her perch on the bottom step of the stairs. 'I'll get it,' she called towards the half-open door of her father's study. *Let it not be another bloody casserole.*

Vivian's death had drawn the most unlikely of people out of the woodwork, some driven by a true sense of duty and concern, most jumping at the chance for a bit of rubbernecking into the sideshow of grief playing out behind the neatly trimmed hedges of number thirty-two. Neighbours her father had never met beyond the nod of a head took turns ringing the bell, offering a few words of bland comfort and a plate of something. No doubt the presence of one of the long-missing daughters of the house had set tongues wagging behind the twitching net curtains. Not that Nee could have cared less what they had to say for themselves.

She paused before the door to squint at the blurred outline of a figure through the privacy glass set in the wood, but the frosted ridges made it impossible to discern much. Taking a deep, composing breath, Nee fixed the politest smile she could muster and turned the latch. Bold as brass, and twice as bloody gorgeous, the last person she'd expected to see gave her a lopsided grin. 'Hello, Mrs Spenser.'

Luke? He looked well; still carrying the summer tan he must have picked up at Butterfly Cove. The sun looked to have added a few paler highlights to his wayward blond curls, but the melting heat in his dark-brown eyes was as familiar as ever. Never one to consider herself the fainting type, Nee had to grip the edge of the doorframe until her knuckles turned white to stop herself from sliding to the floor. 'You . . . you're here?'

'I heard about your mum,' he said, as though that explained anything at all.

His breath condensed in the air and she became aware of the November chill leeching in through the open door. Acting on autopilot, she stepped to the side. 'You'd better come in.'

Catching a hint of the clean, sharp scent of his aftershave as he passed her, she closed her eyes against a sudden rush of memories. Luke, nuzzling the spot just beneath her ear as he whispered

47

some private jest to her. The untidy sprawl of his limbs taking up more than his share of the bed. The wink he'd given her when they broke for air after sharing their first kiss in an alley next to The George, less than an hour after setting eyes on each other.

The ground shifted beneath her, the way it always did when he was near, and the brittle shell she'd wrapped herself in over the past few weeks spider-webbed with cracks. A painful knot formed at the top of her breastbone and she tried to swallow it down, knowing if she let it out she'd start crying. And maybe never stop.

A gentle brush against her cheek forced her to open her eyes as Luke cupped her cheek. 'I'm only here to help, nothing else, okay?' He sounded so sincere, so forthright and honest, so *Luke*, she wanted nothing more than to tumble headlong into the comfort he offered.

'I need you.' Her lips could barely form the words, but it was enough. He reached past her to quietly close the door and then he was there – all reassuring warmth and that big, solid frame that seemed shaped to perfectly enfold her own. A hint of the crisp, winter air clung to the soft wool of his coat beneath her cheek and she breathed deeply. The scent of disinfected death that had infused every breath for what felt like weeks vanished in that first fresh inhalation.

She'd tried so hard to hold it all together, to tell herself she owed Vivian no tears, no regrets. God, she'd become so good at lying to herself about everything. The spiderweb of cracks shattered and the first wave of grief burst through, would have taken her to the floor had he not been there to hold her up. But he was there. How, why, she didn't know, didn't care. Her world narrowed down to one square foot of pale-green carpet beneath her feet and the feel of him against her.

Noises came from her throat, ugly and raw, as she cried. And, God, she cried. For the little girl who'd never known a mother's proper love; for the loss of her art, snuffed out by the bitter realities of life; for all the promises the man holding her embodied that she'd discarded. Luke said nothing – just wrapped her in his arms and absorbed it all, standing sure.

A quiet cough, the familiar noise of her father clearing his throat, sounded nearby, and she would have raised her head had Luke not stroked his hand over her hair and urged her closer against him. 'Hello, Mr Thorpe,' he said, his deep voice vibrating under her ear. 'I was very sorry to hear about your wife's passing. I thought you both might need some help over the coming days.'

'That's very kind of you, Luke. I must say it's good to see you again. Nee's been doing a wonderful job of sorting things out, but another pair of hands certainly won't go amiss. It . . . it wasn't entirely unexpected, but it's still difficult.' There wasn't even a ripple of surprise in her father's voice, like her estranged husband turning up out of the blue was the most natural thing in the world. That familiar cough of his came again. 'Right, well, I think I'll put the kettle on. Will you have something, Luke?'

'Cup of coffee would be brilliant, thanks, Mr Thorpe.'

'I think we're past time for you to call me George. Coffee's only instant, I'm afraid, we've run out of pods for the machine. Lots of visitors, you see. Everyone's been very kind. Come on through to the kitchen when you're both ready.'

Laughter sputtered through her tears at their exchange of mundane pleasantries, as if she wasn't falling to noisy pieces in front of them. She grabbed for the laugh, tried to hold on to it and bring herself back under control, but now acknowledged the grief wouldn't be denied. Luke pressed a kiss to the top of her head. 'Take all the time you need.' She nodded, all she could manage before the tears swamped her again.

When she finally felt able to lift her face from the now-sodden front of his coat, she'd lost track of time. Limp, exhausted, like she'd cried for a week. Luke tucked a stray strand of hair behind her ear, an infinitely tender gesture, but she couldn't bring herself to meet his eyes. Silence hung between them as he waited her out, broken only by the faint strains of her father whistling along to some classical tune on the radio. China rattled against wood, followed by the metallic clink of cutlery. If her dad was laying the table still, they couldn't have been standing there as long as she'd thought.

Inertia held her in its claws. She should move, step back and at least give Luke a chance to take his coat off. But if she broke the moment, she'd have to deal with all the bitter truths she'd just wept out on his shoulder. That was the trouble with life. It didn't wait for you to catch your breath, didn't care if you were ready or not, it just kept coming at you. *Move. Drop your arms. Take a step back.* Her fingers clung stubbornly to the back of his coat, her feet glued to the spot.

A loud grumble rolled from his midriff, and Luke chuckled as he continued to smooth his hands up and down her back. 'My stomach smells whatever your dad's toasting.'

'Probably crumpets.' She'd made a trip to the supermarket that morning, anything to get out of the house for a little while. They hadn't needed much – mostly refills for the coffee machine, which was the one thing she'd forgotten, of course – so she'd wandered aimlessly up and down the aisles grabbing random things that wouldn't take much thought and even less effort to prepare. She couldn't remember the last time she'd had crumpets, but they'd appealed to her enough to end up in the trolley.

He gave an exaggerated groan. 'Have pity on a man. Next you'll be telling me there's strawberry jam to put on them.'

'You always had such a sweet tooth.' She saw him in her mind's eye, covers pooled at his waist, Sunday papers strewn across the bed as he munched his way through a mountain of jammy toast and endless cups of coffee. His breath whispered against her cheek, and it would be so easy to turn her head, to seek out his lips and pretend the past year had been an aberration. But this wasn't one of those time-slip stories. She couldn't wish herself back to another point in time and tread a different path.

Tasting the bitterness of that truth on the back of her tongue, she stepped back. His arms lingered, a brief resistance to her attempt to retreat before he let her go. And so he should. Luke might be here with the best of intentions, but she didn't deserve the easy comfort of his presence. People didn't just forgive and forget, and even if he believed he was different in that, she wasn't the hopeful girl he'd fallen in love with. 'Let me take your coat, and we'll see what Dad's rustled together for tea.'

He ducked his head, trying to catch her eye, but she fixed her gaze at a point over his shoulder as she held out her hand. Tension filled his frame for a moment, before he released it on a sigh and quickly unbuttoned his coat. She busied herself with hanging it on the row of hooks, fussing at the soggy mess she'd made on the front until he caught her hand and pulled it away. The firm grip on her fingers told her he wasn't about to let go in a hurry, so she chose to ignore the way her palm slotted perfectly into his as she led him down the short hallway.

The gilt-edged frame of a mirror caught her eye, but she ignored that too, knowing she'd see nothing good in it. Her eyes itched, that awful dry-burn that came after too many tears, and the skin around her nose felt raw. Fixing the best smile she could muster on her lips, she entered the kitchen, pausing when she saw the feast laid out on the table. 'Oh, Dad, this looks brilliant.'

George shrugged a little awkwardly. 'It was no bother, and I thought Luke would probably be hungry after his journey.' He turned to Luke who was pulling out the chair next to the one she'd chosen, 'You came up on the train? The service from London is pretty good, I find.' Another attempt by her dad at polite small talk, she assumed, because she might not have seen him for a few years, but he'd always been a creature of habit and trips to the capital weren't something she ever remembered him making.

Luke nodded. 'Euston's pretty easy access for me, too, which helped.' He reached for the mug George held out to him. 'Thanks. Nee's right, this looks great.'

George passed a mug of tea to Nee then took a seat opposite.

'Please, help yourselves. I didn't know what you would want, so I put a bit of everything out.' His smile faltered. 'Everyone's been very generous, we've more food than I know what to do with. If you'd prefer something hot . . .'

He made to stand, but Luke waved the hand already gripping a crumpet at him. 'No, no. This is perfect, honestly.'

Nee added a dash of milk to her tea and watched in silence as the two men filled their plates with a selection of sandwiches, cold meat and, in Luke's case, a slab of fruit cake to go with the crumpet already dripping in jam. He paused, the crumpet inches from his mouth, fixing a determined look on her. 'Eat something.' Order given, and it was most definitely an order, he stuffed about half the crumpet in his mouth and closed his eyes with a happy sigh.

It was on the tip of her tongue to refuse him, a tiny spark of heated indignation breaking through the suffocating weight of sadness blanketing her, but two things stopped her. Firstly, she was bloody starving for the first time in days. Secondly, he'd come when she hadn't known she needed him, when she'd given him no reason to ever want to be near her again.

Helping herself to some fruit and cheese, she ate in silence as Luke told her dad about the newest addition to Aaron and Kiki's family, and the 'surprise' party they'd thrown for his brother the previous month. It sounded like he'd had a great time with everyone, reinforcing her decision to leave Butterfly Cove as the right one, even if it caused a pang of regret at the same time.

He cut himself another slice of fruit cake, adding a thinner piece to her plate at the same time. Raising an eyebrow at his presumptuous action got her little more than a cocky grin in return. Damn him for knowing how much she loved fruit cake – they'd treated themselves to a Fortnum's one as part of their homemade wedding supper. Memories of that day swamped her, bringing the fresh sting of tears to her eyes. His smile faltered and she bit the inside of her cheek to hold back the waterworks. 'I'm okay. Thanks for the cake.'

'I'm being bossy, sorry.' He didn't try too hard to look contrite, whatever his words.

'It's fine.' She didn't examine her own motives for acquiescing so easily. Being taken care of was too bloody nice.

'In that case, when you've finished that, I'll make you another cup of tea and you can take it up to bed with you.'

Give a man an inch . . . 'I'm going to have a bath.' A pathetic little rebellion, but she wouldn't let him push her around too much.

He nodded. 'Fine. Bath, then bed.' She rolled her eyes, but couldn't keep the corner of her mouth from twitching in amusement.

'I think we could all do with an early night,' her father interjected with a slightly desperate attempt at diplomacy. 'There's clean bedding in the airing cupboard so it won't take me two minutes to make up one of the other rooms, unless . . .' George trailed off, colour rising in his cheeks.

Oh. God. He couldn't possibly think she and Luke would be sharing a room, could he? Nee gaped at her father, feeling her own blush heat her skin. Luke surely wouldn't expect it . . .

She didn't dare wait for him to respond. 'I've already made up Kiki's bed ready for tomorrow, but Luke can use Mia's old room.' Her elder sister had decided to stay with Pat and Bill, the parents of her late husband. They remained close and had welcomed Daniel into their family with a graceful ease few possessed. The couple would be spending Christmas with their other children and grandchildren, so Mia wanted to catch up with them whilst she could. Kiki's children were staying home with Madeline and Richard, who had also agreed to look after the couple of artists staying at the studios until Mia and Daniel returned. No one had mentioned Luke to her when they'd been making arrangements, and she wondered whether they even knew he'd shown up. *They'll find out soon enough when they arrive.*

Needing to escape, she pushed back her chair. 'I'll make up the bed whilst my bath is running.'

The bland expression on Luke's face told her nothing. 'Thanks. I'll fetch your tea up in a minute.'

Chapter Six

Luke waited until he could hear the water running upstairs, then stood to clear the table. George rose and began to work beside him silently, although Luke could tell he had something on his mind. He refilled the kettle, wiping down the spaces on the kitchen table as the older man cleared them and bided his time. Now he'd set his mind to things, he had all the patience in the world. Nee was his, until the day she said otherwise, and nothing would stand in the way of that. He'd had a long chat with Mia on the phone before he'd travelled up, and though she'd issued a number of outrageously dire warnings to him, she'd eventually come onboard with his plans.

The kettle bubbled and steamed and the loud click of the automatic cut-off switch set Luke into motion, rinsing their cups out, going through the familiar ritual of tea-making. 'Coffee?' he asked George, with a quick glance across to him.

'Tea, please. I think I'll take it upstairs with me, if you don't mind?' George brushed a few imaginary crumbs off the front of his neatly buttoned cardigan, then set his shoulders in a way that told Luke he'd made up his mind to speak. Abandoning the tea for now, he put his back to the kettle, giving his father-in-law his full attention. Face to face, he could see the girls had inherited their brown eyes from him, as well as a certain stubbornness around the jawline.

George folded his arms with a sigh. 'I'm probably the last man with any rights to behave like a protective father, but I'm going to anyway.' Luke nodded. He'd learned about the difficulties within the Thorpe family over the past year, as neither himself nor Nee had spoken much about their backgrounds during their madcap courtship. 'She's lost all her spark, my poor girl, and I need to know whether that is down to you.'

A reasonable assumption, given all the man knew was that his daughter had walked out on her husband. 'She wasn't like this last summer, I swear. Kiki thinks it's to do with whatever happened in New York. Has Nee said anything to you about it?'

'Not a word. She spent most of her time at the care home, before, you know . . .' A tight, painful expression crossed George's face. 'I went when I could, but I had to sit outside the room to avoid upsetting Vivian, and it didn't seem fair to leave her alone.'

Luke tried to imagine the agony of it, especially for someone as self-contained as George. The excruciating embarrassment as people speculated and gossiped about the man who couldn't even enter his wife's room. 'I'm very sorry for your loss.' Such inane, pathetic words, but they were all he had.

George shook his head. 'It's a relief, truth be told, and my soul be damned for saying so. We were never suited, though I loved her once. Love's not enough, though. Not if you don't know how to take proper care of each other. I wanted her all to myself, and Vivian was always such a social butterfly. I held her too tightly, crushed her wings.' A shudder rippled through the older man's frame and he raised a hand to cover his face briefly. 'My therapist says I need to be more open about things, but it's never come naturally to me. I was raised in a household where one didn't, you see.'

Luke blinked at the idea of George seeking therapy, and hoped none of his surprise showed on his face. The older man took a deep breath, then raised his head. 'My Eirênê's happiness is more important than my own discomfort, though, so I'll elicit a promise from you, here and now. If you can't help bring the fire back into my daughter, you must let her go. For both your sakes.'

He spoke sense. Luke might believe he and Nee were meant to be, but if the connection between them had broken irrevocably, they'd be doomed to repeat the mistakes of the past. He'd said as much to Aaron when they'd talked late into the night after his birthday party, but damn it, he wasn't giving up without a fight. 'Give me until the New Year.' If his plans for Christmas didn't work out, he doubted anything would.

George nodded. 'Thank you for hearing me out, and for coming here today. I hope you have more luck in figuring things out than I ever did. Now, I think I'll take my tea and get out of your hair.'

Breakfast the next morning was an easier affair than the previous night's meal. The radio was tuned to Radio Four and Luke flicked through one of the two daily newspapers that had been delivered, whilst George hid behind the other. Nee looked better – whether from the cathartic release of her tears or just a decent night's sleep, it relieved him to note the dark circles under her eyes had faded somewhat. There was still something off about her, but he couldn't put his finger on it. She chatted to them both about the day's plans, deciding which of the many meals in the freezer could be combined to feed everyone once Kiki and Aaron arrived that afternoon.

He watched her flip back and forth through a notebook, double-checking the arrangements for the funeral, and George's measured responses to her questions were in marked contrast to his agonised tone the night before. The spiky blonde cut she'd sported during the summer had begun to grow out, softening around her face. She reached up to brush impatiently at the full fringe when it fell into her eyes, only for it to slip straight back into place again. A good inch or more of dark roots showed, giving a glimpse of the rich brown colour he thought suited her better than the harsh bleach job. Not that he would say anything. She could dye it pink as a baboon's arse for all he cared – she'd still be beautiful to him.

Her pen tap-tap-tapped on the notebook, and the missing piece tumbled into his brain. Frowning, he glanced around. *It had to be there somewhere . . .*

'Lost something?'

Startled, he met Nee's curious gaze. 'Where's your sketchbook?' In the time they'd been together, the battered A3 spiral-bound book had never been more than a couple of inches from her hand.

The colour drained from her face and the tap-tap-tap of her pen ramped up to machine-gun speed. 'I've not really been in the mood to draw.'

Not in the mood? Art was an extension of Nee's very being, an essential component of her make-up. George curled one corner of his newspaper down to stare at Luke across the table. His expression was shielded from Nee, but Luke read the shock in it loud and clear. Making a mental note to have a quiet word with Kiki when she arrived, he shrugged in what he hoped was a casual manner. 'You've had a lot on your plate lately, so that's not surprising.' God, he couldn't lie for shit. Hastily changing the subject, he grabbed his plate and mug. 'Anyone need another drink?'

'Coffee, please, if you're making one,' George said, still nose-deep in his paper.

Nee shook her head as she started paging through her notebook again. 'Not for me. So, just family flowers, and the vicar will make an announcement about donations for the Alzheimer's Society.'

They'd already covered the point not five minutes before, but George responded as though it was something new, his voice patient as they discussed the wording on the back of the Order of Service handouts, which had already been delivered to the funeral director for distribution. On and on, she chattered like a magpie and Luke forced himself to keep clearing away the breakfast things, keeping busy, keeping his jaw clenched to hold back the words bubbling on the back of his tongue.

His self-lauded patience hadn't returned by the time he'd loaded the dishwasher and handed George his coffee. With a quick glance out of the window, he folded the tea towel into a neat square and placed it on the board beside the sink. 'If you don't need me for anything just now, I'm going out for a run.'

Nee kept her eyes on her notes, so it was George who answered him. 'I think we're all set for now. If you turn left at the end of the street, it'll take you onto Park Road. You should see the entrance a few hundred yards further on. We should still be here when you get back, but there's a spare key in the top drawer of the bureau in the hallway, help yourself.'

Luke nodded his thanks and headed out of the kitchen. Glancing back over his shoulder proved a mistake. The sight of Nee hunched almost into a ball as she diligently scribbled in her notebook clawed at his guts. There was something seriously wrong with her, and he was going to get to the bottom of it before he returned to London. Pushing her now would be for his own selfish benefit. He could hold his tongue for a couple more days, let her hang on to whatever bit of strength she had to get through the funeral first. Forcing his feet to keep moving, he jogged upstairs to get changed, hoping the bitter November cold would help temper the anger roaring inside him.

Vivian's funeral was about as awful as his somewhat limited experience had led him to expect. Poor Mia had turned up looking whiter than Nee's hair and as miserable as a kicked puppy. Daniel muttered something about a flu bug and kept her tucked close into his side throughout the service. They'd left the wake after less than an hour, and it had surprised everyone, except probably his brother, when Kiki had taken charge of proceedings in her absence.

Luke had been set to work making endless pots of tea and coffee, whilst Aaron manned the drinks cabinet, offering sherry or port to those who wanted to take the chill off after an hour in the freezing church. The enticing aroma of mulled wine bubbling from a large saucepan soon filled the air and a noticeable increase in conversational volume soon followed. Nee had been put on sandwich duty, although that involved little more than unwrapping and setting out the trays delivered that morning by a local catering company.

Returning from his latest round of refills, he paused by the hob to lean over Kiki's shoulder and inhale the rich red wine and zesty orange fragrance rising from the pan. 'Smells amazing. Everyone seems happy enough, next door. If you keep spoiling them with treats like this, we'll never get rid of them.'

She glanced up at him, a sad smile upon her face. 'I need to keep busy, and the company seems to be doing Dad good.'

He nodded and squeezed her shoulder. 'I get it, Kiki, really. You might want to take a break and rescue Aaron, though. Mrs Hardy from next door has taken a shine to him, or maybe it's the sherry bottle. Either way, he was looking a bit hemmed in.'

Kiki laughed, as he'd intended. 'I'll just get this transferred into some jugs and then go and see.'

'Here, let me.' He stepped in, lifting the heavy pan before she could do it, following her careful direction as he poured it into a couple of large ceramic jugs Kiki had set out on two trays together with a selection of mugs.

'Can you do outside, if I take the other tray next door?' she asked.

He glanced out the window. 'Sure.' A few hardy types had escaped the crowded confines of the house for the kitchen patio, and it was difficult to tell who amongst them were the smokers from the way everyone's breath frosted in the air. Spotting a lone figure at the far end of the garden, he set his jaw. 'I'll just get my coat.'

Shrugging into his dark wool overcoat, he made sure to grab

the silver-coloured down jacket hanging next to it and tucked it under his arm. A slap of cold air hit his face the second he stepped outside the back door, and he muttered imprecations about foolish bloody women under his breath. The tray of mulled wine was greeted with enthusiasm by the occupants of the patio, and he set it on a small, wrought-iron table and left them to sort themselves out. Growing more annoyed with every step, he marched down the neat flagstone path.

'Put this on, you'll catch your bloody death.' He thrust the jacket at Nee, who was visibly shivering from the cold. 'What the hell are you playing . . .' The words died on his lips at the look of utter desolation on her face. Bundling her into the coat like a small child, he zipped it up to her chin, then tugged the faux fur-lined hood up for good measure. 'What is it, sweetheart? What's wrong?' *Apart from the bloody obvious, of course.* 'Is it your mum?' He chafed his hands up and down her arms, trying to get her warmed up as quickly as possible.

She shook her head. 'I just needed to get out of the house. One of Dad's former colleagues from the university asked when my next exhibition was going to be, and I didn't know what to tell him.' She laughed, and there was more than an edge of hysteria to it. 'I couldn't tell him the truth, could I?'

Luke slid his hands up her arms to cup her shoulders, keeping her facing him when she would have otherwise turned away. 'And what truth is that?' He kept his voice whisper-quiet.

'That there isn't going to be one. That there's no more art, not now, not ever!' It was as he'd suspected, though her admission still shocked him.

He pulled her unresisting body closer. 'Talk to me, darling. Let me help you.'

A strangled laugh escaped her throat, but she snuggled closer into his chest. 'Why on earth would you want to?'

'You're my wife, Nee. We might have rushed into things, but I wasn't messing around when I exchanged those vows with you.'

'Ah, God. You're determined to make me feel worse than I already do! You owe me no loyalty and even less consideration for the way I walked out on you.'

'You had your reasons, I'm sure.' With her tucked into his shoulder, he didn't have to hide the clench in his jaw. He hoped, whatever they were, he could forgive her as much as his heart wanted to.

'I was horribly selfish. And stupid.' She sighed.

'Yes, and maybe. I'll reserve judgement until I know more.' Her shocked laugh lifted his hopes.

'It made sense at the time, or perhaps I just needed to convince myself it did . . .' Her voice trailed off towards the end, as though talking more to herself than him.

Damn, she was more cryptic than the Sunday crossword. Having first sworn to himself he didn't care why she'd left, he was now painfully desperate to know – it had to have been more than a simple change of heart. *Or maybe that was his pride speaking.* It was one of the possibilities his talk with Aaron had raised; Nee saying it had been a mistake to leave could have referred to the manner in which she'd done it.

Spotting an old wooden bench under the leafless branches of a tree, he loosened his hold on Nee and led her towards it. Testing the wood, he found it cold-damp rather than truly wet and, tucking his coat beneath his legs, settled himself on one end of it. She sat beside him, not close enough for his liking, but he didn't get chance to slide closer before she popped back onto her feet and began to pace. 'That bloody email . . .' she muttered.

'Email?'

'You don't understand, Luke! I'd given up all hope of hearing from them and there it was, completely out of the blue. He made me choose, and when it comes to working at the Reinhold, there is no choice. Not if you want to be taken seriously. I tried!' The words tumbled from her lips, her tone as agitated as the way she stalked up and down before him.

Tucking his hands into his pockets so he wouldn't reach out and drag her down beside him, Luke tried to fathom his way through what she was telling him. 'When did you get the email?'

She threw her hands up, a gesture of pure frustration. 'That's what I'm trying to tell you! It came through that evening. You'd fallen asleep, after . . . well, you know . . .' Her cheeks flushed, and he swallowed a smile. Their wedding celebrations had been somewhat enthusiastic. Images floated through his mind of champagne-infused kisses, but he dragged himself back as she continued to speak. 'I couldn't sleep so I was just fiddling around on my phone, and there it was. He told me I had a place, and my flight was leaving first thing in the morning.'

'He who?' Luke didn't realise he'd said it out loud until her head snapped up.

'Devin.' So much nuance packed into a single word. Awe, fear, more than a little disgust. He racked his brain trying to recall what he'd read about the Institute during his Google search. He had a vague recollection of an older guy appearing in several photos with A-list celebrities. He couldn't picture a face, per se, more an impression of the kind of perfect white teeth you only got in America, and a rather bouffant hairdo.

She heaved a sigh, a deep breath that shuddered her entire frame. 'He played me from the start, I see that now. I messaged straight back, explained we were literally just married, and he cut me off. Said he was sorry he'd made a mistake in thinking I was serious about my art and withdrew the offer instantly. I . . .' She turned her back to him, leaving him with no way to see her expression thanks to the deep hood of her coat.

When she spoke again, her voice was so soft he had to lean forward to catch her words. 'I panicked. Begged him to reconsider, told him working at the Reinhold, studying beneath his guidance, was my dream. I . . . I told him I'd do anything for a second chance, and he said the only way to get him to change his mind was to prove my commitment to my art. He said he wasn't interested in silly girls in love. He wanted serious creatives who had no room for anything in their hearts other than expressing the truth in art.' She huffed out a breath. 'Pretentious bastard.'

Luke had to agree. The guy sounded like a complete arsehole, and not just because he finally had a target for his own hurts and disappointment. Hearing her say it, the admission from her own mouth she'd made a choice and he'd been on the losing side, hurt. Jesus, did it hurt. Like a knife in his guts, and he didn't know in that moment if he had it in him to put that pain aside and give her a fair hearing. He enjoyed his job, had certain ambitions for his career, but it didn't set his soul on fire. One of the things about Nee that had drawn him to her had been her absolute passion for art.

Trying to put himself in her shoes for a moment, he wondered whether, backed into a corner as she seemed to have been, he wouldn't have done the same thing. He shook his head. He'd never really know. Bracing himself, he asked the one question that might sink his hopes for ever. 'Is that the only reason you left me?'

She whipped around, her hood falling back in the process, and he could see the tracks of fresh tears on her cheeks. 'What?'

He swallowed the taste of bile from the back of his tongue. That wasn't an emphatic denial, and he had to know. 'Was the ultimatum the only reason?'

64

Chapter Seven

Nee glanced down at the thin-soled black shoes she was wearing. Tracing a pattern back and forth in the frost-white grass, she kept her eyes averted. 'I got scared,' she admitted. 'Scared I would grow to resent you if I didn't go; scared we'd rushed into things, that we didn't really know each other well enough to make such a big commitment. The more I thought about it, the more I convinced myself the email was a sign.'

She made herself look up, though it was a struggle to meet his eyes, to be honest with him, and with herself. 'I was just making excuses, though, trying to justify my decision.' God, this was so hard. Why was he putting them both through it, when it wouldn't make any difference? It was too late; what was done was done. In coming to support her, he'd only managed to drive home how much she didn't deserve him. It was why, even after she'd fled New York, she hadn't dared approach him. He needed to move on, to find someone who could love him unconditionally, someone who would protect that big, generous heart of his, not trample it into the dirt.

Needing to put an end to the conversation, Nee shoved her freezing hands into her pockets. 'I'm cold. I'm going to go in.'

He stood immediately, putting paid to any hopes she had of

an easy escape. 'I shouldn't have kept you out here so long. We can continue this inside.'

Shaking her head, she backed away from him. 'There's no point in continuing, Luke. This isn't going to get us anywhere.'

A stubborn frown shadowed his dark eyes. 'Don't keep running away from me. You haven't told me what happened in New York.'

No, she hadn't, and she intended for it to stay that way. He already thought badly enough of her as it was. 'That's because it's none of your business. Not any more.'

He reached for her. 'You're still my wife, Nee.'

'Only on paper, Luke. It's over. We're over.' Shards of pain stabbed beneath her ribcage, as though her heart had shattered into pieces and the splinters dug into her flesh.

'Do you still love me?'

'My feelings for you are irrelevant. I appreciate what you've done for me, Luke. Coming here, supporting me when I needed it. I can never repay your kindness.'

Luke made a chopping motion with his hand, cutting her off. 'Stop it! I'm not one of the bloody neighbours you can dismiss with pleasantries. Answer the damn question.'

Frustration welled inside her and she balled her hands into fists. 'Yes, of course I bloody love you. I've never stopped loving you, and probably never will. That's not the point!'

Hard hands grabbed her arms, dragging her forward until she tipped off balance and fell against his chest. His mouth crashed down onto hers, in a fierce kiss that curled her numb toes. Taking advantage of her gasp of shock, Luke slipped his tongue between her lips, sending sparks shooting through her numb limbs. She grabbed for his shoulders, intending to regain her footing and push him away, but somehow her fingers ended up clenched tight into the wool of his coat.

The kiss went on and on, robbing her oxygen, her ability to think, erasing the litany of reasons why this was a terrible idea. When he finally let her come up for air, she tried to gather her

66

scattered wits. For the first time in months, the terrible ache inside her faded. The heat in his brown eyes chased all thoughts of the cold from her mind, and a tender smile teased at the corners of his lips. His head dipped forward, lashes lowering, indicating his intention to deliver another of those brain-scrambling kisses. She turned her head, intent on avoiding his mouth, not realising her mistake until his soft lips began to nibble along the edge of her jaw and down inside the neckline of her jacket. 'Luke . . .'

'Shh,' he murmured against the side of her throat. 'You talk too much.'

Her laugh ended on a breathy sigh. 'You were the one who wanted to talk.'

'I changed my mind. This is much more fun.' God, how she'd missed his cheeky humour, the easy, teasing banter between them that came as easily as breathing. Her fingers crept into the curls gathered at the nape of his neck and she pressed him closer, just for a second, before tugging at his hair until he lifted his head. He gave her the full effect of his puppy-dog eyes. 'You're going to ruin the moment, aren't you?'

'This doesn't change anything, you know.' No matter how much she might want it to.

The gentle humour in his eyes disappeared in a flash. 'You love me. You've admitted it not just in words, but in the way you kissed me just now. I love you too, so bloody much. I've been in hell this past year without you. There's nothing stopping us from being together . . .' His arms around her back slackened. 'Unless there's somebody else.' A look of suspicion crept into his eyes. 'It's that guy you mentioned, isn't it? Devin Whatsisface.'

A wash of guilt flowed through her, ridiculous given the circumstances, but she couldn't help it. 'Not in the way you think.'

His hold tightened. 'I don't know what to think with all your cryptic shit. Just tell me what the hell happened in New York!'

Pulling free, she paced away to the end of the garden. He wasn't going to let it go, that much was clear. The gnarled branches of the trees stood stark against the washed-out grey sky, reaching towards her like twisted fingers ready to drag her back to the worst night of her life. *Courage, Nee.* She'd been picking around the edges for too long; it was time to rip the top off the festering scab and see how bad the wound really was.

'From the moment I arrived, he dictated my every move. There was a strict schedule to be followed, because he had a show to prepare for. I spent most of my waking hours in the studio, which wouldn't have been too bad if I'd been allowed to work on my own projects, but we had to focus entirely on stuff for the show. From painting backdrops to days recreating hand sculptures from designs he sketched out for me.' She laughed. 'All those rich Manhattan folks coughing up a small fortune for one of his pieces and they're lucky if he did more than dip it in the glaze bucket.'

Warmth blanketed her back, and she allowed herself to lean into the strength of Luke's body as the memories swirled before her unseeing eyes. 'He's a master of the entire medium, that's what sets him above the rest of us. From throwing, to hand-shaping, to slip-casting, most of us are adept at one method above the others, but not Devin. Or so I believed, along with everyone else. That's how he chooses his students, though. Each one of us specialises in different methods so he can pass off our work as his own. He says it doesn't matter, that people are buying his "concept", his "vision" and no one challenges him because, once you've worked under him, your own price tag goes up.'

Luke's voice sounded soft against her ear. 'So, no one says anything and he keeps getting away with it.'

She nodded. 'Exactly. Anyone who spoke out would be easily dismissed as jealous, or lacking in talent. Who's going to listen to some no-name beginner over the great Devin Rees?' As she'd found out for herself.

Memories surged, carrying her back to that dizzying, crazy time. 'And when you're not in the studio, you're at a party in his loft surrounded by celebrities and critics, or attending premieres and restaurant openings, or whatever event needs a bit of the Devin Rees magic sprinkled on it to make it special. I don't think I slept a full night for two months straight. We finally got everything ready for the exhibition, and he promised me it was time to look at my own stuff. I was so excited . . .' Nee took a deep breath, letting the cold air brace her for the next part.

'I should have suspected something was wrong when I walked in and the lights were low. I even made a joke about the candlelight, and believed him when he said he needed something soothing after so many days in the harsh lights of the studio. That didn't explain the wine sitting in an ice bucket, though, or the music playing in the background. The fact it was just the two of us, alone in his private space. All those seminars at uni about being aware of your surroundings and looking for hints or triggers, and I waltzed right in. I knew something was off, but I didn't want to blow my big chance at finally getting started on *my* art.' God, she'd been such a bloody idiot.

Luke's arm curled across the front of her shoulders, holding her to his chest as he whispered against her hair. 'Oh, Nee.'

She could have stopped there. It was obvious from his tone he understood enough of what was coming next. She'd never told anyone, though; not let herself really think about it since the final humiliation of the following morning. Just let it squat in the corner of her mind like some poisonous toad. 'When I asked him where Amber was, he told me she had a book-club meeting and would be back later.'

'Amber?'

'His wife. A Glamazon ex-model with a successful fashion line.' A bitter laugh caught in her throat. 'You can trust the married ones, right? Anyway, he handed me a glass of wine and then took my portfolio off me and started to go through it. That was the thing that let me relax. He barely glanced at me, kept all his focus on my work, asking questions, pushing me to talk about what I wanted to do next. Talking's thirsty work, and before I knew it, my glass was empty. He offered a second one, and when I asked for a glass of water instead, he fetched it straightaway.' A cynical realisation struck her. It was so she couldn't even accuse him of trying to get her drunk.

'You don't have to . . .' Luke's voice trailed off as she raised her hand to grip his arm where it crossed her chest.

'I do. For me.' She felt him nod against her cheek. 'It got really hot. I remember that much, and then it's pretty hazy. The next clear memory I have is waking up in only my T-shirt and pants in an unfamiliar bedroom.' Her voice hitched and she had to wait a few seconds before she could continue. 'I was on my own and the rest of my clothes were folded on a chair by the bed. When I sat up, the room started spinning and I thought I might be sick. When I finally felt well enough to get dressed and leave the room, he was sitting on the sofa like nothing had happened.

'He asked me if I was feeling better; said I'd had some kind of dizzy spell and asked to lie down for a bit. It sounded plausible enough, but I knew something wasn't right and I just wanted to get out of there. He offered to call me a cab, but I said I'd get one on the street. He lives in the heart of Manhattan; you can't walk two feet without seeing one. I got my coat and left, and it wasn't until I was in the taxi that I realised two things – I'd forgotten my portfolio, and I wasn't wearing my bra.'

Nee closed her eyes, catapulted back to that confusing journey home. The smell of old fried food from a crumpled wrapper on the floor, the constant drone of the driver's monologue about a recent political debate, the bile she'd swallowed back over and over as she prayed for the cab to just get her home. The knowledge that something bad lurked behind the black hole in her memory. 'It wasn't with the rest of my clothes on the pile, and the logistics of taking my bra off, putting my T-shirt back on and folding my clothes so neatly when I was out of it just didn't ring true. I still felt really woozy and could hardly drag myself up the stairs to my apartment when I got home. I woke up late the next morning face down on top of my bed, still dressed, with the worst headache I've ever had in my entire life.'

She'd had a shower, checked every inch of herself, but hadn't found anything beyond a strange bruise on her left hip and a scratch across her lower back. With an aching void in the evening's timeline, she hadn't known what to think. 'The phone rang, and the administrator from the Institute asked me to come in and see her immediately. I tried to call Devin, but his phone went straight to voicemail. When I walked into the administrator's office, he was already there, with Amber.'

The tears started then: ugly, shuddering sobs that shook her body. When Luke led her over to the bench, she crawled onto his lap and let him rock her as the shock and humiliation of that encounter rose as hot and fresh as if it had happened only yesterday. After the worst of it was over, she managed to tell him the rest. How Devin had sat there hand in hand with Amber, sympathy in his eyes as he told her he'd done his best to shield her, but after Amber had found her bra under a cushion he'd had no choice but to tell the truth. With an absolutely straight face, he'd told the administrator she'd turned up uninvited, and acting strangely, like she'd been drunk or taken some pills. How he'd gone to fetch her a glass of water only to return to find her almost naked and tried to fight her off without hurting her.

On and on, he'd woven a web of lies and half-truths whilst she'd squirmed under the accusing glare of Amber and the disappointed frown of the administrator. Then Amber had started on her. Telling her how sick she was of starstruck young girls misinterpreting his naturally caring nature for something else. How embarrassed she was for Nee for making such a fool of herself. How she couldn't believe Nee would betray the friendship and support both Amber and Devin had offered her. They'd left the room after Amber started crying, and the administrator had taken over. Said if Nee resigned from her placement and

71

left immediately, Devin had agreed to withhold his harassment complaint against her. Unless she could provide an alternative explanation for her actions.

'And that's when I knew, that this wasn't the first time. That I wasn't the first one this had happened to. But what could I tell her? I didn't know what had happened, had no physical proof he'd done anything other than put me to bed. The bruise and scratch could have been from when he claimed to have fought off my advances. It was my word against his. And why would a man married to a gorgeous, successful woman like Amber look twice at some bony little thing like me?'

Luke's arms tightened around her. 'You're gorgeous, Nee, the most beautiful girl in the world and he's a low-down dirty bastard. I could kill him.' The fierceness in his voice cut through her misery. He sounded furious, but not with her.

'I was so ashamed, I just wanted to get out of there, so I kept quiet. The administrator said I could keep the rest of that quarter's allowance and suggested I use it for a plane ticket home. So that's what I did. I spent the next few weeks dossing on the floor at a friend's place, until she started to get serious with her boyfriend. I found a cheap bedsit, picked up a couple of part-time jobs, and basically drifted.'

'You should have come to me.' Luke still sounded pissed off.

'And said what? Sorry I dumped you for the sake of my career. I've totally screwed that up so, hey, wanna try again?' She leaned her head against his shoulder. Lord knew, she'd had exactly that conversation in her mind a dozen times or more. It had been unthinkable, though, an act of utter hubris. 'Besides, I thought you'd moved on.'

He sat up, almost knocking her off his lap with the suddenness of his movement, and she took the opportunity to slide onto the bench beside him. Being held in his arms felt too good, and she couldn't keep indulging herself in his comfort like that. Turning sideways on the bench, he stared at her. 'What made you think I'd moved on?'

She ducked her head. Damn, she'd said too much. She might not have been able to summon the courage to go and see him, but it hadn't stopped her from visiting places they'd frequented together, hoping to catch a glimpse, to at least convince herself he was okay. Only, she'd got more than she bargained for. Squeezing her eyes shut against the squirm of embarrassment, she forced herself to confess. 'I saw you last Christmas, in The George. You were with a woman with red hair and I saw you kissing.'

'Christ, Nee! It *was* you! I drove myself half-mad thinking I was seeing you here and there.' Luke scrubbed his face with his hands. 'The woman you saw was just someone from work. I was lonely and feeling absolutely crap about everything so I agreed to go for a drink with her. They'd pinned a sprig of mistletoe above the bar and she made a joke about it and kissed me. It was something and nothing. The moment our lips touched, I knew there was no point in leading her on because I wasn't interested.' He shook his head, a bleakness in his eyes that made her want to flinch away from it. 'She wasn't you.'

'Luke . . .' If he kept this up he was going to break her heart, break his own again in the process. He still didn't get it. He loved Nee Thorpe, passionate artist, a woman full of hopes and dreams. He didn't understand she was just a husk, a woman who'd spent most of the past year serving lunchtime drinks in a rundown pub and clearing up rubbish in theatre stalls in the West End in the evenings.

She'd hoped a change of scene would do her good, that spending time with Mia would help her to heal, especially when she'd seen the incredible studios Daniel had created. Her hands ached at the memory of sinking into a fresh block of clay, the blinding fear as her fingers sank deeper into the thick brown mass whilst her mind remained blank and empty. 'There's nothing left of the woman you knew. I'm broken.'

'Is that it? Is that the best reason you've got for giving up on us?' Luke shook his head. 'Not good enough, darling.'

Frustrated, she jumped to her feet and jammed her hands on her hips. It might have had more effect had she not been wearing a shiny, silver puffa jacket. Her fingers sank into the quilted material making her look like a miniature version of the Michelin Man. 'What the bloody hell is it that you want from me?'

Sitting forward on the bench, he rested his elbows on his knees and fixed his hot-chocolate eyes upon on. 'I want you to fight for us, Nee. I want you to get some help, find someone to talk to about everything you've just told me. Get some proper support to deal with what that bastard did to you.' He took a breath and softened his tone. 'You can talk to me, of course, as much as you need to, and I'll do my damnedest not to let my feelings get in the way. Right now, I want to jump on a plane and hunt the fucker down, which wouldn't help at all.'

Such a threat of violence probably shouldn't have comforted her, but it did. She gave him a small smile. 'It might.'

Luke laughed, then sobered again. 'I had a bit of a chat with Aaron because I was feeling all messed up about you. It helped me a lot. Have you talked to Kiki or Mia about what happened?'

She shook her head. 'I wouldn't know where to start.' Wouldn't know what they might think about it, might be closer to the truth.

He stood, watching her warily as he might a frightened animal. When she didn't move, he closed the distance between them. 'Same as you did with me, sweetheart. One word at a time.' His thumb brushed her cheek. 'You didn't judge Kiki when she talked about her ex, did you?'

'Of course not!' He didn't reply, didn't need to, the *well then* expression on his face said enough. Needing to think about it a bit more, she changed the subject. 'Putting everything else aside, how do you suggest we make a go of things? I can't just up and move in with you again. We already did that and made a hash of it. We're not the same people we were a year ago, Luke. I wasn't joking when I said I was broken.'

She might have hoped to catch him off-guard, but the gentle

smile quirking his lips told her he'd already thought about it. 'Christmas. I want you to spend Christmas with me, as my wife. Let me love you again, Nee. Come back to Butterfly Cove, and maybe I can help you put the pieces back together.'

It sounded so good, so tempting. A dream she'd longed for, but feared was for ever out of her reach. 'My art's gone, Luke. And I don't know how to live without it.' She choked on the last words, but swallowed back the tears. There'd been more than enough self-pity already.

'Look at Daniel. His art nearly destroyed him, but he found a way back. With your sister's help. You don't have to do this on your own, Nee. You've punished yourself enough, don't you think?' His soft words stunned her. Had that been what she was doing? She didn't know any more.

'Christmas. I can't promise you anything more than that. And you must promise me, if it doesn't work out between us, you'll let it go. You'll let me go.'

He closed the tiny gap between them, drawing her into the too-delicious warmth of his embrace. 'I promise.' She wasn't sure she believed him, was even less sure she wanted to, whatever happened.

Kiki folded the tea towel she'd been using to dry the last of the glasses. 'Are you sure that's what you want?'

Using a cloth to wipe the soap suds off the edge of the sink, Nee shrugged. She hadn't quite plucked up the courage to raise the subject of Devin, but had mentioned to her about Luke's request to spend Christmas with him. 'I don't know what I want, only that this is more than I ever expected him to offer me and I have to try.' Luke and Aaron were doing their best to persuade the last stragglers to leave, but a couple of their dad's former colleagues seemed determined to make the most of their access to the drinks cabinet.

Footsteps sounded on the tiles, and she turned, hoping to see Luke with the last few glasses, only to be faced instead with a florid-cheeked man whose name she'd forgotten, but not the lingering, damp handshake he'd given her when they'd greeted the mourners after the service. 'Ah, this is where you're hiding, Kiki.'

Nee caught the stiffness in her sister's shoulders, but there was no trace of strain as she stepped forward and smiled. 'Hello, Giles, not hiding, just busy behind the scenes.' *Giles.* The name prompted Nee's memory. Her father had introduced him as the provost at the university.

'Yes, of course. Well, I must say you're looking well, all things considered.' Nee didn't like the greasy edge to the man's smile, and instinct made her move to Kiki's side.

Kiki tilted her head to one side. 'And what things have you been considering, Giles? The unfortunate death of my alcoholic mother, or my recent divorce from an abusive, cheating husband?'

Nee wasn't sure who gaped the most, herself or the provost, whose jaw dropped almost to his chest. She turned towards Kiki, who regarded her with one coolly raised eyebrow. Damn. This was a whole new confident Kiki, nothing like the timid, quiet girl who'd let people ride roughshod over her to avoid making a fuss. A fierce pride filled Nee, and she flashed her sister an approving grin.

The provost shook his head and did his best to recover his equilibrium. 'Forgive me, I meant no offence. I . . . I had no idea.'

Kiki folded her arms. 'I don't know what explanation Neil gave, and I don't much care. I'm just glad to be free of him. You might consider reminding him about the university's policy on fraternisation, though.'

'Indeed. Well, if you will excuse me, ladies, I must just say goodbye to your father.' In a flurry of flustered tweed, the provost took to his heels.

'Who are you, and what have you done with my sister?' Nee kept her tone light, but didn't try to hide the admiration she felt.

Colour spotted on Kiki's delicate cheekbones, proving some things about her hadn't changed. 'Oh, I know that was rude, but

I couldn't help myself. He always was a patronising git. I talked to Aaron on the journey up about what I would do if one of dad's cronies started digging for dirt, and I swore I would just ignore it, but when it came down to it, I couldn't. It's not my shame to bear. Goodness knows the problems in our marriage weren't entirely one-sided, but I did nothing to deserve the way Neil treated me. I covered things up for too long.'

'I thought you were brilliant, Kiki Dee.' Nee slipped her arms around her sister's waist and gave her a hug. 'I'm so glad you're here.'

Kiki pressed a kiss to her cheek. 'I'm always here, darling, and Mia would say the same.' She pulled back to cup Nee's face. 'I hope you and Luke can work things out, but there's no pressure from us. You're our sister, first, last, and always, and nothing will change that.'

Tears prickled the back of her eyes. 'Thank you. I've missed you all so much, and I'm so tired of trying on my own. Christmas with everyone around sounds like more than I deserve, but everything I need.'

'Then we'll do everything we can to make it the best Christmas ever.'

If she wanted things to work out, she would have to do what Luke had asked and fight for them. And that would mean trying to deal with the emotional fallout of what she'd been through. Screwing up her courage, Nee crossed the kitchen and closed the door to ensure they wouldn't be disturbed. 'I need to talk to you. It's . . . it's about what happened whilst I was in New York . . .'

Chapter Eight

'So, as everyone's going to be arriving at different times, we're agreed that a buffet for Christmas Eve is the most practical option.' Mia Fitzwilliams looked up from her newest project book and glanced at Kiki then Madeline. The two women nodded, making notes of their own. With less than a week until the festivities were due to start, the three of them were meeting to finalise menus and put together shopping lists. Their male counterparts had been dispatched to source the trees and decorations. Multiple trees had been her husband's idea – three months married and her heart still thrilled whenever she thought of Daniel that way. It had been a long time since he'd been able to enjoy a family Christmas, and she swore he was more excited than her nephew and niece. They'd already ordered a real tree, which would take pride of place in the corner of the dining room, but he'd persuaded her a couple of artificial trees for the sitting rooms would be nice. And, in truth, she hadn't taken much persuading. She'd missed out on enough of her own special family holidays to be excited about creating something magical for everyone. 'Go big, or go home' had been their agreed motto.

'Daniel spoke to Maggie this morning and she's definitely joining us.' Her husband didn't have any living relations, and the woman who'd helped him establish his photography career by hosting an early show at her gallery was the closest thing he had to family. She'd been delighted to be included, which only proved Mia's instincts had been right to ask her. The only people missing would be her former in-laws. Pat and Bill would leave a hole in their group, but Jamie's brothers and their children had first claim on their time at such a special time of the year. At least they would be joining them to ring in the New Year.

She placed a tick beside Maggie's name on the list. 'So that takes us up to . . .' Mia stared up at the ceiling as she mentally counted off her list. *Kiki, Aaron and the kids is four, Madeline and Richard, Dad, Maggie, the Spensers, us and Luke and Nee.* ' . . .Fourteen?'

Kiki winced at the number. 'Are you sure you want to do this, Mimi? We can have Brian and Cathy at the cottage if you'd prefer.' *Bless her for trying to sound enthusiastic at the prospect.* Things were still a bit fragile between Aaron and his stepmother, although, from what Kiki said, they'd both been making a real effort. They'd been added to the Christmas group after a successful weekend visit recently. Mia had offered to put them up at Butterfly Cove because she had the room, the guest house being closed for the winter. She also hoped it would take the pressure off Kiki and Aaron, who were still negotiating the early stages of their relationship.

'It's fine. More than fine, and it'll give you all a bit of breathing space should you need it.' She tapped the end of her pen against her lips, wondering if she should put voice to her biggest concern. She was beginning to regret going along with Luke's madcap plan. Only he would think the two of them trying to reunite in front of both their families would be a good idea. She sighed. 'Besides, if we keep your spare room free, it gives us an option for Nee.'

'Oh, good point.' Mia's concerns were mirrored in her sister's gaze.

'Come on, you two, where's your sense of romance? I think our Luke's plan is marvellous. Anyone with eyes in their head could see the two of them were smitten with each other at the wedding.' Madeline sipped her tea, then grinned at them both. 'Although you were both somewhat distracted, come to think of it.'

Mia laughed. Much as she'd promised herself that she would catalogue each and every moment of her wedding day, it had passed in a blur of love and laughter. Rather than a home movie, she had mental snapshots of specific moments – the look on Daniel's face when she'd stepped up beside him; her tiny Wonder Woman bridesmaid cartwheeling across the garden; Richard and Madeline putting them all to shame on the dance floor when Luke's playlist hit a Sixties medley; the tremble in Daniel's fingers when he'd unbuttoned the back of her dress.

And Kiki, of course. Going from confusion, to shock, to incandescent happiness when Aaron declared his love for her in front of everyone. She smiled to herself. The Spenser men had a thing for grand gestures.

A wave of heat and nausea wiped the smile off her face. She'd picked up a flu bug the last few days, and couldn't seem to shake it. Daniel had nagged her to make an appointment to see the doctor before he'd left that morning, but she didn't see the point. It was winter and people got coughs, colds and lots of other nasty bugs. Once things settled down a bit and she had a chance to catch up on her sleep, she'd be right as rain.

They'd been so busy it was no wonder she felt rundown, and her mother's death had knocked her more than she'd expected it to. She'd found her face wet with tears more than once in the month since the funeral. Taking time to rest had been out of the question. She and Daniel had been flat-out, clearing and closing up the studios for the winter. Once the final guest had departed from the guest house, she'd moved straight on to giving all the rooms a thorough clean. She and Kiki had worked like demons, taking down the curtains, shampooing the carpets with a monstrous machine hired from a local DIY store, washing down the paintwork so Daniel could touch up spots here and there.

They'd done the same with the teashop, although it had only

been open a handful of weeks. Everything had been deep-cleaned, and the chairs and tables covered for the winter. The contractors they used had fashioned shutters for the windows and the place was sealed up tight against the worst of the weather.

Once she'd started, Mia kept finding other things that needed doing; she wanted everything shipshape before Christmas. There was method to her madness. She hadn't told him yet, but Mia had arranged with the others that the first two weeks of the New Year would be for her and Daniel alone. No guests, no friends or family, just the two of them and lots of peace and quiet. She rubbed a hand across her clammy forehead. She really ought to give the doctor a ring and see if he could squeeze her in before they switched to their emergency timetable for the holidays.

'Still feeling peaky?' Kiki reached her hand across the table and gave her hand a sympathetic squeeze.

Mia nodded. 'I really must call Doctor Laing. It's a miracle Daniel hasn't picked this up from me. The last thing I want is to risk spreading it around when we've got a houseful.'

Madeline raised an eyebrow. 'I'm not sure what you've got is catching, darling girl.' She turned her attention back to her notepad. 'I'll do a couple of large quiches and some sausage rolls for the buffet. What else? A rice salad, perhaps?'

Sitting back in her chair, Mia frowned at her friend, still stuck on her cryptic comment. It was true that Kiki had spent long hours with her over the past couple of weeks, but they'd been cleaning frantically so any germs from her bug wouldn't have stood a chance against all the household sprays and bleach they'd used. Daniel had ignored her suggestion that one or other of them move into another room as she'd crouched miserably in front of the toilet that morning. Thankfully the worst of her symptoms tended to wear off during the day . . . *oh.*

Apparently not noticing her silence, Madeline continued to discuss menu options with Kiki. They debated the pros and cons of a cold roast chicken versus gammon or perhaps a selection of seafood. Mia swallowed hard over the thought of prawn cocktails. 'Can you pass my bag, Kiki Dee?'

Her sister unhooked the miniature backpack from the seat beside her and carried it around the table to crouch next to her. 'You're very pale. Why don't you go and lie down for a bit? Mads and I have got this in hand.'

Ignoring the gentle hand Kiki pressed against her forehead, Mia scrabbled through the contents of her bag until she found her purse. Undoing the stud fastener, she dragged out the jumble of cards filling the slots. Discarding her debit and credit cards, a loyalty card for a coffee shop she hadn't visited in a year or more, and half a dozen folded receipts that should have been filed with her business accounts, she stared at the mostly white card gripped between her bloodless fingers. The handwritten numbers were slightly blurred, but still readable. *Date of insertion: 28/09/14. Date for removal: 27/09/17.*

With trembling fingers, she passed the card to Kiki and forced herself to meet Madeline's eyes. 'It completely slipped my mind. It was a couple of months before Jamie . . . and I tend to avoid thinking about anything around that time.' How could she have been so stupid? What the hell was she going to tell Daniel? They'd talked about it and children were definitely on the cards, but not for a year or two. They had plans, a schedule to keep to.

Kiki's hand gripped her knee, and she glanced down at her. 'This card is for your contraceptive implant, yes?' Mia nodded mutely. 'Oh. *Oh.*' Her sister's eyes widened and she nibbled at her bottom lip. 'Did you . . . well, obviously not . . . you might not be . . .'

Mia swallowed. 'You don't believe that, though, do you?'

'I think you'd better make that appointment, straight away.'

'Well, Mrs Fitzwilliams, I don't think there's any doubt about it.' Doctor Laing nodded to the ziplock bag containing half a dozen tests she'd placed on his desk after sitting down. 'We need to remove your implant immediately. Once that's done, I'll do some routine health checks, blood pressure and the like, and then you can pop down the corridor and the practice nurse will draw some blood. Given what you've told me, it's hard to pinpoint an accurate date, although they generally don't expire immediately. We need to get you booked in for a scan.' He frowned at the calendar. 'I can try and get you an appointment for next week, but with it being Christmas week, perhaps very early in the New Year might be easier?'

'I've got guests arriving tomorrow and through until the New Year, so beginning of January would be better, if you think that will be okay? I haven't told my husband yet, you see.' She gave a little shrug. 'I'm still trying to get my head around it all. I feel so stupid.' She gulped against the sudden lump in her throat, not wanting to start crying in front of him.

The doctor smiled. 'Take a deep breath and we'll deal with this one step at a time. Take your jumper off so I can access your arm, and make yourself comfortable on the bed . . .'

Head spinning and with her handbag stuffed full of useful leaflets from the practice nurse, Mia started the car and eased her way out of the narrow entrance to the surgery car park. The weather was bright and clear, and frost glittered on parts of the pavements still in shadow. Suddenly terrified of hitting a patch of ice, she started to crawl along the side street until the angry honking of a car horn behind her startled her. Giving herself a mental shake, she waved in apology to the irate man glaring at her through the rear-view mirror and increased her speed. Luck wasn't on her side when she turned left and the tailgater followed her onto the main road. The bright orange sign of a superstore beckoned to her and she steered into the slip road to her left. Still not satisfied, the man who'd been following pulled up next to her to shake his fist and mouth something obscene from the way his mouth twisted before he roared away. Flicking him a surreptitious 'v' sign, she turned her attention to the Herculean task of finding a free parking space outside a supermarket on the day before Christmas Eve.

Clutching a takeaway hot chocolate from the in-store café, Mia steered her small trolley one-handed through the bedlam. There was enough food in the pantry, fridge and freezer at Butterfly House to survive a month-long siege, and likely the same amount in both Madeline's and Kiki's kitchens too, but somehow, between them, they'd managed to forget a few things. Turning into one of the chiller aisles, she took a deep breath and began to edge her way patiently towards her first target. A frazzled-looking woman with a baby carrier strapped in her trolley gave her a weary smile as they did the obligatory two-step shuffle, trying and failing to get out of each other's way.

'You first,' Mia wedged herself into a small spot beside the cheese, and the woman's expression brightened.

'Thank you! I don't know what I was thinking coming in here today.' She paused next to Mia then nodded behind her. 'Sorry, could you grab me a block of cheddar? Medium if you can see it?'

Mia twisted around, found the right cheese and handed it over, taking the chance to peek inside the carrier at the little bundle inside. 'Someone's first Christmas, I see. How lovely.'

'We've gone a bit mad with the presents, even though she's too young to have any idea what's going on. I made the mistake of looking in the clothing aisle just now. Nick's going to kill me when he sees the outfits I've picked up for her.' The doting smile on her face said *Nick* would be doing no such thing. A man behind them tutted, and Mia's new friend raised her eyebrows. 'We're causing a traffic jam, I'd better get on. Happy Christmas!'

'Happy Christmas!' Mia stayed where she was until the crush in the aisle thinned out enough for her to grab a couple of tubs of brandy butter, then she escaped into the main thoroughfare of the store with a sigh of relief. Digging out her list, she checked on the rest of the items she needed and turned left. Something sparkly and pink caught her eye and she paused by the children's clothing aisle. *Maybe just a quick look . . .*

'Hey, there you are!' Daniel jumped up from his chair to grab the carrier bags from her hands as she staggered through the back door. He dumped the bags on the table, then turned back to cup her cheek. 'You look knackered, love. Put your feet up, and I'll make you a cup of tea, yeah?'

Sinking into the seat he pulled out for her, Mia studied him from the back as he pottered around making them a drink. The first hints of the silver she loved in his beard were starting to gleam in his hair now too. Not many, just the odd glint as he turned his head and the overhead light caught a strand or two. Months of hard work around the guest house and then the barns had added bulk to his shoulders, though he'd never be considered broad compared to Aaron.

'The tree came whilst you were out and it looks fantastic. Aaron gave me a hand to set it up, and then we put the artificial ones in the sitting rooms.' He smiled at her over his shoulder. 'We decided to leave the decorating to the experts, though.' She returned his grin; Kiki, Aaron and the children were coming over first thing to make a start on the big tree. 'But I thought it might be nice if you and I did the one in our front room.'

She caught the faintest hint of a blush on his cheek, and melted a little. They'd decided to use both the smaller, private sitting room she and Daniel used as well as the larger one reserved for paying guests. Theirs would be designated adults only, a place for anyone needing a bit of peace and quiet from the impending mayhem. In the happy chaos of arranging everything, it would be easy to lose sight of the fact that this was their first Christmas together too. 'I'd like that. We could put on a cheesy movie, and I'll make us some hot chocolate with marshmallows.' Next year, things would be very different, their whole life together transformed.

Plonking down a couple of mugs, he hooked the chair next to hers with his foot and dragged it close before sitting down. Spreading his knees, he leaned forward to tug her seat even closer. 'Come here, Mrs Fitzwilliams, I haven't seen you all day.' He pressed a sweet kiss to her lips, the strands of his beard soft against her face.

She gripped a playful handful of the bushy growth beneath his chin. 'You look like one of those mountain men.' An exaggeration, perhaps, but he was several weeks past a trim.

'I'll clip it tonight, before we go to bed.'

The gleam in his stunning eyes sent a lick of heat through her, and she grinned. 'You've a one-track mind, Mr Fitzwilliams.'

He sat back in his chair with a grin. 'I can't help it. My wife's too damn distracting to think of anything else.' His gaze must have caught on the shopping bags, because he reached to drag one closer. 'Unless you've brought me a present?'

An unconscious hand strayed to her stomach. Would the baby inside her have brown eyes like her, or green as a storm-tossed ocean to match her daddy? She suddenly couldn't wait to tell him. It might be a shock, might be a huge spanner in the works of their carefully laid plans, but they'd done something incredible – created a new life. 'Daniel . . .'

'Who eats this bloody stuff?' His nose wrinkled at the jar of brandy butter in his hand.

Mia took a deep breath and tried again. 'Try the other bag.' Her voice cracked on the last word and she coughed to clear the sudden tension in her throat.

'Hmm?' He stacked a couple of boxes of savoury biscuits on the table next to the butter.

She inclined her head. 'There's something for you in the other bag.'

'A present? It's not Christmas yet.' His mouth quirked, but he pulled the second bag closer. 'What's this?' He lifted out the tiny white bodysuit and turned it backwards and forwards, flashing the embroidered teddy bear holding an 'I ♥ Daddy' banner between its paws. '*Mia?*'

Unable to speak past the lump in her throat, she could only nod in response.

'But . . . but, how?' The little suit looked tiny in his hands as he waved it like a flag.

The utter confusion in his voice made her laugh. 'The usual way. I know it's not what we planned, and I'm so sorry for that. I made a mistake with my implant dates. I know you wanted to get at least one full year of running this place under our belts.' The words babbled out of her until she ended on an apologetic shrug.

Still clutching the baby suit, he twisted back in his seat to face her. 'Are you telling me the most organised woman I've ever met has made a mistake? That my wife, the queen of schedules and planners, has been caught off-guard by Mother Nature?' The gentle tease of his words soothed any lingering doubts she might have had over his reaction.

'So, you don't mind?'

Leaning forward to grip her hips, he lifted her off her chair until she straddled his lap. 'Mind? You've given me the best bloody present a man could ever ask for.' His hands glided from her hips to her shoulders, then higher to cup her face. 'Merry Christmas, Mrs Fitzwilliams.'

Chapter Nine

'Can you manage that one, Eirênê?'

'I'm fine, Dad. You get the black one, I think it's the heaviest. What on earth have you brought with you?' Nee waved off her father's concern as she hauled the suitcase down from the luggage rack at the end of their compartment. Thankfully, the little station at Orcombe Sands was the end of the line so there was no mad rush to unload their bags. Just as well, because George wasn't the only one who'd gone overboard with their gift shopping. With each round-robin update email from Mia about arrangements, Nee's list of things to buy had expanded. Luke had suggested they collaborate on gifts, which had made her a little uncomfortable at first. He'd talked her round during one of his evening calls, presenting a seemingly unending list of logical arguments, until she'd laughingly surrendered.

They'd done a lot of laughing over the past few weeks. One call to check up on her after he first returned to London had turned into two, three, until it became clear he was going to call her every day. He never raised any heavy topics, didn't talk about *them* in any context other than relating to the events Mia and Daniel were planning.

He knew she'd spoken to Kiki about New York, but hadn't pressed for further details. Just as well, because she didn't think she'd be able to talk about the conversations with the crisis helpline Kiki's counsellor had recommended without breaking down. They'd barely scratched the surface, but she'd reached at least one important milestone in the process – it didn't matter what had or hadn't happened in those lost hours. Devin had betrayed her trust, had acted without her consent, had raped her regardless of the biological reality of their encounter. Having a label to pin on it, without feeling she had to dismiss her feelings because she didn't meet some random legal definition or because she'd been left physically unscathed, had come as a relief. They still had some way to go, but with acknowledgement had come the strength to compartmentalise.

She'd begun to look forward to Luke's calls, even planning her days around that precious hour when she could forget the sadness of sorting through her mother's belongings as she helped her father go through the house. George was toying with the idea of selling up and moving somewhere else – somewhere closer to Butterfly Cove, she suspected, although he hadn't said as much. She couldn't blame him; had already decided that, whatever happened over Christmas, she wouldn't be returning with him. Too much had happened beneath that roof for her to ever be able to consider it home.

She'd barely opened the train door before Daniel was there, all smiles in a bright-green elf cap. 'Hey, give me that,' he said, taking the heavy bag from her hands. 'Merry Christmas, Nee!'

'Merry Christmas. What do you look like?' She leaned forward to tug the white bobble on the end of the cap before stepping aside to give her dad room to haul his bag to the door. Skirting around him, she grabbed their holdalls, then a final, smaller suitcase, dropping them by the door for the men to lift down.

She let Daniel hand her down the steep steps onto the platform and found herself swept into a bear hug. 'You look good.' He smacked a kiss on her cheek then tugged the knitted cap off her head. 'Wow! I'm loving the new look!'

Raising a hand to her shiny chestnut cap of hair, Nee smiled shyly. 'It looks better, doesn't it?'

Luke's comment after the funeral about punishing herself had sat with her for a long time. Not being able to stand her reflection in the mirror, she'd decided to totally change her look almost as soon as she'd returned from New York. The bleach-blonde hadn't suited her, but it made her look harder, less like the stupid, naïve girl who'd let herself be taken advantage of, so she'd kept it. A recent trip to a sympathetic stylist had resulted in a colour much closer to her original, and a retro-style bob which brushed her cheekbones.

Her dad smiled over at them. 'I told her she looks like a flapper girl, just needs a string of pearls and a feather in her hair.' And with that, he gave her the perfect idea for New Year's Eve and the fancy-dress party Mia had planned. She shook her head. Her big sister seemed determined to throw everything but the kitchen sink into the celebrations – as well as the fancy-dress party, there was to be Secret Santa, and what was gearing up to be an incredibly competitive games night. The boasts and bets thrown around in their email group had grown progressively more outrageous and the losing pair were taking a midnight skinny-dip in the ocean. Bloody Luke had been behind that ridiculous suggestion. He'd just better be as good at Trivial Pursuit as he'd promised her!

Snatching her hat back from Daniel, she tugged it back over her ears. The sky was the palest of blues, and a bitter wind funnelled along the platform, making her shiver even in her warm, padded coat. She tipped her head back to study the fluffy white clouds overhead. 'I hope it stays like this for the next few days.' It could be as cold as it liked, as long as it stayed bright.

'We should be so lucky. Forecast for tomorrow and Boxing Day is horrendous. At least we'll get everyone home and settled before then.' Daniel grabbed the handle of the largest case and began towing it along the platform. 'Luke and his folks arrived about an hour ago, and Mags is due in about half-two.'

Letting her dad fall into step with Daniel, Nee trailed behind them, tummy full of nervous butterflies. Agreeing to spend the holiday with Luke had been this nebulous concept she'd been aware of but had avoided thinking about too deeply. A terrible mistake, she realised, now the prospect of being face to face with him once again loomed. *And his parents, too.* Goodness only knew what they must think of her.

Luke had broken the news of their marriage to them not long after Mia's wedding, but he hadn't been very forthcoming about how much they knew. He'd travelled down to their house the previous day, and driven down with them to Butterfly Cove that morning. With so many people around, an extra car would come in handy. Luke had called her just before she'd gone to bed and promised her everything would be fine. She could only wish for a tenth of his confidence. It was too late to back out now, even if she wanted to, and nerves or no, she didn't want to. Those nightly chats had only served to underline how much he had to offer her. Eight days to sort herself out and see if she could find enough of her spirit to be equal to that offering.

Despite the coldness of the day, the back door stood ajar and the air filled with the scents of spices and buttery pastry. Following Daniel's instructions to leave everything in the car for now, they entered into a scene of organised chaos. Mia was pulling the source of the delicious aroma from the oven, chatting with Madeline, who stood at the sink, washing up in what looked to be a pair of leopard-print rubber gloves. A mini production line was set up at the kitchen table, with Richard and an older couple she didn't recognise busy peeling, chopping and adding a variety of vegetables to bowls of cold water. Luke's parents, she assumed, knowing she was right when the man glanced up and offered her a smile which displayed a very familiar set of dimples.

Chairs scraped back and Nee found herself in a whirlwind of hugs, kisses and handshakes as she and George were welcomed into the room. A soft hand on her arm was followed by the fragrance of expensive perfume and she found herself under the critical examination of a slender blonde in her early sixties. 'So, you're her.'

Her insides squirmed under the censure clear in Cathy's eyes, but Nee forced a smile. Getting off on the wrong foot with Luke's mum would be the worst thing imaginable. 'I'm Nee, yes. You must be Cathy, Luke has your eyes.' Was that a slight softening in the cold glare from her? God, she hoped so.

The silence between them seemed to stretch on into infinity, although it couldn't have been more than a second or two before Brian Spenser stepped up beside his wife to hold out a hand to her. 'Nee? Delighted to meet you. Luke's in the dining room helping Aaron and the little ones decorate the tree.' He released her hand then hooked his arm around Cathy's shoulder. 'Come on, darling, there's still about a hundred weight of potatoes to get through.'

Grateful for the rescue, Nee took his cue and escaped the hubbub of the kitchen. Perhaps Luke had asked his dad to run interference between her and Cathy, or perhaps she was reading too much into everything. The sounds of laughter and Bing Crosby crooning 'White Christmas' came from the open door of the dining room, drawing her like a magnet. Aaron balanced on a footstool, one arm stretched out holding an angel with a wonky halo and a glittering silver-white dress. A green hat, twin to the one Daniel had been wearing, perched on the top of his head. Kiki and her two children knelt beside the tree, sorting through thick strands of tinsel and boxes of baubles. It was like a scene from a Hallmark movie, and she ached to take her place within it.

Luke stood barely two feet in front of her, a pair of faded jeans clinging to his hips beneath a blue and red striped polo shirt. They must have bought a job lot of those silly hats, because he wore one too. 'Left a bit, no, no, too far, right a bit, steady now.' She could hear the teasing laughter in his voice as he issued what were supposed to be helpful instructions to his brother. He sounded so happy and relaxed it did nothing for her nerves.

What if she let him down in front of everyone? Nee clenched her fists against the creeping self-doubt. If she couldn't find enough of her own confidence, she'd have to borrow some of his for now. *Fake it 'til you make it.* Putting her shoulders back, she took a step into the room.

'When I get down from here, you're going to be sorry, Spud,' Aaron mock-grumbled as he tried to straighten the angel who'd taken on something of a drunken tilt.

Her nephew, Matty, turned to say something to his mum and caught sight of her. Nee quickly raised her finger to her lips to shush him. He ducked his head to cover his smile, but kept his head turned towards her, watching as she crept up on her target. Luke had his hands propped on his hips, leaving her enough space to slide her arms around his waist and squeeze a startled exclamation from him. 'Hello, Mr Spenser.'

His hands curled behind her back, holding her close against him. 'Hello, Mrs Spenser. Glad you could make it.' He lifted his left arm, giving her room to slide around his side. Easy as that, her whole body relaxed. Luke believed in her and that was all that mattered right then.

Unable to contain his excitement any more, Matty jumped up and ran across to throw his arms around her legs. 'Aunty Nee, Aunty Nee, it's Christmas tomorrow!'

She cupped the back of his head and hugged him close. 'Yes, it is. I'm very excited. Are you?'

He nodded against her thigh. 'Did you bring me a present?' Trust a seven-year-old boy to cut right to the heart of the matter.

'Yes, sweetheart. I've got presents for you and Charlie, and Mummy too.' At the mention of her name, her little niece scrambled to her feet and squirmed in beside Matty for cuddles. Kiki's eyes met her sister's over their heads. 'Hello, Kiki Dee.'

Eyes sparkling, Kiki sat back on her heels and spread her hands to show the tangle of decorations around her. 'Thank goodness you're here. I need someone with a bit of artistic flare!'

Nee swallowed. Kiki hadn't meant anything by her throwaway comment, but she couldn't help the pang inside her.

As though reading her mind, Luke flexed his hand on her shoulder, tugging her a fraction closer towards him in a purely protective move. She let her head drop against him for a moment, acknowledging then releasing the little flutter of panic. *No pressure, no rush.* Hanging a few baubles on a tree wasn't beyond her.

Shoving the angel none-too-gently onto the upright branch at the top of the tree, Aaron hopped off the footstool and gave her a wave. 'Hey, Nee. You and your dad have a good journey down?'

'Yes, thanks. He's still in the kitchen, I think.'

Matty tapped her leg and she looked down. 'Grandad's here?'

She nodded. 'Yup. Why don't you go and say hello to him?' Grabbing his sister's hand, her nephew zoomed off, leaving the four of them alone.

Kiki stood up. 'Well, let's get your coat off, if you're staying.'

It was one of those silly expressions families had rather than any kind of a question, but Nee glanced up at Luke, pursing her lips as though considering it. 'I've not had a better offer yet, so I suppose I'm staying.' Aaron snorted and she couldn't fight her smile.

Luke tapped her nose with one finger, then followed it with a quick kiss. 'Cheeky girls don't get presents.' His eyes strayed upwards from hers. 'Hey, what's this?' Tugging her hat free, there was no hiding the admiration and approval in his bright-blue gaze as he studied her new look. 'There's my girl.'

Feeling suddenly shy at the warmth in his voice, she busied herself with unzipping and removing her coat. 'I'm glad you like it.'

He closed the short distance between them. 'I love it.' If he didn't stop looking at her like that, Nee would be a puddle on the floor. She licked her lips as his head lowered a fraction closer.

'Please tell me I'm not going to have to watch you two smooching all bloody Christmas.' Face on fire, Nee took a step back, catching the filthy glare Luke tossed at his unrepentant brother. Aaron grinned, ducking to the side to avoid the elbow Kiki aimed at his ribs.

'Behave!'

Aaron shook his head at Kiki. 'And miss out on the chance to wind him up? Not happening.' He dodged the punch Luke aimed at his arm and ran laughing from the room, with Luke in hot pursuit. Brothers would be brothers, no matter how old they got.

Kiki rolled her eyes. 'At least we didn't fight like that. Quick, come and help me with this mess whilst it's quiet.' She held her hand out to Nee, who took it and returned the affectionate squeeze.

'We didn't fight, but I seem to remember some world-class sulking.' Laughing, they settled down next to the tree and began sorting the jumble of decorations into groups by colour.

'I never sulked, that was Mia,' Kiki said as she held up a pink bauble, looking for a space to hang it on the tree.

'What was me?'

Nee giggled at the guilty look on her middle sister's face as Mia crossed the room towards them. Kiki had always been an open book. Shuffling to the side, she made room for Mia to join them. 'Kiki Dee was pointing out how you were the sulker in our family.'

'Oh, you traitor!' Kiki's outrage only made Neé laugh harder. And sisters would still be sisters. The thought warmed her right through.

Apparently opting for the moral high ground, Mia ignored them and studied the tree with a critical eye. 'So, what's the theme here?'

Nee sat back on her heels and surveyed the riot of mismatched balls, bells and tinsel. The tree was a million miles from the elegantly dressed ones she remembered as a child, when Vivian had still had interest in things outside the bottom of her glass. From the wonky angel, to the group of branches entirely covered in red decorations, it was a terrible mess. And the most glorious thing she'd ever seen. 'It looks like the elves got drunk and vomited Christmas on it. I hope nobody's got OCD.'

Mia laughed. 'It's making my fingers twitch a bit, but that's a good thing. I need to relax and enjoy myself, and looking at this will serve as a good reminder that no one cares about matching napkins for every meal, except me.'

'Napkins, seriously?' Nee scoffed.

'I know, I know. Daniel gave me a serious talking to when he found me at six this morning counting how many packets of cocktail napkins we had.' Mia gripped each of them by the hand. 'It's been so long since we were all happy, I just want everything to be perfect.'

Nee blinked at the moisture gathering in the corners of her eyes. Mia had always been the one who'd taken care of them; she might have known she'd try and take this responsibility upon herself. 'It doesn't have to be perfect, Mimi. It just has to be us, all of us, here together in this beautiful home you've made for us.'

'No tears, no tears! Bloody hormones.' Mia tugged her hand free to wave it in front of her face. What miserable timing for her to be getting her period right on top of Christmas. Unless . . . Nee watched as Mia gave her tummy a funny little pat.

One look at her eldest sister's beaming smile, at the bright-eyed nod from Kiki on the other side of her, and Nee clapped her hands to her cheeks. '*Mia?* Oh, that's wonderful!' And it was, because no one deserved a family more than the woman who'd nurtured them and held them all together whilst still a child herself. Nee's brain flipped from delight into complete panic mode. 'Don't you need to rest? You shouldn't be on your knees like this. Let me get you a chair.'

'I'm fine. Stop fussing, or you might set Daniel off. He's been remarkably calm about it so far.' Mia started packing loose decorations back into the plastic boxes they'd come from. 'We only had it confirmed yesterday, so we're still a bit shell-shocked. I know we should wait until after the scan before telling everyone, but Kiki and Madeline were already in on the secret, and I wanted you to know too.'

Nee squeezed Mia's arm. 'I'm sure everything will be fine. Let's not invite any trouble to our door. You must put me to work though, anything you need. Promise me?'

'I promise.' Mia paused, cut her eyes to Kiki and then back to Nee. 'Are you sure about this reunion with Luke? Not that we don't wish you happy, and we love him like one of our own, but I don't want you to feel pressured into anything.' It was the same thing Kiki had told her back at their dad's, and knowing they'd stand with her no matter what helped ease the last of the tension in her belly.

'I want it to work, I hope we can make it work, but I've been in such a terrible mess since New York. If I can't get my head straight then I won't be a burden to him.' She looked at her sisters. Both had made enormous changes in their lives – perhaps there was a chance for her too.

Going up on her knees, Kiki shuffled over until she could hug them both. 'You're not on your own. We'll help you in any way we can. I'm just sorry we weren't there when you needed us.'

Nee leaned into the hug. 'It's my own fault for staying away.'

Mia kissed her cheek. 'Well, we're not letting you get away from us again. No matter what happens between you and Luke. We went through all that nonsense with Aaron trying not to rock the boat, and he nearly lost Kiki in the process.'

Nee hid her face in her sister's shoulder. If it came down to a choice between breaking Luke's heart and ruining his life, she'd turn her back on Butterfly Cove for ever.

Chapter Ten

Leaving the dining room had proven a mistake. Not only had Luke lost sight of Nee, but he'd been collared by Madeline as soon as he entered the kitchen and spent the next half an hour making a salad to a set of very detailed instructions. Why he couldn't just slice a few bits of cucumber, a couple of tomatoes and lob them into a bowl on top of some shredded lettuce was beyond him. Bean sprouts? If there was a more pointless vegetable, he'd yet to discover it. He stared at the pink-stained tips of his fingers and thought she might have warned him about the beetroot. His only consolation was an equally confused-looking Aaron next to him, trying (and failing!) to cut radishes into little flower shapes. With spades for hands, it was little short of torture.

He leaned closer to his brother to whisper in his ear. 'So, what do you think we did to upset her?'

Aaron flicked a wonky radish flower into the salad bowl then met his eyes with a rueful shrug. 'Dunno, Spud. Maybe someone let slip about her Secret Santa present.'

Luke snorted. In the fine tradition of such things, just about everyone had missed the point of the 'secret' part of it and there'd been lots of whispering in corners and trading of names as people begged for clues as to what to buy. Aaron had taken him aside earlier and confessed what he'd bought for Madeline, and Luke thought it was a stroke of genius. He also knew Daniel had drawn his mum's name thanks to a desperate phone call. He'd toyed with the idea of being cruel for about two seconds before suggesting his friend went for a safe option. Not that Cathy couldn't be teased, but he wasn't sure how well she'd react to a joke gift surrounded by people she didn't know that well.

It had taken him several calls and subtle enquiries to discover Richard had drawn Nee's name, and the older man had kindly agreed to trade with him for Charlie's gift. With the kids involved, Aaron and Kiki had needed to help them choose presents for their recipients. They'd also had an additional gift to buy because Charlie had insisted that Tigger be included. He peered under the table. Sure enough, his brother's little shadow lay beside his feet, happily gnawing the toe of Aaron's trainer.

'What are you two whispering about?' Madeline's voice sounded right behind them, sending his heart racing.

A dull blush coloured Aaron's cheek as he glanced over his shoulder. 'Err, nothing, Mads.' Jesus, he couldn't have looked, or sounded, guiltier if he'd tried. Luke rolled his eyes. It had been the same since they were kids, most of their pranks failing miserably as good-hearted Aaron confessed all.

'We were just saying how gorgeous you're looking today, Madeline, darling.' Luke flashed his best smile and batted his eyelashes for good measure. Always stylish, even when wearing something casual, this morning's outfit was a lilac T-shirt with lace trim at the sleeves and hemline, and a pair of black jeans.

'Your brother is a terrible liar, boy, but you'd charm the birds from the trees.' She might shake her head at him, but it didn't stop her brushing a kiss to his cheek. 'Right, I think that salad will be fine. Pop it on the dining-room table for me.' Madeline turned to place a hand on Aaron's shoulder. 'I need you in the pantry.'

Aaron waggled his eyebrows at her. 'Whatever will Richard think?'

Madeline laughed. 'Silly boy. Some idiot put all the pickles on the high shelf and I can't reach them.'

Daniel walked through the back door just in time to hear her comment. 'Idiot? You must be talking about me.' His broad grin showed he'd taken no offence as he lugged in a large suitcase. 'You ladies sure know how to pack. Welcome to the madhouse, Maggie.'

The blonde gallery owner followed on his heels into the room and straight into the welcoming embrace of Madeline. The two women had become firm friends at the wedding, and she'd been added to their ever-expanding amorphous family. 'Maggie! We can finally start the celebrations now you're here. Come and meet Cathy. I know you two will get on like a house on fire.' She led her friend over to where his mum had been standing, unnoticed, by him at least, in the corner. Luke's love and admiration for Madeline ratcheted up to eleven. It was just like her to make sure his mum was part of things, to help her smooth the way as she tried to find her feet in amongst everyone.

Safe in the knowledge everyone was happy for a minute, he grabbed the salad and made good his escape. It was time to track down his wife.

He found Kiki and Mia in the dining room, arranging things on the table for their buffet lunch. They shook their heads when he handed over the salad and enquired after Nee. He tried the large family room next, finding his dad, Richard and George decorating an artificial tree with careful deliberation whilst the two children sprawled in front of some noisy cartoon on the television. No, they hadn't seen her either. The little front room sat empty, which could only mean . . . 'Oh, bugger!'

He charged up the stairs two at a time, down the corridor to the little wing at the side of the house, before coming to a stop at the threshold of the suite of rooms Mia had nicknamed the Harem. The design and layout were down to him, a project she'd given him back in the spring, as though sensing he needed a distraction. He'd decorated the lavish spaces with only one person in mind, and he hesitated at the stiff line of her shoulders as she stood in the doorway of the adjoining sitting room.

Wanting to have things to hand for her if, *and only if*, she somehow found her muse again, he'd set the room up with an easel, sketchpads, paints, charcoals and pencils. They'd be spending most of their time downstairs with everyone else, so his plan had been to let her know there were things there if she wanted them, but to keep the door shut so she didn't have to face them until she was ready. It had never occurred to him he'd get drawn into doing something else and wouldn't be with her when she came upstairs for the first time.

Fearing he'd made a terrible mistake, he tucked his hands in his pockets and took a step inside the bedroom to lean against the wall. 'I'll get rid of it if you want me to. I just thought . . . well, maybe I didn't think. I just wanted you to have what you needed, should you need it. Not that I'm suggesting you have to try, or even that you should . . .'

'It's fine.' He closed his eyes briefly at the deadness of her voice. *Shit.*

Pushing away from the wall, he strode across the room and tugged the door to the offending room closed. 'Forget about it. It was a stupid idea. I'll pack it all away later.' With a gentle hand on her arm, he turned her away. 'Now, did you need me to fetch your stuff up? Maggie's here so I don't think it'll be too long before lunch starts.'

He tried not to take it personally when she eased away from his touch and moved to one side of the bed. 'Daniel carried my bags up for me. I've already unpacked my stuff. I . . . I took this side, if that's all right?' Her hand waved at the right side of the king-size mattress piled high with richly brocaded pillows in shades of magenta, gold and olive-green.

'Whatever you want is fine by me. You had enough hangers and stuff in the wardrobe?' He'd only used a couple for the dark, pin-striped suit and formal shirt she'd asked him to bring for

New Year's Eve. Everything else he'd folded away in the bottom half of the large chest of drawers.

The shining wings of her hair fell forward to shadow her face as she nodded. 'Plenty of space, thanks.'

He perched on the side of the bed, one thigh resting on the mattress, and studied her. Everything about her was wrong – her posture, the slight woodenness to her responses, the lack of eye contact. 'What's the matter?'

Her head snapped up, revealing two very wide doe-brown eyes. 'What? Nothing.' She drew her bottom lip between her teeth, reminding him more of his shy, sweet, future sister-in-law than the fiery, feisty woman he'd fallen hook, line and sinker for. That bastard had snuffed out her fire and Luke wanted to beat him bloody for it. What if there was nothing left? No tiny spark for him to kindle back to life?

The depth of his rage surprised him, and he placed the hand he wanted to clench into a fist flat on the thick quilt beside his leg. There was no place for Devin Rees in this room. He wouldn't allow thoughts of what he might have done to Nee taint their private space. There was a woodpile out behind the barns; he could vent his feelings on a few logs later if he needed to. Shoving the simmering anger down deep, he waited to be sure his voice would be gentle before he spoke. 'Talk to me, darling, please.'

She brushed the hair from her cheek, glancing away and then back, a rosy flush marking the pale skin between the top of her cream, long-sleeved T-shirt and the base of her throat. 'I hadn't thought about the fact we'd be sharing a bed, and now I can't seem to think about anything else.' The blush stole up her neck and across her cheeks.

Ah.

He couldn't say he hadn't thought about it. As each day carried him closer to this moment, his mind had filled with the scents and sights and sounds of her. But his personal desires could take a back seat, could go and stand outside in the freezing bloody cold, because nothing was worth the discomfort written large upon Nee's face. 'I'm not expecting anything from you. I'd like to sleep with you beside me, I've missed you so bloody much, but I'll use the sofa next door if you'd prefer. Or find another room.' Luke clamped his mouth shut before he said any more. If she really wanted him out of the room then it was all over before he'd even had a chance.

'I don't know what to do for the best, Luke. I feel like I'm messing you around. I was so full of hope on the way down here, but now it feels like a terrible mistake. If I can't even look at a bloody easel without having a panic attack, what's the point? What if I never get it back, Luke, what then?' She looked so lost that he didn't care about what happened beyond offering her whatever comfort she would accept from him.

'Come here.' Luke shifted further up the bed until he could lean against the pillows, then lifted one arm.

'Luke . . .'

'Shh. Slip of your shoes, turn off your brain and come and have a cuddle. Whatever else, we're still friends, aren't we?'

Thankfully, she did as she was told and crawled up the bed to curl into his side. 'I hope we can always be friends, whatever happens.'

He kissed the top of her head. 'Whatever happens, darling, I promise.' God, she felt so good in his arms, there was no way he would ever let her go. Unfortunately, it was becoming clear he'd read too much into the sweetness of her earlier greeting. His mind drifted to the Secret Santa gift waiting for her under the tree. Would it make things worse, put her under even more pressure than she was already feeling? He stroked her back, trying to calm his racing thoughts. If they were both second-guessing themselves, they'd never get anywhere.

Her hand crept up to rest upon his ribcage, and he focused on keeping the motion on her back soft and even. 'This is nice,' she murmured. 'I've missed this.' She sighed, then settled a little closer into the crook of his arm. 'I don't suppose we can just hide away out here, though. We can't really miss lunch.'

He laughed. 'You've met your sisters, right? That buffet they've set up will keep us all going for a week. If you want to stay here for a while, no one will mind.' Him least of all.

'Just a few minutes then.'

A few minutes turned into an early afternoon nap, and it was growing dark by the time Nee raised her head from Luke's chest with a sleepy blink. 'You should have woken me earlier.'

Leaning forward, he kissed the tip of her nose. 'You were snoring so prettily, it seemed a shame to disturb you.'

Outraged laughter burst from her. 'I don't snore!'

'Of course you don't, my mistake.' He widened his eyes to his best mock-innocent expression and she rewarded him with a cushion to the face. Still laughing, she climbed off the bed and headed into the en-suite bathroom. The nap had done her the world of good, melting all the tension out of her and giving her whirling brain time to relax. Shame about the terrible case of bedhead it had left her with. Shaking her head vigorously for a few seconds sorted that issue out, though, and she gave her hairdresser a mental high-five for persuading her into such a stress-free cut. A quick brush of her teeth to freshen up, and she felt much more able to face everyone again.

Her tummy rumbled as she re-entered the bedroom and she clapped her hand to it. 'You'd better have been telling the truth about that buffet, or there'll be trouble.'

His laughter as he wandered past her into the bathroom warmed her to the tips of her toes. He really was still the funny, teasing man she'd fallen madly in love with. Her eyes fell on the closed door across the room and her own humour faded. Fear bubbled inside her, but she refused to let herself acknowledge it. Walking over to the sitting-room door, she placed her hand upon it. She would spend an hour in there; not now, but later in the week. One hour. It was the least that she owed him. Luke deserved the very best version of her she could be.

'I'll pack everything up later, I'm really sorry.'

She glanced behind her at his regretful words, then shook her head. 'No. Leave it. I wouldn't have made it this far without you pushing me.' The thought she'd had earlier came back to her. 'But I might need to borrow some courage from you to take the next step.'

'Whatever you need, darling.' Luke crossed the room to slip his hands around her waist. 'Just let me know, and it's yours.'

With perfect timing, her tummy rumbled again. 'Feed me?'

He slung an arm around her shoulders and steered her from the room. 'In this house, that's the easiest task in the world.'

The kitchen was empty apart from a stern-looking Aaron kneeling by the back door having an intense, if one-sided, conversation with a tiny brindle dog. 'I don't care if it's raining, Tigger. We both know you've got a bladder the size of a pea, so get outside and cock your leg right this minute.' The dog put both front paws on Aaron's knee and wagged his tail so hard his entire rear end wiggled.

'No, you don't need me to come out with you.' Aaron sounded a little more desperate now. The puppy barked and licked his hand. 'Oh, damn. Hold on, I'll get my coat.' He pushed to his feet with a sigh.

Nee bit her lip to try and hide her smile, but Luke had no such compunction. 'There's only one alpha in your pack, Bumble, and it sure ain't you.'

Aaron laughed. 'You're not wrong, Spud. Between this rascal and the kids, I'm very much the bottom rung of the ladder.' He didn't sound in the least bit disappointed about it. A look of horror dawned on his face as a gentle patter of liquid on the kitchen tiles came from behind him. 'Oh, *Tigger.*'

Grabbing a newspaper from the table, Nee crouched down to mop up the little puddle and laid a few clean sheets down just in case. 'Look on the bright side. At least you don't have to go outside now.'

After retrieving a bottle of disinfectant spray and a cloth from under the sink, Aaron stared forlornly at the crumpled paper. 'I remember the days when I actually read the newspaper.' Kneeling, he cleaned the spot on the floor then sat back on his haunches. 'You two arrived just in time. I was going to give you a shout any minute because the kids are getting impatient over Secret Santa, and we'd like to try and get them home and into bed at a reasonable time because they're bound to be up at the crack of dawn.'

Nee tossed the wet paper in the bin, then rinsed her hands at the sink. 'Give us two minutes to grab something to eat and we'll be ready.'

Aaron joined her at the sink to wash up. 'Kiki put a plate for each of you in the fridge, or there's afternoon tea set out in the main lounge.' Patting his still-flat stomach, he cast her a rueful smile. 'I'll be the size of a house before the New Year at this rate.'

Clutching her own piled-high plate, Nee followed Luke into the lounge where they were greeted with a chorus of cheers and laughter. Chairs and cushions had been arranged in a loose circle and a pile of gifts sat at the side of Daniel's chair. He'd swapped the green elf hat for a red one, the white pompom on the end dangling next to his right ear. 'So, how are we going to do this then?' he asked, as Nee settled herself on an empty chair whilst Luke sprawled at her feet.

'How about you give everyone their presents first and then we take turns to open them?' Mia suggested to general agreement, so Daniel sorted through the gifts, placing the appropriate one in front of each of them. Small, large, square, flat, even one shaped like a cracker, the presents were as varied as the wrapping covering them. Taking his seat again, Daniel picked up his digital camera and began taking photos, whilst Madeline and Cathy did the same with their smartphones.

Charlie practically vibrated with excitement as she clutched the snowman-covered package to her chest and Nee had to bite the inside of her cheek as Mia surveyed the group with a serious expression on her face. 'So, who's going first?'

'Me! Mememememe!' Charlie shouted. The rest of the them laughed whilst Kiki leaned forward to whisper something into her daughter's ear. With a guilty nod of her head, Charlie added, 'Please, Aunty Mia.'

'Of course, poppet.' Her sister's reply was practically drowned out by the frantic tearing of paper.

Nee sat forward at the first glimpse of iridescent glitter and gave whoever had chosen Charlie's gift a mental pat on the back as the beaming girl pulled free a pair of beautiful butterfly wings with straps to fasten them over her shoulders. Kiki helped her into them and the little girl danced and fluttered around the circle, gathering admiring comments and kisses like the Queen of the May.

Mia nodded to their sister. 'You next, Kiki Dee and then we'll go clockwise from you.' Kiki unwrapped her own present with a little more decorum and there was no disguising the delight in her smile when she held up a page-a-day calendar with daily affirmations on it.

Round the circle they went – Richard had a Bonsai kit, Maggie a collection of luxury tea samples, Aaron a mug with 'I love my dog' on it. Daniel laughed at the home-dye kit for his beard, and Matty stripped off his jumper to proudly wear his new 'Future Astronaut' T-shirt. Brian looked suitably amused at a pair of wind-up racing grannies, Cathy relieved at a miniature set of high-end bath products. Mia clapped her hands in delight at a set of colourful inserts for her planner. And then it was her turn.

Nee couldn't tell much from the size of the silver-wrapped box she held on her lap. Slitting open the flaps at either side, she pulled the paper free to find a plain cardboard box. Intrigued, she removed the lid to find a mass of scrunched-up crepe paper in shades of pink and purple. Digging carefully, her fingers touched a net bag, and she drew it out with a gasp. Hands shaking, she struggled to open the drawstring top and empty the contents onto her palm. 'Oh, God. *Luke.*' There was no mistaking the slender band of gold, looped onto a smooth snake-chain necklace.

His hand closed over hers, trapping the ring between their palms. 'I wanted to give it back to you and thought you could wear it like this for now.' He kept his voice low, pitched only for her ears, and she nodded in response, overwhelmed to have it back in her possession once again. She understood the significance, too. Worn on the chain, it would show him she was willing to try, and if she chose to put it back on her finger, he would know she meant to stay.

A silence fell over the room, even the children picking up on the tension from the surrounding adults, leaving Nee feeling horribly exposed. Luke flicked her a wink, then turned his back on her to make a big show of opening his own present. Laughter echoed around her as he held up a flamingo-pink top, displaying it proudly to the group. His actions took the attention away from her, and she clenched her hand around the ring for a moment before trying to undo the clasp with trembling fingers.

'Need a hand with that?' Mia reached over to take the necklace from her and fastened it easily around her neck. She paused to squeeze her shoulder in silent support, before turning her attention back to everyone else as a fresh round of laughter rose. Her dad held up a 'Senior Moments Workout' puzzle book, and she was pleased to see him join in with the good-natured teasing from the other older adults.

Luke rested his back against her knees and she leaned forward over his shoulder to press a kiss to his cheek, her eyes catching the wording on the bright T-shirt he'd tugged on over the top of his polo shirt. She couldn't help but laugh as he tipped his head back to meet her eyes, a grin of pride on his face as he patted the '*It's hard to be this pretty*' motto emblazoned on his chest. 'Suits you,' she said, leaning further forward to press a kiss to his lips.

'Watch this, it's going to be good.' He nodded towards where Madeline had begun unwrapping her gift.

'Cheeky buggers!' Mads declared as she brandished a junior detective's kit first at Daniel, then at Aaron. 'I know this has to be one of you two!'

'It's to help with your meddling, Mads. Every interfering old bag needs one!' Aaron grinned, totally blowing his cover.

'You should have got me some wings, like Charlie,' she sniffed. 'Everyone knows I'm a fairy godmother.'

The ring nestled on Nee's breastbone, warming in moments to match the temperature of her skin. It felt good, a solid, reassuring weight, and she hoped she'd find the courage to return it to where it rightfully belonged before too much longer.

Chapter Eleven

Aaron lowered himself onto his back with a sigh, tucking one arm behind his head as he settled deeper against his pillow. Kiki pressed her cheek against his other arm, and he lifted it up to let her cuddle in next to him. The novelty of sharing a bed with her still hadn't worn off, and he counted his blessings as the events of the past few months drifted through his mind. So many changes, so many highs and lows, it was hard to equate his life now to where he'd been at the beginning of the year. Icy-cold toes slid under his calf, and he winced before settling his leg more heavily on Kiki's freezing feet. It didn't matter how hot or cold the weather was, they were always bloody cold.

Their aim of getting the children to bed at a decent hour had been an abject failure, and it had taken Kiki threatening to cancel Father Christmas's visit to get them scampering up the stairs. Whilst she sat guard on the landing, he'd spent the next hour retrieving their presents from various high cupboards and other hiding places. Another stack waited beneath the tree at Butterfly Cove, but they'd agreed Christmas morning would just be the four of them. Five, he corrected himself, because Tigger had amassed an impressive collection of gifts too.

Turning his head to brush a kiss on Kiki's temple, he savoured the moment of blissful peace. *Squeak, squeak, squeak.* He closed his eyes. 'When I find out which Secret Santa gave the dog that bloody chew toy, I'm going to kill them.'

Kiki huffed a laugh against his ear. 'If you weren't such a soft touch, his bed would be down in the kitchen where it belongs, and you wouldn't be able to hear it.' It had surprised them both to discover she was the natural disciplinarian of the two. Whether it was indulging the children with an extra bedtime story, or giving in to the piteous whines of the puppy if he left him alone for more than thirty seconds, Aaron Spenser had come to accept he was as soft as a marshmallow. He tried hard to stick to the rules and routines Kiki laid down in the hopes of running a smooth household, but he was so bloody happy, he'd give them anything they asked for – her above all.

No, his life was nothing like he could have imagined it being this time last year. At thirty, he'd assumed his future had been mapped out, that he'd at least settled on certain key fundamentals. A career and a life in the city, to be shared with a wife at some point, who was equally focused on her own job. Nice holidays, dinners out, pleasant socialising with friends. No kids, no pets, nothing difficult. Yet here he was, working for himself in a country cottage full of laughter, noise and messy chaos, thinking life couldn't get much more perfect. Unless . . .

'I saw the look on your face when you were watching Mia earlier.' Such tenderness and sympathy she'd shown when her sister had dashed from the room, face a worrying shade of green. But it had been more than that. Daniel had said something to his wife as he rubbed her still-flat belly and an expression of such wistfulness had crossed Kiki's features, it had set his own thoughts whirling.

'We talked about it, Aaron. Agreed we're happy as we are.' Although their room was pitch-black, he felt her sit up as though to stare at him. 'Didn't we?'

'We did, and I am, absolutely. All I'm saying is, if you wanted to revisit the discussion at some point in the future, I'd be amenable to the idea.'

'You're not just saying that for me, are you? If we did . . . oh, God, I can't believe we're even thinking about it . . . if we did decide to have a baby in the future, then I need you to be one hundred per cent behind the idea.'

Just hearing her say the word *baby* sent a frisson of excitement and abject terror running through him. It would add to the noise, the constant compromise of running their house together, never mind the mess! But how much more joy and laughter would it also bring beneath the cosy thatch of their roof? The smile on his face grew so wide, his cheeks ached.

Using the arm still around her back, he urged her back down until she leaned against his chest once more. 'Whatever you want, my darling love, I'm right there with you. Now, before we consider actually making a baby, I think we should get a bit more practice in first.' He captured her delicious giggle in his mouth, and all thoughts of the future dissipated in the hazy heat of here and now and her.

Aaron blinked at the red digits on the bedside clock cheerily informing him the time was 5 a.m. and bit back a groan. Tigger scratched at the door again, adding the whine which usually signalled his need to go outside. Wincing at the freezing cold air, he hurried into the T-shirt and jogging bottoms that served as pyjamas and tiptoed across the room, trying not to wake Kiki. He scooped the puppy into his arms, receiving an enthusiastic tongue bath for his pains, and inched out of the bedroom. His hand paused in the act of fumbling for the landing light switch as he spotted a stream of light from under Matty's bedroom door. After a quick tap on the frame, he opened the door to find both children tucked under the covers, the contents of the stockings from the ends of their beds strewn across the covers. Matty was reading aloud from a fairy picture book Aaron had spotted the week before and added to Charlie's stocking. The telltale empty wrappers of at least two items from a chocolate selection box were also evident.

'Merry Christmas, early birds.' Aaron kept his voice pitched low and held a finger to his lips when Charlie bounced up and opened her mouth. 'Mummy's still sleeping.'

A grave expression crossed the little girl's face. 'She needs her beauty sleep,' she whispered.

Trying not to laugh, he crossed the room to sit on the edge of the bed, careful not to squash a Batman action figure. 'Where did you hear that saying, poppet?'

Charlie beamed at him. 'Grandad Brian said the same thing to Nanny-Cat last night.' Somewhere in the selection of suitable titles for his dad and step-mum, Cathy's had been abbreviated to Nanny-Cat. She didn't seem bothered about it, so they'd let it go. 'She's pretty, but Mummy is beautiful so she has to sleep more.' Such a perfect piece of child logic.

Reaching out his thumb, he wiped a smudge of chocolate off her cheek. 'I'm going to let Tigger out and get you two a glass of milk to wash those sweets down with.' Worry flickered in the children's eyes, and he cursed himself for his clumsiness. They were still so fragile, Matty especially was always too quick to assume he'd done something wrong. 'If no one's eaten the Crunchie then save it for me, okay?'

The little boy rewarded him with a shy smile, then pulled a face. 'No one likes Crunchies, you're weird.'

Relieved to see them happy once more, he left the room to the sounds of them whispering 'weird' to each other and giggling. He made sure to close the door in hopes the rising volume wouldn't carry down the hallway to Kiki, then negotiated his way through the safety gate and down the stairs. Charlie was probably old enough now not to need it, but it gave him piece of mind to know neither of the children would take a tumble if they got up in the night for any reason. His bare toes hit the tiled hallway, and he cursed, flipped on the light and shoved his feet into a pair of trainers sitting by the front door. Perhaps he'd get lucky and Father Christmas would bring him some slippers this year. 'Aaron, mate, you're an old man,' he said to himself with a laugh, and the puppy yapped as though in agreement. 'Cheeky sod. Let's get you outside before we're both sorry.'

Unfortunately for them both, the storm which had blown in the night before showed no signs of abating. The heavy thatch on the cottage roof had muffled the sound, but man and dog surveyed the lashing rain outside with matching expressions of disgust. Tigger sat down on the inside mat, and Aaron crouched down, bracing himself for another battle of wills. 'The sooner you go, the sooner we can both get back upstairs in the warm.'

The puppy turned his head away and began chewing on his tail, making it clear there was no debate to be had. 'Spoiled little bastard,' Aaron muttered and stamped off to retrieve a golf umbrella from the hooks by the front door. 'I'm going to smash that mug, you know? I love my bloody dog, indeed. I should just chuck you out there and be done with it.' His harsh words fooled no one, least of all the puppy, who waited until Aaron was standing outside with the umbrella open before he trotted out and took care of business beneath his own personal shelter.

Juggling the umbrella and a plastic bag proved impossible, so Aaron had no choice but to abandon it whilst he cleaned up after the dog, who had retreated to his spot on the kitchen mat, tail wagging like he hadn't a care in the world. His T-shirt was soaked in seconds, the icy rain stinging his neck worse even than Kiki's feet finding his in the middle of the night. Still muttering, he stripped it off, found a dry one in the ironing basket and poured a few biscuits into the dog's bowl after washing his hands.

Armed with a tray bearing three glasses of milk, dog at his heels, Aaron made his way back upstairs. The door to their room remained closed, so he left Kiki to sleep and let himself back into Matty's room. The presents had been cleared to one side of the bed, and the children had arranged themselves, and the pillows, along the long side of the mattress resting against the wall. He handed them each a glass and Matty lifted the edge of the quilt. 'We made a space for you too.' *Jesus*. Every time he believed it wasn't possible to love them more, they did something to prove him wrong.

Overwhelmed for a moment, he turned away to place the tray on the floor, taking the opportunity to swipe at the moisture filling his eyes. With a deep breath, he picked up his own glass and climbed into the bed, only to have Charlie thrust her milk into his free hand and clamber over his legs so he had to shuffle over and take the spot in between them. Taking back her drink, she picked up her new fairy book and dropped it in his lap. 'Your turn to read!'

He glanced at Matty, who seemed content enough playing with his action figures. 'All right, little man?'

The boy grinned up at him, then nodded. 'I'm all right.' He paused Superman mid-swoop to hand Aaron a shiny gold chocolate bar. 'We saved this for you. Merry Christmas, Aaron.'

'Merry Christmas, bud.'

Less than two hours after 'a proper breakfast', as Kiki had sternly put it after their chocolate feast, and the mad excitement of the first round of present opening, they were somehow showered, dressed and pulling up outside Butterfly House. The rain eased off enough for them to make a mad dash into the kitchen where they found Mia, still in her ratty old tartan dressing gown, the only occupant. 'Oh, hello! Look at you in all your finery. You've put me quite to shame.'

Crouching down, Mia accepted hugs and kisses from the children. 'Hello, my darlings. Did you get lots of wonderful things from Father Christmas? Uncle Daniel should be finished hogging the shower, so I can go up and get dressed. Why don't you come with me, and you can tell me what you got.' She herded the children towards the door, pausing on the threshold to call back to her sister. 'Come with us, Kiki Dee. I'm having a wardrobe crisis and can't decide between the green or the blue.'

'I thought you'd decided on the blue?' Kiki followed her sister, then popped her head back around the door a couple of seconds later. 'Will you boys be all right on your own?'

Aaron glanced down at the puppy at his feet, who'd not only been coaxed into a bright-red jacket, but seemed inordinately pleased with it. 'What do you say, Tigger? Reckon we can manage unsupervised, don't you?'

Kiki laughed. 'I find that highly unlikely.' She blew a kiss, aimed more at the dog than himself, and disappeared again.

Hands in his pockets, Aaron was strolling towards the main lounge, when the open door to the dining room caught his eye. Peering in, he found his stepmother, looking chic and festive in a forest-green dress, humming along to carols as she laid the table ready for lunch. Things had been much better between them lately, but they hadn't spent much time alone together. By design on his part, and hers too, he suspected. Still, he couldn't exactly walk past without saying something. 'Morning, Cathy. Happy Christmas.'

Startled, she raised the hand clutching a pile of napkins to her chest as she looked up. A familiar bracelet glittered on her wrist, and he felt his throat tighten as he spotted that the gold bead he'd bought for her birthday had been added to the others. 'Oh, Aaron, you made me jump! I didn't hear you arrive.' She nodded at the tablet on the table next to her, the source of the beautiful music. 'I'm just catching up on *Carols from King's* as we missed it last night.'

The service had always been part of their holiday preparations at home, a brief lull in the general chaos created by two rowdy boys. Drawn by the angelic sounds of the choir, he entered the room to stand next to her and watch the screen for a moment or two. 'The Holly and the Ivy' had always been a particular favourite of his. 'Lovely,' he said, as the music drew to a close. Glancing at Cathy, he nudged her arm gently. 'Nearly as lovely as you look this morning.'

'Oh.' She raised a hand to touch the smooth waves of her hair, a faint blush on her cheek. 'Thank you, and you're looking very handsome.' Reaching up, she straightened the collar on his shirt, then patted his chest. He couldn't remember the last time she'd touched him voluntarily, certainly not in an affectionate way. 'You look more like your father every day.' It was a huge concession, because she'd only ever been able to look at him and see the ghost of his dead mother haunting her, though her relationship with Aaron's dad had been entirely platonic whilst Trisha had been alive. Another tiny step along their path to reconciliation.

He coughed to clear the lump in his throat. 'Speaking of Dad, where is he?'

Cathy busied herself with the table once again. 'Oh, he's hiding away with George and the newspapers somewhere. No sign of your brother yet.'

Given her tone, he decided to ignore the topic of Luke; there was no missing that she'd made no mention of Nee. Given how much Cathy doted on her son, any romantic choice of Luke's would face an uphill battle for her approval. Throw in the drama of their secret wedding and immediate break-up, and he didn't fancy Nee's chances much. Taking a handful of the holly-covered napkins, Aaron moved around the other side of the long table and laid them across the empty plates, copying the way Cathy had placed the others. 'Dad and George seem to be getting on well.'

'Yes, he's a very pleasant man. Everyone's been very welcoming.' There was a slight catch in her voice, and he stopped to study her. Even with her skilful, subtle make-up, there was no disguising the signs of strain around her eyes and mouth.

Taking a breath, he forced himself to make his own concession. 'Are you having a nice time? I know we've thrown you in at the deep end with a load of strangers. You can always come and stay with us, if you'd prefer.'

After placing the wine glass she'd been polishing down, she met his eyes and smiled. 'I'm fine. A bit overwhelmed with all the new faces yesterday, but Mia couldn't have been kinder. Our room is beautiful, and there's plenty of quiet spots to escape to if I need a break.'

He laughed. 'You won't find many of those at ours, that's for sure! Which room are you in?'

'Oh, the lovely beach-themed one. Mia tells me we should be able to see the ocean from the window, but no such luck.' They both turned glum faces towards the thick, drizzly rain outside the patio doors.

'It's supposed to clear up tomorrow.' He hoped so, because too many days cooped up would test even the calmest of temperaments. 'The cove is fantastic, a real haven. It'll be good to get out and get some fresh air.'

She nodded. 'And walk off a few calories too. Mia certainly knows how to put on a good spread.'

They continued to set the table; Cathy handed him a box of luxury crackers and they worked in companionable silence for a few minutes. Aaron glanced around to check on the dog, finding him curled up on the tiles next to the fireplace. A pile of logs and greenery sat in the hearth, but for decorative purposes only. The central heating would be more than enough, especially once everyone was packed in here around the table.

Placing the last cracker down, Aaron stepped back and let Cathy add the finishing touches – bright-red tealights in clear glass holders around a central white pillar candle. 'It looks fab.'

She smiled. 'It's the least I could do to help.' Turning from the table, her smile dropped and she stared down at her clasped hands. 'So, what do you think about it all?'

Surprised she'd sought his opinion, Aaron leaned back against the wall and raised an eyebrow. 'Luke and Nee, you mean?' She nodded, and he considered his next words carefully before speaking. Luke had poured his heart out to him for hours after his birthday party as he'd tried to sort through the mess of his feelings. Aaron knew how he felt about Nee, but it was still a struggle to set aside his protective instincts.

'I think he loves her very much. And she loves him too.' Whatever worries he might have about Nee hurting Luke, that much was as plain as the nose on his face. 'As for the rest of it, I think we have to let them get on with it, and hope they work things out.'

Turning her back, she walked away to stare out of the patio windows. 'I'm not sure I can stand by and say nothing. What if it goes wrong and she leaves him again?' He could hear the pain in her voice, knew some of it stemmed from the fact Luke hadn't confided in her when Nee had left him the first time. It was easy enough to recognise an emotion he knew all too well.

'Then we'll help him pick up the pieces and start again.' Pushing away from the wall, he crossed to stand behind her, then placed a hesitant hand on her shoulder. 'We have to let them find their own way, Cathy.'

With a teary laugh, she reached up to place her hand on his. 'Oh, bloody hell, I know you're right.'

He squeezed her fingers. 'Doesn't mean we have to like it.'

'No. We most certainly don't.'

Chapter Twelve

Nee drifted awake in a layer of sensations, the rattle of something more substantial than just rain on the window, the weight of Luke's arm curled around her waist, holding her tight against the heat of his body, the scents of jasmine and rich amber from the infuser on the bedside table. True to his word, he'd made no attempt at anything more intimate than a sweet, lingering kiss before tucking her beneath his arm and falling asleep the previous night. She'd lain awake for some time after his breathing slowed into a regular deep rhythm, savouring the feel of him there beside her. The tension she hadn't been aware of carrying seeped from her bones in slow stages until, feeling lazy and content, she'd tugged her pillow to the perfect angle beneath her cheek and slept.

She might have lain there for hours had her body not reminded her of the reason she'd woken in the first place. Lifting Luke's arm, she began to wiggle out of bed until his fingers hardened on her hip. 'Where are you going?'

'Just to the bathroom. I'll be back in a minute, keep the bed warm for me.' His grip remained for a few seconds before he let her go and shifted over to lie more on her side of the mattress. By the time she returned, he was snoring softly. Deciding her pyjamas were decent enough covering, she slid her feet into her slippers and crept downstairs for a bit of foraging.

A knife and teaspoon resting in the sink and a few stray crumbs in front of the big wooden breadbin were proof she wasn't the first person up and about. The only lights on the ground floor were those she'd switched on herself, and she guessed whoever it was had taken their breakfast back to bed with them.

The clock on the microwave read 06:30, so she set the coffee machine up and let it brew ready for whoever was up next. Although the heating had kicked in, the kitchen was still too cold for her to want to hang around long enough for the percolator to finish. Tea was her preference, and this early in the morning, Luke would be happy with anything caffeinated so she fixed him a strong cup of instant. Loading a tray with the two mugs, glasses of orange juice, and a selection of pastries from the breadbin, she made her way back to their room.

Having put the tray carefully on top of a chest of drawers, Nee switched on the lamp beside it. The burnt-orange shade cast a low, warm light across the bed, highlighting the threads of gold woven into the bottom edge of the magenta quilt cover. From the moment she'd first seen it, the opulent splendour of the room had delighted her. Some might think it gaudy, but the riot of colour, textures and scents created a fantasy world her senses couldn't get enough of. It was a slice of pure escapism, and she adored the boldness of it, particularly in contrast to the subtle, muted tones of the rest of the house.

She put the coffee and a glass of juice on the table beside Luke, then placed a soft hand on his shoulder. 'I brought you a drink.' He grumbled a bit, then rolled onto his back, giving her enough room to reclaim her side of the bed. Wriggling her toes in the toasty warmth his body heat had left behind, Nee propped her pillows up and sipped her tea; the plate of pastries on her lap wouldn't last much longer if he didn't wake up soon. She nudged him with her elbow. 'You've got about thirty seconds before I eat this Belgian bun.'

121

In truth, the sticky icing was a shade too sweet for her, especially this early in the day, but the threat was enough to get him stirring and he lifted his head. 'Wha'?'

'Coffee. Pastries. Happy Christmas.'

He gave her a sleepy smile, all dimples and rumpled curls. God, he looked like a cherub bent on mischief. 'You're here.'

Yes, she was there, and for the life of her she couldn't remember why she'd chosen to be anywhere else. A wave of emotion crashed through her, and a flood of words full of promises she might not be able to keep filled her throat until she thought she might choke on them. The serene depths of her mug of tea held no answers; and though the bedroom might look like an Eastern bazaar, there was no fortune teller here to read the secrets of the future. Not sure where to start, she fell back on practicality. 'Drink your coffee before it gets cold.'

Finally with it enough to sit up, Luke grabbed his drink and settled his pillows on the headboard so he sat shoulder to shoulder with her. 'You brought me breakfast in bed.'

He pressed his leg against hers beneath the covers and she stroked his ankle with her toes. 'I did.'

'Thank you.' His fingers raised to brush the side of her cheek, and she would have leaned in to the touch had he not dropped his hand to snatch up the Belgian bun, which he then appeared to scoff at least half of with a single bite. 'You can have the pain au chocolat,' he said magnanimously once he managed to swallow the mouthful.

'Gee, thanks.'

'Only one, though.' He finished the bun and started on an apricot jam-filled Danish.

The plate soon held nothing more than a few buttery crumbs, and she moved to put it back on the tray, but he took it from her before she could do more than lift the corner of the quilt. 'Stay there, I'll do it. I've got something to show you, anyway.'

Intrigued, she nestled deeper into the cosy warmth of the bed

122

and waited. The faintest hint of daylight showed through a small gap in the curtains, but the unrelenting beat of the rain still spattered against the glass. It would be a few hours yet before Kiki returned, and it had been agreed the night before that everyone would get up as and when they felt like it. Given the pointed looks Cathy had thrown at her throughout the evening, Nee was in no rush to leave the safe cocoon of their bedroom and make polite conversation.

Luke slipped into the sitting room, and she looked away from the half-open door, forcing her mind to focus on the swirling pattern of the canopy suspended over the bed to resemble the inside of a Bedouin tent, rather than thinking about what lay beyond. If only she hadn't left her portfolio behind . . .

That was the worst thing – knowing the oversized leather case which held her most precious treasures was still in Devin's hands. Her whole life had been in that case, not just the glossy images of her favourite pieces, but her sketchpad and ideas book too, along with her favourite pens, pencils and tools. And she'd left it in his apartment when she'd fled into the night. Knowing she'd have to start again from scratch had been the biggest barrier, leaving her paralysed with dread the few times she'd plucked up enough courage to approach her favourite art-supply store.

Carrying a large A4 ring binder, Luke closed the door on the sitting room and returned to bed. He held the binder in his hands for a few moments before holding it out to her. 'Look, I know I sprang your ring on you yesterday, so I thought it might be better to give you this behind closed doors. Nothing's booked, or anything. I've just been thinking about it a lot since I was up at your dad's.'

She stared down at the big black words on the sheet inside the clear front cover of the folder: 'Honeymoon stuff'. *Honeymoon.* They'd never got that far before. Getting married had been a spur-of-the-moment idea, and neither of them had given much thought to what would happen after the wedding – although she was damn sure neither of them could have imagined the actual outcome.

'If it's too much, you don't have to open it.' God, he would tie himself in knots if he kept trying to do the right thing by her all the time.

She placed her hand on top of the one he'd extended to take the folder back. 'I want to see what you've been planning.'

His fingers hesitated on top of the cover before he nodded. There were so many conflicting emotions on his face – hope, worry, love, fear. They were a perfect match for the feelings fizzing in her stomach. Taking a deep breath, she flipped open the thick cover and gasped as an image of the distinctive orange domes and tiled roofs of Florence filled the first page. With a trembling hand, she turned over the plastic pocket to see the stark glass plains of a pyramid illuminated in the courtyard of the ancient Louvre palace. A reproduction of *The Creation of Adam* – the most famous image from the ceiling of the Sistine Chapel. From Gaudi's Gothic cathedral in Barcelona, to the breathtaking splendour of the gold room in St Petersburg's Hermitage, pictures of the finest artistic sites across the continent filled her gaze.

There were brochures too, together with printouts for train timetables, cheap flight options and hotels in each location. Even details of a few cruise ships. She shook her head, speechless at the time and effort he must have gone to in pulling all the information together. 'Keep looking,' he murmured softly, and she turned the page to find a divided section towards the back.

Here, he'd placed details of artist retreats – a French chateau surrounded by ripe vineyards; a small stately home in a wild Scottish glen; a beautiful pastel villa on the shores of Lake Garda. Heart fluttering wildly in her chest, she met his gaze. 'What would you do if we went on one of these?'

He shrugged. 'Go exploring. Laze in the sunshine and read. I wouldn't have any trouble finding things to keep me occupied.' Giving her his best smile, he flexed his arms. 'I might even do a bit of life modelling, if they needed volunteers.'

An image of him posing like some Greek statute before a group of eager-eyed women filled her mind. *Not a chance!* No one was getting the privilege of seeing him naked other than her. He was hers, and she was not going to share him with anyone else. A devilish urge to tease seized her, and she closed the folder with a snap. Shoving it towards the end of the bed, she got up on her knees and studied him. 'Take off your T-shirt.'

His mouth dropped open in surprise, and she folded her arms. 'Come on, if you want to be a model, I need to make sure you haven't let yourself go.'

'Let myself go? I'll bloody show you!' He stripped off his shirt, displaying the fine, broad muscles of his shoulders and upper chest. Doing her best to maintain a serious expression, she poked and prodded, lifting his arm to flex at different angles to trace the definition lines each pose created. There was no hesitation in her fingers, the landscape of his flesh a sense memory she'd never forgotten. There was a smattering of freckles behind his left shoulder; a jagged, faded scar on his right side from a childhood encounter with a barbed-wire fence. As familiar to her as her own skin, as precious, as beloved.

'Nee.' Her name a roughness in his throat to match the stubble on the proud jaw beneath her fingers.

'Yes,' she whispered. 'Oh, yes . . .' And he reached for her, rolled them both until the blissful weight of him pinned her down. With him to keep her grounded, she'd never float away, never disappear into an insubstantial wisp of nothingness. In his eyes, she could see the reflection of the girl she'd once been, the woman she could grow into with him there to hold her dreams safe.

With trembling fingers, he brushed aside the buttons on her top, peeled back the two halves of the material to expose her to the greedy heat of his gaze. He needed to know, and she needed to tell him what she wanted. That this – them together – was something she needed as much as her next breath. 'Touch me.'

And he did.

With exquisite tenderness, and then a rush of hard, demanding strokes, he shattered her completely, and, in the process, made her whole again. By the time she welcomed him into her body with an insistent tug on his hips, her face was wet with tears; his too, she realised, as he settled against her and claimed her mouth. The familiar dance, the give and take of pleasure between them – she knew it to the point where instinct overtook thought. He was hers, she was his. Man and wife. 'I love you.' A breath of sound. 'I love you.' Louder this time, a heated rush against his ear. 'I love you.' The last a cry she turned her head to muffle in the pillow at the last second.

Panting, he dropped his head into the curve of her neck, the sweat from his brow slicking over her skin. 'God. Nee.'

'I know.' It was the best her poor, scattered brain could come up with. 'I know,' she repeated as a fizz of giggles bubbled through her.

Luke pushed up onto his elbows to stare at her. 'Why are you laughing?' She might have worried, if not for the merriment sparking in his gorgeous brown eyes.

'I don't know,' she gasped, before the giggles took her over. But she did know. Hope. It was hope filling every inch of her, expanding until she couldn't keep it contained within her body.

They'd just finished dressing when she heard the sounds of laughter and little feet running on the stairs. Luke tugged down the front of his dark-grey waistcoat then turned from the full-length mirror. 'Will I do?'

The waistcoat matched his charcoal trousers, and he'd teamed it with a white shirt and a tie covered in dancing snowmen. She thought he looked fabulous – smart and sexy, with just the right dash of fun. Stepping closer, she stroked her hand down his chest. 'I think I might have a thing for waistcoats.'

Laughing, he captured her lips in a quick kiss then slid an arm around her waist – and lower to pet her bottom. 'These velvet trousers are certainly making my morning brighter.' She'd teamed the wide-legged black velvet on her lower half with a red camisole beneath a floaty, sheer blouse in the same vibrant shade. Her parents had always dressed up for Christmas Day, and it was a tradition they were all happy to carry on with.

She twisted away from Luke in a way that kept his touch on her lingering as long as possible, until his fingers slid down her arm to capture her hand. Her progress to the door was halted when, instead of following her, he took a step back towards the bed. 'Luke . . .' She threaded the warning laugh with just a hint of regret that they couldn't do as he was hinting.

'Nee . . .' Sweet, sultry and far too tempting.

Turning to face him, she tried to pull him in the right direction. 'Come on, I know you're just trying to duck out of kitchen duty.' With so many people in the house, and everyone wanting to help, Mia had drawn up a rota so things would get done without too many helpers underfoot. She was on the after-lunch squad, together with Maggie and Richard.

'Well, that's not the only reason, but it was surely worth a try.' He flashed her an unrepentant grin and they left their room hand in hand, meeting Maggie at the top of the stairs.

She'd also chosen red for her outfit, although her soft-knit dress was a deep-berry shade to Nee's scarlet. A gold chain-belt encircled an enviably slim waist, matching the jewellery at her throat, wrist and ears as well as the clip holding her ash-blonde hair in an elegant twist. *Oh, to have an ounce of her style and grace!* Nee might have been intimidated by the woman, especially considering the great reputation of her gallery, but she was kindness personified. 'Good morning and Merry Christmas to you both!'

They exchanged a quick kiss on the cheek, then Luke offered his arm to Maggie in a gallant gesture. 'Allow me.'

'Thank you, dear.' She took his arm, glancing back at Nee as they began to walk down. 'So, what do you think of your husband's amazing design skills, then? I adore the pretty room I'm in, but I must say the sheer opulence of the Harem sets my heart racing.

Have you tried out that gorgeous corner bath yet? If I got in it, I don't think I'd ever get out – heaven!'

Almost stumbling in shock, Nee managed to stammer out something about how much she loved the suite of rooms. Her instinct about it not being Mia's style had been right – but, *Luke?* Practical, straightforward Luke, whose own flat boasted the plain, dark colours of a typical bachelor pad? With his natural charm and tendency to turn everything into a joke, it would be easy to take him at face value. That beneath the façade, an imagination full of wild fancy lurked, surprised her. They might be married, but there was so much about him she didn't know. With a silent promise to pay more attention to the things he *didn't* say, Nee followed them into the kitchen.

'Oh, damn. I forgot the tray.' She turned on the threshold, but Luke beat her to it.

'No, no. I'm the kitchen elf this morning.' He jogged back towards the stairs, just in time to bump into Daniel as he came through the doorway, carrying Charlie in his arms.

'Morning, all!' Daniel bent down to set the little girl on her feet. 'Here you are, Your Majesty.' He bowed to Charlie, receiving a little tap on his head with her silver wand in return. Last night's butterfly wings had been teamed with the wand and a sparkly tiara. They were the perfect contrast to the midnight-blue velvet dress she wore with thick, white tights.

'A fairy princess?' Nee guessed.

'That's right,' Kiki said as she came through the door, Mia and Matty on her heels. 'Santa brought you a new tiara, didn't he, darling?'

'Yes! And a pink bike, and Elsa, and fairy stamps, and a rabbit bag, and . . .' Nee shook her head as the dizzying list of presents continued.

Kiki looked between her and Mia, a blush on her cheek. 'Santa might have got a bit carried away,' she whispered, and they all smiled. After the year they'd been through, Kiki and her family deserved a bit of spoiling.

'Right, you lot are in my way.' Mia made a shooing motion with her hands. 'All of you into the front room and let me sort out what's going on.' She checked her watch. 'Lord, I'm at least half an hour behind schedule.'

Kiki led the children away, but Nee hesitated. 'What can I do?'

Her eldest sister smiled. 'Not a thing, darling. I've got Daniel, and . . .' She gestured with her head as Luke appeared carrying the tray. ' . . .This one. I'll be fine. We did most of the prep last night and the turkey's already in the oven. Madeline should be here any minute and she's on lunch duty.' She paused. 'Actually, can you do a headcount and get everyone in the big room? Once I'm back on track, we can serve the Bucks Fizz and open the presents.'

Nee raised her fingers in a cheeky salute. 'Aye, aye, Captain.'

129

Chapter Thirteen

Luke and Daniel made swift work of the breakfast things, and they had the dishwasher loaded and all the boards wiped down before Madeline and Richard came dashing through the back door sheltering under a wide umbrella. 'Bloody filthy rain! What happened to that white Christmas I asked for? Hello, my lovely boy, Merry Christmas.' Madeline offered her cheek to Daniel as he moved to help her out of her coat. She looked around the kitchen, 'Well, don't you all look splendid. You especially, Luke.'

He did a twirl, still wearing the apron he'd put on to keep his clothes from getting splashed. 'I scrub up all right, don't I, Mads?'

'You certainly do.' She crossed the room to give Mia a quick hug. 'Right, what's to do?'

'Turkey's nearly done, so can you get the beef out and into a dish, and then maybe double-check there's enough veg?' Mia glanced over at him and Daniel. 'Do you two want to put some nibbles out, and pour some drinks? Nee was going to check what everyone wanted . . .'

'I'll see to that,' Richard said. 'Morning, lads, everything all right with the world?' He shook hands with them both.

Three parts ecstatic and one part terrified he'd imagined what had been the most incredible start to the day, Luke couldn't hold back a satisfied grin. 'Pretty bloody perfect, thanks.'

'Oh, I like the sound of that. Come and tell me more.' Madeline plonked what looked to him like half a cow on the kitchen table and threw him a saucy wink.

Damn. He adored Madeline, but she picked up on every stray word. Things with Nee were so close to being everything he wanted, he couldn't afford for her to get skittish if they became the topic of conversation. He held his hands up. 'Come on, now. A gentleman never kisses and tells.'

'So, there was kissing, eh?' she said, slyly, and he couldn't stop a rueful laugh.

'I'm saying nothing, Not another bloody word.' He made a zipping motion across his lips, then quickly mimed unzipping them as he sent an appealing look across the room. 'Richard, can you do something about your wife, please?'

'Sorry, son. I gave up trying years ago. You're on your own, I'm afraid.' Grinning broadly, Richard left the room to chase down the drinks orders and, deciding his own retreat was in order, Luke escaped into the pantry to track down the nibbles.

With the lunch preparations back under control and everyone clutching a glass of something fizzy – Bucks Fizz for those who wanted it, and sparkling elderflower for small people and those who preferred to watch what they were drinking – the grand opening of presents began. With his Santa hat back in place, Daniel worked his way through the stack of gaily wrapped boxes and bundles beneath the tree, placing a small pile before each adult, and considerably larger ones in front of the children. Paper, ribbons and labels flew as everyone got stuck in.

'Socks!' Luke brandished the multipack of outrageously striped footwear with a grin. 'Cheers, Mum.'

'Snap!' Richard held up a set of more muted socks.

'Double-snap!' Aaron chimed in.

'Four of a kind!' His dad waved some black socks with fluorescent toes and heels.

'I suppose this makes it a full house.' George gave a shy smile as he too displayed a matching gift. Setting them aside, he picked up a small, square parcel. 'Hankies?' His guess was met with laughter.

'Oh, I think I've got one like that too.' Richard dug around in the stack in front of him.

Madeline dug him in the ribs. 'Well, if your every response when asked what you'd like is '*I don't need anything*', then what do you expect?'

'A bottle of scotch?' Richard ducked when she aimed a swatting blow at his head. 'An all-expenses-trip to the Bahamas?'

Madeline snorted. 'You'll be lucky if I don't send you to the knacker's yard, you silly old fool.'

Although she was shaking her head at him, their devotion to each other was obvious to Luke. He let his gaze drift from the bantering couple to where Nee sat on his left. Bent over a set of instructions for something Matty had received, her short hair had slid forward to shield her face from view. He hooked it back behind her ear, letting his fingers trace the delicate shell, and her head moved to chase the touch, though she kept her focus on the conversation with her nephew. Intrigued, he abandoned the rest of his gifts to shift closer, stretching one leg out behind her back so he could lean across and see what held their attention.

Nee immediately turned and settled into the gap between his legs, leaning her back against his chest and extending her hand so he could read the tightly spaced pages of print. Frowning, he tried to make sense of what he was reading. 'Are you building a space shuttle?'

Matty scrunched up his nose as he looked up at him. 'That's not what one of the pictures is, so I don't think so.'

Nee yielded the booklet to him when Luke gave it a tug, and he flipped it over to study the cover. Pictures of a robot, and four different kinds of vehicles, including a helicopter, boasted the things that could be made from the bucket of Junior Meccano pieces. Memories filled his head of hours spent at the dining-room table with his dad and Aaron as they tried, and sometimes failed, to build similar things. His older brother had been much better than him, his more-patient nature perfectly suited to the intricacies.

Full of energy, Luke had been too easily distracted, too prone to fits of frustrated destruction. Give him a ball and enough space to run himself ragged and he'd been happy. His eyes flicked to the incessant rain drumming against the large picture window, and he bit back a sigh. Somewhere in the pile beside Matty was a beach cricket set he'd purchased for him. If the weather didn't let up, they might not get a chance to try it out. It might be tough to swing the bat bundled up in coats and scarves, but that wouldn't matter. He just hated being cooped up, and was also dying to see what the normally serene cove looked like in the full lash of winter.

Knowing when to admit defeat, he handed the leaflet back to Matty. 'Why don't you ask Grandad Brian to help you? He's an engineer, did Aaron tell you?' Wide-eyed, the little boy shook his head. Luke nodded. 'He's brilliant at this sort of thing, and I know he'd be really pleased if you asked him to show you what to do.'

He still looked a bit uncertain, so Luke glanced over his shoulder towards his dad, caught his eye and tilted his head in their direction. Brian put down the book he'd been holding and crossed to join them. 'What's this?' He knelt down next to Matty and tilted the bright-red bucket back to study the label. 'Wow, I haven't seen Meccano for ages. Is this yours, Matty? You lucky boy!'

Biting his lip in a gesture Luke had seen Kiki do a hundred times, Matty nodded. 'Luke said, you might show me?' His voice was all hesitancy and hope, and it broke Luke's heart anew that, despite his brother's best efforts, this little boy still expected disappointment and rejection.

His dad knew the score, though, they all did, and Luke could read the gentle understanding in his face as he reached out to ruffle Matty's hair. 'I'd love to. Shall we clear a space on the table and have a look now?' Holding the bucket in one hand, and the boy's shoulder in the other, Brian steered a smiling Matty through the chaos littering the floor and over to the table.

Remembering he was still on duty, Luke kissed Nee's cheek. 'I'd better give them a hand to clear the table.'

She stood with him. 'I'll help. If you take the plates, I'll find a bin bag and get rid of all this paper.'

He'd washed the bowls and set them on the rack to dry by the time she joined him in the kitchen with a black bag bulging with wrapping paper and discarded boxes. 'If you stick it in the pantry, we can sort the recycling from it later,' he suggested. Although he was a big fan of saving the environment, there was an ulterior motive to his suggestion. Everyone was busy in the front room, and the pantry was quiet and secluded . . .

'Hey, what are you up to?' Nee asked, although from the way his hands were sliding over her hips, he thought it was pretty obvious.

'Come closer and I'll show you.' Her arms curled around his neck and he boosted her up to sit on the low shelf running along the back wall. She welcomed his kiss with a soft laugh, and he raised one hand to cup the back of her neck, stroking the delicate column of skin.

Touching her, tasting a hint of sharp orange juice on her lips from where she'd drained the last of her Bucks Fizz, he relished every sensation. The eagerness of her response gave him greater hope that, after earlier that morning, they were truly on the road to building a life together again. There was no hesitancy in her kiss, no hint of regret or second thoughts, and though he knew it was too soon to take the wonder of being with her for granted, he couldn't help but let his mind weave dreams of their future.

He thought about his father teaching Matty in his slow, patient manner; remembered, too, the way George had surprised them all at the wedding by enthralling the children with his animated storytelling. And, just for a moment or two, in the sweet tenderness of the kiss, he imagined *their* children in the same scenarios. Not that he was in any hurry to start a family; it was simply the possibility of them, when he'd feared that future lost to him for ever, that sent his head spinning.

'Don't mind me.'

They broke apart, turning to see Daniel smirking at them from the doorway of the pantry, and Luke sent him a glare that only increased the width of his grin. 'A little busy here, mate,' Luke said, giving his back to the other man in the hope he'd take the hint and bugger off. He stared down at Nee, all puffy-lipped and starry-eyed from their kiss, and ducked his head, intent on capturing her mouth once more.

'I'm only the advance party. Mia's on her way to crack on with lunch.' Daniel paused, and when he spoke again there was real amusement in his voice. 'And I think I heard your mum volunteered to help her.'

'Oh, God. Put me down.' Nee shoved at his chest, making enough room to wriggle off the shelf. Her hands stroked frantically over her hair, setting in place the strands he'd mussed. 'I'm already in her bad books as it is without her catching us messing about like this.'

Luke frowned. His mum had been polite to Nee, making a point of thanking her for the fancy face cream and other toiletries they'd given her as a joint present. He hadn't a clue what she used, and it had been Nee's suggestion for him to get his dad to make a list of what was on Cathy's dressing table. She'd seemed genuinely pleased, and Maggie had cooed enviously over the heavy glass jar whose contents promised some outlandish, age-defying miracle. Given his own propensity to play it safe with a spa voucher or some fancy chocolates, she had to know Nee had chosen her presents this year. If there'd been any tension between the two of them, it had been too subtle for him to pick up.

Lifting her chin with a gentle finger, he forced her to meet his eyes. 'Is there a problem I need to know about?'

She turned her head away and slipped past him. 'No. Everything's fine. I was just making a silly joke.' He might have called her on the blatant lie had voices not filled the kitchen at that moment. With a sigh, and a promise to press for a more satisfactory answer once they were alone again, he followed her out.

Of course, the first person he saw was his mum. She raised an eyebrow at him and he followed her glance to see his shirt was partially untucked thanks to Nee's wandering fingers. Shoving the white cotton hurriedly back into his trousers, he straightened his waistcoat then spread his hands as though presenting himself for inspection. With a roll of her eyes and a tut, Cathy dismissed him and turned her attention back to Mia.

Nee leaned close enough to whisper, 'I'm going to see if anyone needs anything next door,' then beat a hasty retreat before anyone thought to comment on the high colour in her cheeks.

Luke hung back for a few moments, until it was clear to him there were more than enough willing hands present. He touched his mum on the arm and gestured towards the hall. Hearing her heels clicking on the tiles behind him, he kept walking until he reached the cosy sitting room which had been designated a child-free zone for the week. A quick peek told him the room was free and he stood back to usher her in, closing the door behind her.

Cathy turned to face him, flicked a non-existent piece of fluff from the sleeve of her blouse and eventually crossed her arms with a sigh when he did nothing more than study her. 'Well, what is it?'

Tucking his hands in his pockets, Luke shrugged. 'I just thought we should have a bit of a catch-up. I've barely seen you since we arrived.' True, they'd been at Butterfly Cove less than forty-eight hours, but now he thought about it, it was obvious his mum had been avoiding him – avoiding Nee was probably the truth of it, but it amounted to the same thing.

She shrugged one silk-clad shoulder. 'It's been nonstop since we got here and, with so many new people to meet, my head is spinning.' Her eyes darted to the left, back to his, then skittered away again. 'Besides, I thought you'd be too preoccupied to be bothered with me and your dad.'

Bloody hell, if they gave out prizes for passive-aggressive behaviour, she'd have enough to fill a trophy cabinet. 'Mum . . .'

'What? What do you want me to say, Luke? You can't just drop all this in my lap and expect me to be okay with it. You got married and never said a word to any of us, for God's sake!' She threw her hands up in a gesture of clear frustration. 'Oh! I know I promised your brother I'd keep quiet about it, but I can't. Not now you've forced the point. She left you – walked out without so much as a word – and now I'm supposed to be thrilled you're suddenly reunited again?'

Damn. He knew it was a lot to ask, expecting her to accept all the surprise news he'd dumped in her lap, but it was like she wasn't even prepared to give Nee a chance. And when had she and Aaron suddenly become confidants? 'She's trying, Mum. You must see that from all the thought she put into making sure we got your presents spot-on.'

Cathy moved closer to reach up and place a hand on his cheek. 'It's not about her, darling. From what I've seen, she's a lovely girl. It's about you.' He tried to pull away, but she raised her other hand to hold his face. 'You're my son, and Aaron might have inherited your father's good nature, but you're as stubborn and as bloody-minded as I am. Once we make up our minds we want something, we go all-out to get it – and the rest of the world be damned.'

Releasing her grip, she moved past him to stare out of the window into the pouring rain. 'From the first moment I saw Brian, there was never any other man for me.' Her fingers pressed against the pane. 'Unfortunately, he'd already met Trisha and there was nothing I could do about it, not unless I wanted to risk losing them both from my life.'

Luke closed the gap between them to place a hand on Cathy's shoulder; he knew the story of how his mum and Aaron's mum had been best friends who happened to fall in love with the same man. He also knew his mum had never said a word to either of them, had stood by and watched them get married, build a life and a family together until that evil bastard of a disease had stolen Trisha's life away.

'When she died . . .' A shuddering breath wracked her slender frame. Cathy took a deep breath and tried again. 'When she died, my beautiful, bright Trisha, it was a relief for us all. So much pain, I've never seen anything like it. She was glad to go in the end, made Brian and I swear we'd take care of each other for her. When she said that, it made me wonder if she'd known all along about my feelings for him.'

His mum turned to face him, and the anguish in her eyes made him flinch. 'That should have made it better, but it didn't. When you've wanted something for so long and you finally get it, your expectations are so high, the reality can't possibly match it. That's what happened to me. I'd built this picture-perfect image of life with your dad and whenever something went wrong, I needed someone to blame.' And that someone had been his poor brother.

Cathy closed her eyes as she drew a long, composing breath, and when she opened them they shimmered with tears. 'I'm not dragging up the past for sympathy. I've no one to blame for any of those difficulties other than myself, and it's to Aaron's credit he'll even speak to me now. I just see that same possessiveness I felt when I see you looking at Nee, and it scares me.'

He took a step back, not liking the comparison one bit. 'It's not like that with us, Mum. Nee and I have talked things out, and I understand why she left. I've forgiven her.'

'Just like that?' She laughed, a harsh crack full of disbelief. 'You might have convinced yourself that's true, but I'm not buying it. I *know* you, Luke.'

Anger burned bright in his veins, and his hands clenched into fists at his sides as he fought to keep his voice low. 'Maybe you don't know me as well as you think. Everything between me and

Nee is great. I've forgiven you for a lot of things, but I swear if you try and come between us, I'll walk away and never look back. And that's the *truth*.'

Cathy held up her hands in surrender. 'All right, all right, darling, the last thing I want to do is fall out with you. I won't say another word, and I'll make sure Nee feels welcome into the family. I really do like her, you know.' When she touched his arm, he was still so angry it was all he could do not to shake her off. She tightened her grip until he forced himself to meet her gaze. 'If I'm wrong about this, Luke, then nothing would make me happier. And that's *my* truth.'

Chapter Fourteen

As they made their way to the dining-room table, Nee found herself caught in a friendly, though persistent, pincer movement by Brian and Cathy, which resulted in her sitting between them and opposite Luke. Their sudden interest in her couldn't be a coincidence, not after her conversation with Luke in the pantry earlier. She glanced from side to side then widened her eyes at him across the table, but he just flashed his dimples in response. That wide-eyed innocent look was fooling no one.

Deciding to accept the olive branch, if that was indeed what this was, she turned slightly in her seat to angle her body towards Cathy. Time to make some small talk and see where it led. The table looked beautiful with red-and-white accents offset by the vivid green holly decorating the napkin set across her plate. Seizing on the décor as a suitably neutral topic, she gestured to the candles set in the centre of the table. 'Doesn't this look great?'

'Your sister bought all the accessories, so it was an easy job, and I enjoyed the chance to do something,' Cathy said, as she unfolded her napkin and smoothed it over her lap. She smiled at Nee, a look that held considerably more warmth than she had become used to from her. 'I think Mia would spoil us all rotten given half the chance.'

Nee nodded in agreement. 'She's always been that way, for as long as I can remember. Like a little mother hen fussing around us. I'm so used to it, I have to make a conscious effort to stop her from doing everything.' Her gaze travelled to the end of the table where her sister had been pressed into her seat by Daniel to stop her from carrying armfuls of heavy plates and dishes from the kitchen. She saw Mia frown as an oven-proof dish full of roasted vegetables was placed in a position that was probably contrary to whatever mental layout she'd had in her mind, and looked away with a smile. Leaning closer, she lowered her voice to a confiding level. 'Poor Mia, she might burst something if Daniel keeps fussing at her.'

'I'm sure she'll make her feelings known if he oversteps the mark. I doubt any of you have any problems expressing yourselves. I've seen Kiki handle Aaron well enough, and she's not someone who strikes me as confrontational.' Cathy took a sip from the water glass beside her plate, and there was something about her expression which made Nee wonder if Kiki might not have handled Cathy too. She might be the shiest of the three of them, but Kiki could be fierce when it came to defending what was hers. Her confrontation with the provost at their mother's wake had proven that.

Cathy tilted her head sideways, pinning Nee with a steady look. 'If Mia's the boss, and Kiki's the mediator, what does that make you?' There was no malice in the question – she could read only genuine interest in her eyes – but it struck to the heart of the problem. Who was she? With her sisters taking the burden of their parents' failings upon themselves, she'd been free to fly, free to strike out in the world and follow her dreams. They'd filled her with confidence, a belief she could conquer whatever challenge she faced, and she'd been foolish enough to believe it. Everything had fallen easily for her, so running headlong into failure had left her utterly shattered.

She knew they still believed in her, and that Luke, too, would

141

encourage her to reach and grab for every opportunity, but she had no confidence in herself any more. Full of arrogance, she'd believed herself invincible, above risk or threat, not the easy, pathetic prey she'd turned out to be. The sounds of conversation, glasses clinking and cutlery against china faded into the background as she took a deep breath and whispered, 'Lost. I'm lost.'

Cathy's hand moved to clasp hers tightly. 'But not alone, dear. Try and hold on to that at least.' After another quick squeeze, she released her fingers and turned her attention to Richard sitting on her other side. 'Could you pass me the potatoes, please? They look heavenly and I've put on a loose pair of trousers especially for this feast.'

With a casual brush of her hand, Nee knocked her napkin off her lap, giving herself the chance to duck under the table and retrieve it. *Bloody hell!* She had no idea what had possessed her to make that confession – and to Luke's mum of all people! A flash of black and tan stripes caught her eye and the sight of Tigger trying to wriggle under the table was enough to ward off the rising panic. The puppy froze the instant he realised he'd been spotted. He tucked his face onto his front paws, tail wagging like a windscreen wiper on the highest setting.

The tablecloth stirred beside her and she glanced sideways at Brian, who'd bent down beside her. 'Everything all right?' he asked quietly, and she nodded towards the dog with a grin. 'Ah.' Brian's face disappeared, to be replaced a few seconds later with his hand, a sliver of turkey breast dangling from his fingers. Tigger shuffled forward until he perched directly under the juicy titbit and sniffed it warily. The meat dropped to the floor, and he pounced on it, tail a blur of happiness.

Feeling a little more settled, Nee sat back up to find Luke frowning at her. *'All right?'* he mouthed at her, and she nodded before accepting a plate laden with slices of roast meat from Brian. He tipped her a wink which she returned. *Not alone.* She grasped the promise like a lifeline.

With everyone's plates loaded, it was time for the crackers. Arms crossed in front of them like they were about to break into 'Auld Land Syne', they attempted to pull them all at once, with varying degrees of success. Nee ended up with two stub ends and no prize, whilst Luke whooped with delight over winning a miniature deck of cards and a pocket bottle opener.

'If I didn't win, that means I don't have to wear a hat, right?'

Nee's question was met with hoots of derision as Daniel picked up a still-furled orange hat and flicked it across the table at her. A bright-pink paper crown already adorned his black cropped hair at a jaunty angle. 'Get it on, you party pooper.' A quick glance around showed she was the only one without a crown – even Maggie had one set delicately atop her perfectly set and styled hair. Laughing, Nee unwrapped the hat and put it on to a round of applause.

'Can we eat now?' Aaron's plaintive appeal and hangdog expression made Kiki shake her head at him.

'It's been, what, an hour since you last ate?'

He cast her a bashful smile. 'Maybe ten minutes. I might have sampled a couple of sausages wrapped in bacon. Quality control and all that.'

Kiki mock-sighed. 'If you fed any to the dog, you're staying up all night with him, not me!' From the corner of her eye, Nee saw Brian duck his head as though fascinated with the food on his plate. She fixed her eyes on her own, knowing if she glanced his way for a second they'd give the game away. Lucky for them, Matty sent a spinning top he'd been trying to master flying off the tablecloth to land with a plop in the gravy boat. Silence reigned over the table for a long moment.

'Nice shot.'

Nee goggled. Of all the people to step in and rescue the boy, she'd never have expected it to be her dad, who'd always been a stickler for good manners at the table. Whatever scolding words might have been on Kiki's tongue froze as she stared across the table at Nee, her jaw dropping open and the shock in her eyes reflecting Nee's own. Giving Matty a quick glance which said she'd speak to him later, Kiki used a teaspoon to fish out the toy and place it on the saucer below the gravy boat. 'Shall we eat?' she asked. 'Before all Mia's hard work goes to waste?'

Stuffed to the gunnels, and probably another mouthful past that, Nee was grateful to be on clear-up duty as it at least gave her the chance to stand up for a few minutes. Together with Maggie and Richard, she ferried the serving dishes and dirty plates from the dining room to the kitchen. Pausing to survey the mess, Maggie sighed at the scene of devastation before them. Taking an apron from the back of the door, she carefully hooked it around her neck, then straightened her shoulders with a look of determination on her face. 'Right, I'll sort out leftovers. Nee, do you want to scrape and stack, and Richard can rinse and load whatever will go in the dishwasher?'

'Sounds good.' Nee smiled her thanks when Richard handed her an apron, before taking a pink, frilly one for himself and putting it on. He placed the scraps bucket for the compost within easy reach for her and started collecting the cutlery – leaving her a large serving spoon to use. They worked in companionable silence, broken only by the soft strains of something classical coming from the radio. Ever-organised, Mia had left a stack of plastic boxes with snap-lock lids on the board next to the fridge for the leftovers, and they were soon full and stored in the fridge.

'I call that a job well done,' Richard said after rinsing the last plate, stacking it and turning the dishwasher on.

Daniel appeared loaded with dessert bowls. He plonked them down with an apologetic smile. 'A job half done, sorry. Aaron's on his way with the glasses too.'

'I knew it was too good to be true. The bowls can wait for the next load, but we'd better deal with the glasses.' He snapped on a pair of rubber gloves. 'Right then, Nee, my darling. I'll wash and you dry. Deal?'

'Deal.'

'Is there something I can use to wipe down the boards, whilst you two do that?' Maggie asked. Richard stepped to one side to give her room, and Nee retrieved some kitchen spray and a clean cloth from beneath the sink, and then they were off again. By the time Mia and Kiki walked in with the remains of a chocolate log and half a trifle they were done.

'Oh, I can't believe how great it looks in here. Thank you!' Mia's relief at not facing a mountain of tidying up was palpable.

Nee stepped forward to take the dish from her hands. 'I think we'll just wrap this and put it in the fridge as is. Someone's bound to want some more at teatime.' She studied the fine lines bracketing her eldest sister's eyes. 'You look done-in. Why don't you go and have a nap? We can sort out coffee if anyone wants one.'

Mia's mouth pursed in a look of stubborn determination, and she might have protested had Kiki not stepped in. 'Go on. Dad's eyes were drooping at the table. If you have a lie-down, then anyone else who wants one won't feel so bad.'

Knowing she was beaten, Mia raised her hands up in surrender. 'I suppose you two are going to bully me until I agree?'

'Absolutely.'

'Count on it.'

Nee and Kiki spoke over each other, and they all laughed.

With Mia dispatched upstairs, together with an ever-watchful Daniel, Nee and Kiki made their way to the front room. Maggie and Richard headed for the sitting room to watch the Queen's speech after Kiki informed them Madeline and George were already in there. They walked into the big, family room to a clatter of plastic and Matty's exasperated shout of his sister's name. 'I told you not to touch it!' Red-faced and with angry tears glittering in his eyes, Matty scowled at the little girl, who promptly burst into noisy sobs.

'Oh, God.' Kiki dashed forward to scoop Charlie up, whilst Brian leaned over to speak in a low, soothing voice to Matty.

'But she ruined it,' Matty half-wailed.

'I know, I know, but we can put it back together again. She just wanted to play.' Brian lifted the boy and settled him on his lap. 'Look, this section's mostly intact. It'll just take a few minutes to set things right again.'

Charlie continued to cry like her heart was breaking, unintelligible words punctuating her sobs. Nee gestured to her harried-looking sister. 'Let's take her upstairs for a minute.'

'Good idea.' Kiki followed her back into the hallway. 'Can you grab the holdall for me, and then check Matty's okay? It's so unlike him,' she said over her shoulder to Aaron, who'd joined them.

Retrieving a blue bag, Aaron handed it to Nee, then paused to stroke a finger down Charlie's damp cheek. 'He tried to tell you you were too little to play with the Meccano, didn't he, poppet?' The little girl buried her head in Kiki's shoulder and wailed some more.

Kiki raised her eyebrows at him over Charlie's head. 'And she wouldn't be told, am I right?'

'Yep. You know our girl, stubborn as a mule.' After pressing a quick kiss to Kiki's temple, Aaron returned to the front room, and Nee led the way upstairs to her room.

Her sister waited until the door was shut behind them before setting Charlie down and kneeling in front of her. 'Stop that, now.' The firm tone was not one Nee had often heard from her usually gentle sister, but it did the trick. After a couple more indignant sniffles, her niece subsided into silence.

'Good girl. Now then, did Matty ask you not to touch his Meccano?'

Charlie ducked her head, muttering, 'I wanted to play.' Nee had to admire the little girl's spirit. Worried she would ruin Kiki's masterful handling of the situation with an ill-timed smile, she went into the bathroom to clean her teeth.

By the time she returned, Kiki had Charlie out of her dress and into a cosy-looking onesie with an adorable set of bunny ears on the hood. 'All better?'

Kiki nodded. 'I think so. Miss Charlie understands her brother is very good at sharing, but that he's also allowed to keep some things just for himself, don't you, darling?' Charlie didn't look entirely convinced, but she nodded in agreement.

Nee bent down to pick up the discarded clothing, folded it up and put it in the holdall. Straightening up, she showed Charlie the DVD she'd found tucked inside the bag. 'Why don't we go downstairs and watch something nice on the telly?'

'Elsa!' All smiles in an instant, Charlie let Nee pick her up and they trooped back downstairs. As soon as they re-entered the front room, there was only one person on Charlie's mind. 'Aaron, Aaron!' She held out her arms to him, straining to be let go. Nee put her down quickly before all the wriggling caused her to drop her, and the little girl dashed across the room to where Aaron and Luke sat side by side on the wide sofa.

'Here's my little bunny!' He scooped her up and held her close so they could rub noses. 'All right, now? No more fuss?'

She shook her head, a solemn look on her face. 'No fuss.'

'Good girl. Have you said sorry to Matty for spoiling his robot?' Biting her lip, she shook her head again.

Matty crossed the room to plonk himself down next to them as soon as Luke shifted up to make a space for him. 'It's all right, silly bunny. I didn't mean to shout.'

'Sorry.' She wiggled over to put one arm around her brother's neck and a soft sigh of relief whispered around the adults in the room at disaster averted and the return of peace.

'What've you got there?' Luke nodded to Nee, and she held up the *Frozen* DVD with a grin.

'I've never seen it, have you?' Her excitement was met with a groan from both brothers, making her laugh. 'I want some snow on Christmas Day, even if it's only on-screen.' The never-ending rain was still pouring down outside.

Cathy glanced up from the huge crossword she'd found in one of the newspapers. 'Oh, I haven't seen it either. Put it on so I have an excuse to put this wretched thing down.' She glared in disgust at the crossword, then held the paper out to Brian. 'You'll have to finish it off.'

Her husband settled on the arm of the chair, put on a pair of dark-framed glasses and frowned at the puzzle. 'That's not how you spell "myrrh", my love. Should be two r's and one aitch.' He jumped up again as she went to swat him with the paper and he snatched it off her with a laugh. 'Don't worry, I'll fix it.' Nee couldn't stop her own laugh when Cathy stuck out her tongue at his retreating back.

She set the DVD up, and joined Luke, who'd slid from the sofa to sprawl on the floor, settling herself between his stretched-out legs, her back to his chest. The kids were snuggled into Aaron, eyes already glued on the screen, and Kiki climbed over her and Luke to join them on the sofa.

Luke's arms closed around her, tugging her closer still. 'This is nice,' he whispered in her ear, and she nodded. Content, a little drowsy and surrounded by the warmth of her family, she rested her head on his shoulder and let the magic of Disney sweep her away to a magical land of ice and snow.

Chapter Fifteen

Gritty-eyed, Luke studied the canopy above the bed in the room he'd designed for the woman beside him. The incessant rain pattered against the window, adding to the restless feelings which had been stirring in his gut since the conversation with his mum before lunch the previous day. He loved Nee, and she loved him – had told him, and shown him as much. So why wasn't he curled around her in the warm cocoon of their bed and dreaming of their future?

Because maybe his mum had a point.

He'd convinced himself his intentions had been entirely honourable when he'd proposed they spend Christmas together. That he'd be helping heal the bonds between Nee and her family, as well as with him. Lying there, in the stillness of the dark, it was hard to hide the truth from himself. He'd hoped that by showing her how good life was with everyone they loved around them, she'd find it too difficult to walk away. Christ, he was a manipulative bastard.

As though sensing his tension, Nee stirred and placed a hand on his arm. 'What's the matter?'

Here was his chance to admit the truth and give her a choice. All he had to do was say the words, admit the dark truth behind his intentions, give her the honesty he'd demanded from her time and again. 'Nothing. The rain woke me up, that's all.' A coward, and a bastard.

'Bloody weather,' she mumbled, already mostly asleep. 'Snuggle down and forget about it.' She curled her back into his side, nudging against his hip until he rolled and pulled her against him. 'Mmm, better?'

'Much better.' He kissed the back of her shoulder. 'Go back to sleep, darling.' In the morning . . . he'd talk to her in the morning. Or the day after at the latest. Definitely before the end of the week.

Breakfast was a lazy affair, with his mum stepping in to man the frying pan when Mia bolted from the room after the scent of bacon got too much for her stomach to handle. Daniel rose to head after her until Cathy brandished the spatula at him. 'Sit down and give your poor wife five minutes' peace, for goodness' sake.' The threat might have held more weight had she not been wearing a pink sweatshirt bearing a picture of a cute polar bear and the motto *Ice love you*. Luke glanced down at his own jumper covered in dancing Christmas trees and decided not to say anything. Mia had decreed the dress code for Boxing Day would be themed tops and jeans.

Abashed, Daniel sank down into his chair, though his head remained turned towards the half-open kitchen door. The expression on his face was a perfect match for the puzzled-looking reindeer on his T-shirt. Cathy flipped the bacon onto a piece of kitchen paper and added another packet of rashers to the pan. 'I think this will be the last lot,' she said to Nee, who stood beside her buttering bread to make sandwiches.

'Here, you go, Dad.' Nee placed a plate in front of George, and then a second in front of Daniel. 'Stop pouting and eat. If she's not down in ten minutes, you can take her up some ginger ale, okay?' He nodded forlornly and it was all Luke could do not to smirk at the pathetic state of his friend.

150

'Ten across, "*Or What You Will*" in seven and five.' His dad peered over the top of his glasses. 'Come on, Luke. Prove I didn't waste all my money on your education.'

Luke shook his head. 'Give it a rest, Dad. At least until I've finished my coffee.' He hooked his arm around Nee's waist as she approached his side of the table with a doorstep sandwich. 'Thanks, gorgeous.'

With a kiss to his lips, she leaned in to his embrace for a moment. 'I gave you the extra-crispy bits.' Her hair was held back from her face with a fluffy white headband that had two fat, jolly Santas attached to springs sticking up from it. They matched the larger one on her white jumper perfectly. It shouldn't be possible for her to look sexy, but he couldn't take his eyes off her. Here was a glimpse of his Nee – funny, sassy and just a touch outrageous. Maybe he'd just let his mum project her own worries onto him and he wouldn't need to have that conversation with her after all.

He must have been staring because she waggled her head to make the Santas bobble around. 'What? I thought you liked it well done?'

He nodded. 'I do. I just wasn't sure you'd remember.'

She laughed, negating his sudden panic that he'd said the wrong thing. 'Of course I remember. I've put extra tomato ketchup on it, too.'

With a sense of dread, he lifted the corner of the top slice and sighed in relief at the dark, spicy slick of HP sauce on the bacon. He hated tomato ketchup almost as much as she loved it. Their first argument had been over a portion of fish and chips they'd shared on a bench on the way home from the pub one night. Starving, because they'd been too busy chatting to get around to ordering a meal, Nee had darted into the chip shop and returned with the greasy, heavenly treat wrapped in paper. Mouth watering at the smell of fried fish, salt and vinegar, he'd almost wept at the horror of red sauce coating everything. She'd settled back to gleefully stuff her face, leaving him to trudge back up the road to get a second, unsullied portion.

She patted his cheek for falling for her ruse, then leaned across to study the crossword in front of his dad. 'Twelfth Night,' she said, then returned to her spot beside his mum, putting an extra swagger in her walk. If she'd been a cat, her tail would've been swishing.

'Of course it is, clever girl.' Brian blew her a quick kiss and filled in the answer. 'Did you know your wife was a Shakespeare aficionado, son?'

Nee turned back and gave a little curtsy. 'Brains, as well as beauty. What can I say?' She winked at Luke.

'Didn't you study *Twelfth Night* as the set text for your GCSEs, Eirênê?' George asked mildly, before taking a bite of his sandwich. To all intents and purposes, his entire attention was fixed on his breakfast, but there was a definite gleam in his eyes. Although a more subdued effort, the navy cardigan he wore over an open-necked shirt had a wide band of snowflakes at the hem and wrists.

'Dad! You're supposed to stick up for me, not give away my secrets.' The Santas on her headband wobbled in outrage.

'Sorry, dear.' George put his sandwich down and met Luke's eyes in a solemn gaze. 'My youngest daughter is an intelligent, most attractive young woman and you are lucky to have her.' He rather spoiled the sincerity of his declaration by turning to Nee and adding, 'Happy now?'

Whatever pert response was forming on her lips was avoided by the timely arrival of Madeline and Richard bearing a new stack of daily papers. 'Ooh, is that bacon I smell?' Richard's eyes lit up as he slid into a vacant chair at the breakfast table and poured himself a cup of tea from the large pot in the centre.

'You'd think I never fed him!' Madeline scoffed as she crossed to greet Nee and Cathy with kisses. 'What's on the agenda today?' She peered out of the window at the rain. 'The forecast is promising this will clear up soon. They're even threatening snow overnight, although I'll believe that when I see it. What were they calling it, darling? Something terribly dramatic.'

'An Arctic blast,' Richard supplied, and she nodded. 'That's it. Goodness, they love a bit of drama on the weather these days with their amber warnings and suchlike. We've had a couple of nasty freezes in the past, but I don't remember more than a few flakes falling. Certainly not enough to stick.'

'Well, if we get snowed in, there's enough food to last at any rate.' Cathy added more bacon to the pan, paused and glanced at Madeline. 'Am I adding enough for you, too?'

Madeline bit her lip before giving a quick shrug. 'Oh, go on. It'd be rude not to!'

Luke stood up and held the back of his chair. 'Here, have my spot. I'm finished and I want to get a few things set up next door.' He met Nee's curious gaze. 'Want to give me a hand?' She took his hand and he led her out of the kitchen to a chorus of speculative remarks. They'd hardly cleared the doorway before the legs of a chair scraped on the floor and Daniel shot past them and sprinted up the stairs, a bottle of ginger ale in his hand.

'Poor chap, he's suffering almost more than she is.' Nee turned to face him. 'So, what did you want to show me?' He couldn't help but laugh at the cheeky grin on her face.

'Well, yes, that, but we'll save that for later.' He led her towards the large Welsh dresser in the dining room and knelt down before the lower cupboards. 'Look, I had a chat with Mia after I suggested we spend this week together because I thought if we did something fun it might help you get your creative spark back. Now, though, it feels like maybe I'm heaping too much pressure on you, so if you'd rather not, we can get some of the board games out and play those instead.'

Nee crouched beside him and pressed a finger to his lips. 'You're babbling, Luke. What are you talking about?'

Taking a deep breath, he opened the cupboard doors and showed her the arts and crafts supplies. There were jewellery-making kits, some paint-by-numbers sets for both children and adults, and a box of ceramic tealight holders shaped like lighthouses with paints for decorating. Nee picked up one of the boxes and studied the instructions on the back. 'And this was your idea?'

All the guilt he'd been feeling in the middle of the night came rushing back like a freight train, and he sat down with a miserable thud, knowing he deserved the bruise the parquet flooring would likely leave on his backside. 'I'm sorry. It's too much, I'm being too pushy. I wanted something that would keep the children entertained and you did such a great job helping Charlie decorate the place settings for the wedding.'

'It was bloody hard work, even doing that,' she admitted, eyes still fixed on the back of the box. He would have taken it from her and shoved the damn thing back into the cupboard had she not held it out of reach when he grabbed for it. 'But once I let myself forget about the fact it was "art" it became a lot easier.'

Putting the box down carefully, she took his hand and wrapped her fingers around it. 'Thank you for thinking of me. For trying so hard to help me with everything. It means the world to me.'

She pulled him closer, and he let himself be drawn into her embrace, shielding his face in her shoulder. He couldn't bear to look at her, to see the gratitude in her voice reflected in her eyes, not when he knew the truth of it now. He was a selfish git. Yes, he wanted Nee to be happy and whole again, but only because it suited his own desires. If he truly loved her the way she deserved, he'd have found a way to do all this for her without any strings attached. Perhaps he was more his mother's son than he'd realised.

Self-awareness was an absolute bitch.

They'd wound the dining-room table out to its furthest extent, covered it in a plastic sheet and several layers of newspaper and set everything out by the time Aaron and Kiki arrived with the children. Mia and Daniel had returned and, as Cathy had predicted, she looked right as rain once again. Luke got his iPod set up and found a playlist of classic Christmas hits to keep them entertained as everyone settled around the big table. Madeline, Maggie and his mum commandeered the jewellery-making kits, whilst Nee and her sisters settled with the children at the other end to decorate the lighthouse candle-holders. Mia had bought enough for the tables in the tearoom, and Luke had to agree they would add a charming, homely touch to the place.

His dad and George sat opposite each other, tackling an ambitious paint-by-numbers picture of Nelson's flagship *Victory* at the Battle of Trafalgar, and Richard contented himself with the papers he'd brought with him. Aaron fiddled with his smartphone, keeping them apprised of the cold front as it made its way slowly down the country from Scotland. He seemed nearly as excited as the kids at the prospect of snow reaching them. Not really in the mood to settle to anything, even though the crafting had been his idea, Luke kept himself busy, opening the windows as the smell of the paint grew; fetching drinks for those who wanted them, an extra cardigan for Nee to throw over her shoulders when she shivered in a draft from the window.

Cackling laughter rose from where his mum and the other two older women were sitting, loud enough for Richard to lower his newspaper and observe they sounded like the opening scene from *Macbeth*. Madeline glanced towards the children and, seeing them occupied, flipped a quick 'v' sign at her husband, who blew a kiss in return.

Luke circled the table to peer over her shoulder and barked out a laugh. The three of them were making friendship bracelets, but instead of the recipient's name, or something cute, theirs spelled out 'old fart', 'grumpy git' and 'dusty fossil', in between the bright rainbow of beads. 'You three are incorrigible,' he said, brushing a kiss on his mum's cheek when she turned her grinning face up to his.

She winked at him. 'I don't suppose its fizz o'clock yet, is it? This is thirsty work.'

He checked his watch. 'Close enough for those that care about propriety.'

'Not us then!' Maggie's wry comment sent the three of them into fits again, and he beat a hasty retreat to the kitchen to sort out aperitifs and some snacks to go with them.

Trying to carry everything in one go, he just about made it back into the dining room before the packed tray in his hands started to wobble a bit. 'Give us a hand, Bumble.'

Quick as a flash, his brother jumped up to steady the tray, and between them they set it down on the sideboard without any mishaps. They circled the table in opposite directions, clearing coffee cups and replacing them with glasses of Cava, small bottles of beer and soft drinks. Brushes, bags of beads and pots of paint were shoved aside to make room for small bowls of peanuts, crisps and the like as everyone abandoned their projects for a break.

Charlie made a grab for her cherryade, knocking a small pot of red paint over in the process. Nee righted the pot before much of the contents had spilled, and quickly balled up the sheet of paint-covered newspaper. Luke held out his hand and took it from her to dispose of in the kitchen rubbish bin. The music had changed by the time he came back – the gentle strains of Bing's 'White Christmas' replaced by the raucous, rowdy lyrics of 'Fairytale of New York'. Daniel was slurring along in a pretty accurate impression of Shane MacGowan, with Maggie, of all people, giving him hell as she fired back Kirsty MacColl's biting lyrics.

The smile on his lips froze as Luke caught sight of Nee's pale, stricken face. The significance of the song, with its tale of shattered dreams and betrayal, hadn't even occurred to him when he'd primed his iPod earlier. It was just a Christmas song, like all the others. *Shit!* He dived for the iPod and flicked on to the next track, drawing shouts of protest. Giving Daniel a sharp jab in the shoulder, he nodded across the table at Nee, who was staring down at her lap. 'Oh hell, I didn't think,' Daniel muttered. 'Sorry.'

Nee appeared oblivious to everyone around her as Luke hurried around the table to her side. By the time he reached her, she was on her feet clutching a sheet of Friday's newspaper in her shaking hands. The main article was one of those 'Top shows to look out for in 2017' pieces, and featured a prominent, familiar face beneath the byline.

'Christ.' It hadn't been the stupid song that upset her, but the image of *fucking* Devin Rees, all blow-waved hair and shiny, capped teeth set in a mocking grin.

'That's mine,' she whispered, turning limpid eyes swimming with pain to him. He stared down at the photograph of a painting next to that wanker's picture. There were two figures, anonymous, but clearly masculine and feminine, on a stark white background. The male was turned away from the female, who stretched her arms towards him, fighting against a sea of hands that clawed at her body. Scrawled in bright red across the hands were words like 'ambition', 'pride' and 'deception'.

Confused, Luke turned his attention back to Nee. 'What d'you mean it's yours? Did you paint this?'

She shook her head, hand convulsing on the sheet of paper until it crumpled in one corner. 'No. This isn't one of the works I produced from his designs. This is much worse.' A tear spilled over and rolled down her cheek. 'This is personal. Private. From my sketchbook.' The paper drifted to the ground as she grabbed for his arm. 'This is *us*, Luke.'

Anger rushed through him, thick and black as bile. She'd told him Devin passed off his students' work as his own, but to see proof of it in stark colour stunned him. His own fury was nothing in comparison to the rictus of pain her delicate features had twisted into. Shoving it aside, he reached for her, but she stepped back, letting the sheet of paper drift to the floor between them. 'No.'

Her denial struck him like a body blow. How could one word hurt so damn much? Maybe it wasn't him she repudiated, but she might as well have. 'Nee.'

'No. No. *No.*' She turned blindly, almost tripping over the leg of Madeline's chair in her haste to escape the room. To escape him.

Questions whirled behind him, and he heard the sound of at least one person standing. 'No. Leave her,' he snapped, without turning around. If someone needed to go after her, it was him, but not like this, not until he had some sense of control back. Feet rooted to the floor, he stared down at the grinning face of Devin Rees and wished the man himself was in front of him – a proper target for the useless, impotent rage surging in his veins.

Aaron came to stand beside him, nudging Luke with his shoulder just enough to make his presence known. He studied the picture. 'Who's that?'

He had to say something, offer some explanation to the others without betraying Nee's confidence. 'That's the reason she left New York.' Drawn by his master's presence, the puppy crawled out from beneath the table and sniffed at the fallen sheet of newspaper. Turning in a circle, Tigger cocked one leg and peed on the grinning, smug-faced bane of Luke's very existence.

A flash of red in the garden caught his eye. 'I've got to go.'

Chapter Sixteen

Out. She had to get out. The word pounded in her brain as she made a dash for the kitchen, skidding across the floor in the thick woolly socks she'd chosen to match her jumper. A pair of muddy Wellington boots stood beside the back door, and she paused only long enough to shove her feet into them before she ran out and onto the driveway. The gravel crunched beneath her heels, a mocking echo of the time she'd run crying from Luke after their run-in at the wedding. Running away. She was always bloody running away. Hating herself, but unable to stop her headlong flight, she ran for the steps that would take her to the relative privacy of the beach.

Pausing at the top step, she dashed the moisture from her face, found it warm, not cold, and understood the rain had finally stopped. With one hand on the rail, she blinked away the still-falling tears enough to see her path and clattered down to the dark, wet sand. It sucked at her boots, threatening to pull her over until she slowed her pace. The tide was in, white horses pounding the shoreline in charging waves, a match for the swirling riot of emotions riding inside her.

He'd gone through her things.

The thought was enough to bring a wash of bile to choke the

back of her throat. Her portfolio was one thing – those were images she'd chosen to present to the world, parts of herself she'd been willing to put on display for people to view, and judge, and comment upon. Her sketches, though . . . oh, God.

She bent at the waist, gasping for breath, heart racing a mile a minute in the same panicked confusion of that night she still couldn't remember clearly. Fighting the panic, she ran through the list of what she did recall, as the helpline had suggested as a way of countering the crushing pressure of not knowing. She'd found no trace of him upon her, no physical proof or sensation he'd done anything other than remove some of her clothing. Enough to convince herself there'd been no physical violation.

This felt almost worse somehow. Like he'd reached his filthy hands inside her mind, inside her very being, and rummaged around to take whatever he wanted. He knew everything, all her hopes and fears, her most intimate desires, her darkest secrets. Some people kept a diary, but she'd used art as her therapy, always had.

A warm hand settled on the bare skin of her nape, a familiar touch she should have welcomed, but she flinched beneath it. In letting her sketches fall into Devin's clutches, she'd betrayed Luke all over again. Everything she'd felt about him, from those first heady days to the heart-wrenching despair of having thrown away their marriage for a chance at fame, was laid out in charcoal sketches and pencil drawings. Bile rose again, hot and bitter, and she swallowed hard against the urge to vomit. He maintained that gentle connection throughout, anchoring her.

'Stand up a minute,' Luke urged, and she forced herself to straighten. Unwilling to meet his eyes, she studied the rest of him, and the corner of her lips tweaked in a wry smile at the sight of his thick navy bomber jacket. At least one of them had had the sense to dress properly. The rain might have stopped, but the chill of Aaron's prophesied Arctic blast rode the wind buffeting off the sea. A shiver rippled through her, and he shrugged out of his coat to wrap it around her shoulders.

She tried to twist away from the glorious warmth of the coat, from the never-ending kindness and consideration this man kept giving to her when she deserved so little of it. 'Don't. Don't be nice to me.'

He gripped the edges of the collar closed around her neck, refusing to let her wriggle out of it. 'Shut up and put it on. I never heard such bloody nonsense.'

His gentle, steadfast gaze was too much to bear, and she closed her eyes, but didn't resist as he guided first one, then the other of her arms into the too-long sleeves and zipped up the jacket to the tip of her chin. Lifting a hand above her head, he flicked one of the springy Santas attached to that stupid bloody headband she'd put on this morning. She'd seen them in an accessories shop on the high street a couple of weeks previously and hadn't been able to resist the ridiculousness of them. She'd had hope then, a belief she was ready to take the next step and move on with her life, that she could put the past away and forget about it. The acid gnawing inside her said she'd been a naïve fool at best for believing so. Worse still, she'd let him believe she was ready. 'You don't understand, Luke.'

'Ah, if only that were true, my darling, I could just keep on pretending.' Her eyes flew open at his cryptic comment, but he pressed a finger to her mouth before she could speak. 'Stop it. Stop jumping to conclusions, Nee. God, you're like an open book, did you know that? Just as well you never decided to be a professional poker player because you just let it all hang out there, don't you? Every thought, every emotion, you just put it out there for the world to see. It's magnetic . . . and terrifying.'

The admiration in his voice twisted like a knife in her guts. She'd prided herself on her openness once, had thought that's what she needed to be a great artist – to bare her soul. But then she'd met him, and understood some things were too precious to share, so she'd hoarded it, like a dragon curled protectively around her treasure.

And now it had all been stolen.

'You weren't for sharing.' The words caught in her throat, so she tried again. 'You were meant to be just for me, but he's spoilt that now. Ruined everything.' God, she sounded like a petulant child.

Luke's hand cupped her cheek. 'Only if you let him.' She shook her head in denial, and he lifted his other hand to her face, holding her firm, making her meet his gaze. 'Think about it, Nee. What's he taken from us that can't be replaced? He's like a leech, a vampire, draining the vitality of others to replace what's missing from his own heart. What must it be like to stare in the mirror every day and see a fraud? See a sham, a hollow façade with all the wealth and trappings, and none of the talent?'

'If he's a vampire, then he won't see anything in the mirror.' How the hell she could laugh at a time like this, she had no clue. 'And it's not that simple. He has talent, has the vision; he just uses others in the execution of those ideas.'

He scoffed at her words. 'Really? I don't see it. It's *The Emperor's New Clothes*. He's strutting around with his arse on show and everyone's too afraid to call him out on it.' His hands shifted from her face to cup her shoulders, giving her a little shake. 'He stole from you, Nee. He took something of yours and tried to pass it off as his own. That's not vision, that's not talent, that's plagiarism.'

She knew he was right, but still. 'He'll get away with it, though. No one will know.'

'Bollocks! You'll know, and I'll know. And everyone else in your life who's worth anything will know.'

A bitter laugh escaped her. He made it all sound so bloody easy, like she should just be able to shrug it off and walk away. 'He took everything from me!'

Luke's arms dropped to his sides and she missed the warmth of him instantly. 'What did he take, Nee? Nothing that can harm us, nothing that can *change* us. Not unless you let him. Those

162

pictures weren't your feelings, they were representations of them, that's all. Your heart's still beating, everything that makes you the person I love, is still right here in front of me.'

He was right. Her heart was still there. She could tell because it hurt so bloody much she wanted to rip it out of her chest and throw it on the ground. Why hadn't she stayed away? Why had she let her loneliness overcome her good sense and jumped on the train to attend Mia's wedding? If she'd never come here, she'd never have seen Luke again. Could have stayed in the safety of the numb cocoon of self-pity she'd wrapped herself in since leaving New York.

But she had, and here he was. So full of life and love, blazing like an inferno. At first it had been a relief to warm herself again, to melt a little of the ice, just enough for the good things to slip through. Only the fire kept on burning, and now there was nothing between her and all the ugliness – and it hurt. It hurt. It hurt so *fucking* much, she wanted to shred the skin from her bones to let it all out.

'Too much,' she gasped. 'Too much.'

'I know, my love. I know.' He pulled her into his arms and she clung like a limpet as all the ghosts of the past whipped and screamed at her, trying to pull her away, to drag her back under their control. He tightened his embrace for a few more precious moments before releasing her and taking a step back. 'When I said to you before that I understood, it had nothing to do with Devin. It didn't really have anything to do with you either. It's me.'

He shoved at the wind-tossed curls straggling over his forehead. 'This is going to seem like the worst, shittiest timing, Nee, but I'm going to let you go.'

Oh, she'd been wrong when she'd thought it had hurt before, because that pain, *that pain*, was as insignificant as a mosquito bite compared to the wrenching torment of this new assault. She couldn't survive it, couldn't see how her body could remain corporeal as his words detonated inside her. His lips were still moving, but she was deaf to anything but the screaming voice inside her. The world swam, and she staggered sideways before he caught her.

'Nee? Nee, look at me! You didn't listen to the rest of what I was saying, did you?' She shrugged, dully, because what was the point. He shook her again, a little harder this time, and she raised her hands to push him away.

Releasing her shoulders, he snatched for her fingers, chaffing the cold from them between his warm palms. 'I love you. I love you so much it's hard to see beyond it, but I did this all wrong. I tried to force you to do what *I* want, to be who *I* want you to be, and you're not ready. Worse still, I did it in front of everyone else just to make it that much harder for you to say no.' His face was wet, and that wasn't from the rain either.

She tried to free her fingers to catch the tears, but he kept them trapped between his own. 'Luke . . .'

'I won't go far, and I won't go for ever, I promise. I'll stay at Aaron's, give you some space to breathe, to work things out without me putting pressure on you.'

What was he saying? That he was leaving her, but he wasn't? 'I don't understand. You're the one good thing I have going for me, Luke. Don't take that away from me too.' If he did that, she'd be nothing.

Why was he shaking his head? Why was he letting her hands go and walking away from her? He couldn't leave her alone like this, with all these emotions she didn't know what to do with. Goddamn him! He'd forced her to feel when she hadn't wanted to and now he was just walking away? How dare he?

Bending her knees, she scooped up a handful of wet sand and threw it at his departing back. 'You bastard!' The clod struck him squarely between his shoulder blades, staining the bright wool of his sweater. He didn't pause, and his hunched posture as he walked away was so like the worst of her fears she had to close her eyes as she sank to her knees.

Wet soaked through her jeans in seconds, reminding her of the last time she'd been on this beach. The day she'd decided to leave Butterfly Cove; the day her dad had called to say Vivian was dying. If he hadn't phoned, if that call had come just a day later, she wouldn't be in this mess. Her hands clenched in the cold sand. *No.* No more lying to herself, no more running away from the pain.

In three short months, she'd come full circle and was back in exactly the same spot. Letting Devin hurt her; letting Luke walk away from her. Her life slipping through her fingers like the grains of sand she clawed at. Only this time, there was something different.

This time, she was mad as hell about it.

By the time she returned to the house, her sister's car was missing from the driveway, and realisation slapped her full in the face once again. A tiny part of her had decided Luke only meant to shock her, that he would be here waiting for her with an apology on his lips and the reassurance that he would stand beside her. But the moment she stepped into the quiet kitchen and found Mia waiting for her, face creased in concern, she knew. He'd really gone through with it and moved out of Butterfly House. Grasping the surge of bitter understanding, she shoved it into the growing pit of anger in her belly, feeding it, stoking it higher.

'Are you all right?' Mia shook her head at herself as soon as she'd spoken. 'Of course you're not bloody all right. How could you be?' She circled the table, intent on grabbing Nee into a hug, and for a second she wanted to let her. To let her big sister take over, fill the gap her husband had left and take care of everything. So tempting. So easy. *So cowardly.*

'Don't, Mimi.' She couldn't keep the bite from her words and snapped her mouth shut quick, afraid the anger would boil out.

Appearing nonplussed for a moment, Mia stopped in her tracks, then gave herself a shake. 'Okay. No fussing.' Her fists clenched. 'Damn it, Nee. You can't expect me to stand aside and do nothing. Give me something to do to help you.'

The anguish in her voice helped Nee rein in her temper. Poor Mia. None of this was her fault, and making her go against her natural instincts to take care of her would just be punishing the wrong person. 'Make us a cup of tea? It's bloody freezing out there.' Nee sank down into one of the wooden chairs, grimacing at the way the wet denim of her jeans clung to her legs. 'Where is everyone?'

'The grey army are in the lounge, filled with a burning need to watch *The Sound of Music*, apparently.' The way Mia rolled her eyes told her what she thought of that excuse. 'And Daniel's out behind the barn destroying the wood pile.' A plate loaded with sandwiches and a slab of cake landed on the table in front of her, together with a steaming mug of builder's-strength tea. 'Are you going to tell me what's going on?'

The anger roiled inside Nee, a living beast ready to escape, but this wasn't the time or the place to unleash it.

Just a few minutes more.

She shook her head. 'I need to do this on my own.' Luke had been right about that much at least. Picking up the cup and plate, she rose. 'Thanks for this.'

Mia walked with her out into the hallway, but stopped at the door leading towards the stairs. 'Looks like I have a date with Captain Von Trapp then. You know where I am if you need me.'

'Thanks, Mimi.' Nee began to climb the stairs, a very out-of-tune version of 'Doe, a Deer' echoing behind her. The forced cheeriness in her sister's tone was unmistakable, but Nee forced herself to ignore it. If her resolve broke now, she might never do what needed to be done. Every step was an agony of indecision, but she forced herself to keep moving.

A brass lamp by the bed sent a soft glow over one corner of the room, a drawer hung half-open, empty now of its contents. All little signs, little reminders that Luke had been and gone.

Abandoning the plate and cup on the dressing table, she ghost-walked into the bathroom, seeing only the empty spaces where his toothbrush and deodorant had sat next to hers. A pale, pale girl stared back at her from the mirror, a mocking caricature of seasonal joy with her festive jumper and those bloody Santas bobbling around on her head.

Ripping off the headband, she tossed it in the empty bathtub, the jumper and her soggy jeans following soon after. Clad in nothing but a thin vest and shorts, there was nothing to hide behind now, and she stared at her reflection. *A sham . . . a fraud . . . none of the talent . . .* Luke's words rolled through her mind as she forced herself to look deeper, beyond the image, past the anger, and into the heart of the young woman staring back at her.

'Who are you?' she whispered, and the answers echoed back.

She was Eirênê Thorpe. Neglected daughter, always hungry for acknowledgement and affirmation.

She was Nee Thorpe. Failed artist, allowing the opinions of others to build her up and break her down to nothing.

She was Nee Spenser. Runaway bride, letting happiness slip through her fingers.

'No.' She'd been all those girls at some point, but now it was past time to grow up and take control of her life. To be the person she wanted to be, a person she would happily face in the mirror every day.

And she didn't have to do it alone.

For wasn't her father downstairs right now, trying his best to make up for his failures? Hadn't her sisters given her all the love she'd ever needed without limitations? She'd only failed as an artist because a man who should have been a mentor and protector had betrayed her in the cruellest of ways. And hadn't Luke told her he loved her, even after everything she'd done? Wasn't his only sin trying too hard to make things right between them?

If she wanted to be worthy of those efforts, she had to purge the ghosts holding her back. Acknowledge the failures, mourn the losses and the hurts, then put them aside to heal. With a deep breath, she left the bathroom. A scrap of pale-grey caught her eye and she crouched down to retrieve a rumpled T-shirt from under the bed. It was the one Luke had used as a pyjama top, and she pulled it on, catching the faded hints of his crisp aftershave and the indefinable essence of *him*. 'He hasn't gone far, and not for ever.' She whispered the reassurance to herself.

The cup and plate sat on the dresser, and she gulped down the lukewarm tea and ate the sandwich with precise, careful bites. She'd neglected herself for too long, and that would end too.

Straightening her spine, she strode towards the closed door of the sitting room and pushed it open without hesitation. The art supplies were exactly where he'd placed them – the easel angled beside the window to catch the fading afternoon light, a stack of sketchpads and pens on the table next to the decadent elegance of the red-velvet chaise-longue. Closing the door behind her, she chose the chaise. Feet curled under her, the cloud-soft throw from the back of the seat tucked over her legs, she reached for a sketchpad and flipped it open.

The next time she left these rooms she would be Nee Thorpe-Spenser. And that woman could be anything she damn well chose to be, because she would reclaim the power she'd put in other people's hands and shape her own future. Head down, absorbed in the images spilling from the end of her pen across the paper, she was oblivious to the gradual darkening of the sky and the silent fall of the first flakes of snow drifting gently past her window.

Chapter Seventeen

Luke perched on the windowsill in his brother's spare bedroom watching the fat flakes of white dance and whirl in the glow of the front porchlight someone had left on when they'd come to bed. There was something about snowfall that made the world seem quieter, like it muffled everything in its soft blanket. Even the litany of doubts racing around his head eased as he watched the silent, hypnotic curtain fall. He wasn't sure how long he'd been sitting there, but the roof and bonnet of Kiki's little blue car had already disappeared under several inches, and there was no sign of it abating. They'd had the devil's own job getting the children to bed, but they'd eventually settled with the promise of a snowman-building competition in the morning.

Charlie had commandeered him on the landing, all sleepy-eyed and smelling sweetly of the lavender bubble bath she'd been coaxed into by her despairing mother. The hot water and calming fragrance appeared to have done the trick as she'd smothered an enormous yawn whilst offering him the raggedy brown toy he now clutched in one hand. 'Mr Bunny is very good at taking the sad things away,' she'd assured him. It had been all he could do not to bawl like a baby as he'd bent down to give her a kiss goodnight. *It was the right thing to do.* How many times had he told himself that in the past few hours? A shiver warned him he'd been sitting beside the glass for too long. Even the radiator beneath him had lost the last of its warmth. He glanced across at the bed, dressed in a thick quilt with a fleece blanket folded neatly over the bottom half, and cursed himself for a fool. He could be curled up with his beautiful wife watching the snow from the cosy haven of their canopied bed. But no. His conscience had landed him in self-imposed exile. It was ridiculous to feel so sorry for himself because of something he'd put into motion.

Had he made a huge mistake? Staked too much on that flash of anger on the beach? Only time would tell. When she'd sworn at him, then hit him with that lump of sand, he'd almost wanted to laugh. Not at her, but because it was exactly the kind of thing she would have done when they'd first met. She'd been too subdued, like a black and white version of herself. Even when she'd taken him inside her body, he'd sensed something missing. He wanted *his* Nee, in all her Technicolor glory, not the pale shadow she'd become.

Perhaps this was just another example of his own selfishness and, in leaving Nee, he'd merely replaced one ultimatum with another. Perhaps now he'd been made aware of it, it would always be with him – a permanent flaw, something he couldn't change any more than he could stop his hair from being curly. Having turned it over and over in his mind, he still didn't know for sure, but he wanted to believe that, this time, he'd only had Nee's best interests at heart. She needed to find her own way to put the past behind her. Getting back together whilst she was still so vulnerable wasn't the right answer. It might work for a bit, but the business with Devin was too deep a wound for a sticking plaster and it would eventually fester if left unaddressed.

So, he would wait. And try to control the panic and his own need to make everything perfect. It might take her a month, it might take a year, but there was no one else for him, so he would make himself be patient. Crawling under the duvet, he propped the toy rabbit beside his head then reached for his phone to check if there'd been any response to the quick text he'd sent her earlier. *Nothing*. With a sigh, he tossed it back on the bedside table and rolled onto his side. The empty expanse of mattress beside him seemed to mock him. What if, when all was said and done, Nee decided she needed to put all of her past behind her? *Including him.*

He punched his pillow in frustration, barely missing poor Mr Bunny in the process. He tucked the rabbit under his arm and closed his eyes. Patience and self-sacrifice might have their limits.

His phone remained stubbornly silent, and though Mr Bunny had done his best, the lack of communication from Nee worried him more than he tried to let on to the others. The snow must have stopped not long after he'd gone to bed, because although the grass and driveway had been completely buried, the happy toot-toot of a horn let them know his parents had managed the short drive from Butterfly Cove without too many problems. Aaron had informed him as he'd sat down for breakfast they were coming to the cottage in a change of plans. He waved off Luke's attempt at an apology for the disruption as he rose to answer the door. 'Look, it's fine. Easier for us not to be lugging a load of the kids' stuff back and forth every day.'

He might have known Aaron would find the bright side in the situation. He was good at taking things in his stride. A quiet sniff from over by the sink told him he'd have to work much harder to get back in Kiki's good books. Finishing up his toast, he carried his plate towards the dishwasher next to her, but she was already moving away towards the kitchen door. Deciding to leave it alone for now, he made himself busy tidying up as he listened to the children greeting Brian and Cathy's arrival with great enthusiasm.

Whilst Kiki urged the children upstairs to swap their pyjamas for warm clothes, his mum and dad followed Aaron back into

171

the kitchen. 'Want some coffee?' His brother moved towards the kettle when they nodded, giving Luke a pat on the shoulder as they passed each other.

At least his mum would understand. Luke let the thought bolster him as he bent to accept a hug and a kiss from her. 'Hello, Mum.' He pulled out one of the chairs he'd just tucked away for her to sit on. Hanging her padded coat on the back of the seat, she removed the thick, faux-fur band she'd been wearing to keep her ears warm and shook her fingers through her hair to settle it back into perfect waves. She smoothed the front of her thick polo-necked jumper then placed one booted foot on the seat of the chair and stood up on it.

Confused, Luke gaped up at his diminutive mother and was rewarded with a resounding thump on his ear. 'Ow. What was that for?' He retreated out of harm's way whilst Cathy held her hand out to his dad so he could help her down from the chair.

'What do you think it's for, you stupid boy? We've left the house in chaos. Poor Mia's beside herself because Nee's locked herself in her room. Maggie's escaped with Madeline into Exeter to do some shopping in the sales and George has buried his nose in some incomprehensible textbook. You persuaded us all to go along with your madcap scheme and now you've done a runner the moment you hit a bump in the road.' She plonked herself down in the chair with a huff.

'Hey, that's not fair! You were the one who warned me about being too possessive. I haven't left her, I just backed off a bit to give her some space to breathe.' He looked to his dad for support, but Brian had pulled a chair up close to his wife and fixed him with a frown.

Cathy slumped back in her chair, a hand raised towards her mouth. 'Oh, goodness. You did this because of me?'

Luke rubbed the last of the pain from his throbbing ear as he sank down opposite her. 'No. Not really. But what you said did set me thinking and I realised I'd put her in an impossible situation.'

Aaron served the coffee then took the remaining chair. 'You might have thought about that before you got us all involved. This is exactly the kind of issue I was trying to avoid with me and Kiki.'

Luke nodded. His brother had almost lost a chance at the wonderful life he now had by being too cautious. To keep everyone else happy, he'd tried to persuade himself that simple friendship between the two of them would be the best option. Luke had done the complete opposite – he'd rushed in all guns blazing. 'You were trying to do what was right, same as I am now.'

Aaron took a sip of his coffee, then gave a wry laugh. 'And I was an idiot. Something which clearly runs in the family. You'd better hope and pray forgiveness for it is a trait all the Thorpe women possess, not just mine.'

'Forgiveness? Nee will understand once she's had time to think everything through. That's what I'm trying to give her – time.'

There was sympathy in the smile his brother gave him, but it didn't do much to lessen the body blow as he gave voice to Luke's greatest fear. 'And what if once she's taken that time to think everything through she decides she's better off without you?'

Cathy sniffed. 'And who would blame her after this little stunt of yours? Well, as you're both idiots, it must come from your father, so it can't be my fault after all.' She shoved her chair back as she stood. 'I'm going to see if Kiki needs a hand.'

'Hey, what did I do?' Brian protested towards her retreating back.

Even with a lump on his head and the more uncomfortable knowledge of his father's disappointment, Luke continued to cling to the conviction that he was doing the right thing, and not only because he didn't have much option. Nee was where she belonged, safe in Butterfly Cove with her family around her. If only she'd contact him.

Shoving his hands in his pockets, his hand closed over his phone and he resisted the urge to pull it out and check for a message. He'd texted her a couple of times during the day. Nothing too heavy, just that he was thinking of her, then a little anecdote about something that had happened with the kids. Proof he was keeping his promise about not going far, letting her know he was there when she was ready. If she was ready. She'd not responded to any of them.

'Stop moping about and give me a hand with this, will you?' Kiki's sharp tone called his attention away from the back door. His parents and Aaron were still outside in the garden with the children, but he'd come in to change his top after a large snowball, shaped by the children and wielded by his mother, had been shoved down the back of his neck. Making a start on lunch, Kiki had given him a look that made it plain he was still in her bad books. He'd been halfway towards the back door when she'd spoken and he regretted not moving faster.

She'd hardly said two words to him since breakfast. Around the children, she mustered the usual smiles and sweet sense of humour he was used to, but the moment they found themselves alone like this, she either ignored him or barked instructions. He couldn't blame her. His presence was causing tension between her and Aaron too, as his brother's default reaction was to leap to Luke's defence.

Turning, he saw her stretched up on tiptoes, fumbling for a large bowl on the top shelf in an overhead cupboard. 'Here, let me.' He leaned over her and lifted the dish down to her waiting hands.

With a muttered word of thanks, she ducked past him to place it on the board next to her weighing scales. When she turned back to get something else down and huffed at him for being in the way, he held up his hands and retreated to his previous spot by the door. A muffled shout came from the garden and he stared through the glass to see Charlie and Matty racing around in the snow, Tigger bouncing and yapping at their heels. He'd been decidedly unsure about the strange, white stuff on the ground, but secure in a fetching tartan coat (another Christmas gift), the lure of the children playing had been too much for the puppy to resist.

The glass misted from his breath, blurring the scene. He supposed he should go out there, the temperature likely warmer than the chilly atmosphere between him and Kiki, but then he'd have to face another woman who was royally pissed off with him. However cross Kiki might be, she had nothing on his mother, and she was still furious with him. As the snowball down the back had proven.

A musical chime sounded behind him and he was halfway to the table before Kiki had fished her phone out of the pocket on her apron. Angling her hands away from him, she studied her handset, tapped a response and tucked it away again. 'Did you want something?'

Jesus. Anyone who thought Kiki was the soft, gentle sister should have seen the look she was giving him right then. He had to know, though. Patience be damned. 'Is she all right?' he blurted out. 'That's all I want someone to tell me. It's not like I've walked out and left her without a word.'

Kiki folded her arms and gave him an appraising look that about blistered the skin from his face. 'So, is *that* what this nonsense is all about? What goes around comes around, yeah? She left you and now it's your turn to get your own back? Coax her with all your promises and declarations of love and then leave her stranded so she knows how you felt when she did it to you? Only you had to go one better and show her up in front of everyone! At least when she did it to you, none of us knew anything about it.'

Horror filled him as every harsh word struck him like a blow. *How could she possibly think him capable of that?* 'God, no, Kiki! Punishing Nee is the very last thing on my mind.'

She threw up her hands in a gesture of pure frustration. 'Then what the hell were you thinking, because I can't make any sense of your behaviour. You want to know if she's all right? Well, the answer is no! Whilst you're skulking around here feeling sorry for yourself, she's locked herself away in that bloody sitting room

175

upstairs. Mia's only held back from having Daniel kick the door down because at least she's eating whatever meals they leave for her outside.'

'The sitting room?'

'Yes, the one that's part of the suite of rooms you were staying in. Won't say a word to Mimi other than that she's fine and to please go away.'

Oh. *Oh.* He had to clutch at the edge of the kitchen board beside him as a wave of euphoric hope washed through him. Light-headed, he let out a little whoop of triumph.

'What's got into you? I've just told you Nee's turned herself into a virtual hermit and you think that's something to celebrate? Oh . . .' Kiki's diatribe broke off as he grabbed her around the waist and span her around. 'Put me down!'

Aaron opened the back door, letting in a blast of frigid air. 'What's all the shouting about? The kids can hear you two. Hey, put her down, Spud! Just because you abandoned your own wife doesn't mean you can try and steal mine.'

Luke set Kiki down, then planted a kiss on her cheek. 'Don't you see what it means? I bought her a load of art supplies and set them up in the sitting room. Part of my stupid masterplan to fix everything. If she's locked herself away in there . . .'

Understanding dawned on her face and Kiki flung her arms around him. 'Then maybe she's painting again? Oh, Luke!' He clung to her, knowing it was too soon to be celebrating, that they could be jumping to conclusions, but damn it, it was Christmas and he was going to believe in miracles. The muscles in his face ached from how hard he was grinning, but nothing could dampen his mood. Not even when Aaron grabbed him in a headlock and dragged him outside before shoving him headfirst into a pile of snow that had been swept off the path. Abandoning the very wonky Olaf-shaped snowman they'd been building, the children rushed over and jumped on top of him, driving him further into the freezing mound. He held out his hand to his dad to get a lift up, and Brian obliged, but only lifting him far enough to give his mum access to shove another fistful of snow down his neck. 'Bloody hell!' He fell back on his backside with a thump.

'Language!' Brian folded his arms with a tut.

'Language!' Matty parroted, copying his granddad's exact tone and actions, which sent Charlie off into a paroxysm of giggles. Living up to his name, Tigger bounced over and jumped up to lick a trickle of melted snow from his cheek.

A snowball caught him on the side of the head, and a second, smaller, one on his chest, sending the puppy running in retreat. The five of them formed a semicircle around him, all with more snowy projectiles in hand and still he couldn't stop grinning. Knowing when he was defeated, Luke dropped onto his back in the snow and accepted the freezing onslaught.

Changing his top had been a complete waste of time.

Thankfully, the one-sided snowball fight relieved a lot of the tension between himself and the rest of the family so the rest of the day proved a much more relaxing affair. The forecast had threatened a sharp freeze and more snow overnight, so his parents headed back to Mia's before dark in case the roads became too tricky. Charlie had rewarded his efforts in building her a snowman with permission to use her special-edition *Frozen* bubble bath, which had done wonders to soak the chill from his bones – even if it had left him smelling of strawberries.

After a light supper, he'd even talked Kiki into agreeing to one of his favourite treats as a kid and the five of them were camped out on the living-room floor in a huge bed made from the quilts and pillows they'd dragged downstairs. It wasn't even seven o'clock and the children were already heavy-lidded as they watched a stop-motion cartoon about Santa's reindeer. Propped up on the far side of the temporary bed, Luke finally understood something that had escaped him before.

His mum had made it seem like a treat because of the apparent effort it had taken to talk her into it. Quilts had normally only been allowed downstairs if either he or Aaron had been unwell. In reality, they'd always ended up so relaxed and sleepy, an early night had inevitably followed, leaving his mum and dad to enjoy a quiet evening. He offered a silent salute to her for being so sneaky.

By the end of the cartoon, sweat was popping on his brow. He kicked the mountain of covers off his legs and sat up – too quickly from the way the room swam before his eyes. It was too hot, he needed a cold drink, something to ease the ache in his throat. He got halfway to his knees before deciding it might be too much effort.

Aaron sat up with a frown. 'All right, Spud? You look a bit peaky.'

'He looks like Robbie,' Charlie piped up.

'Robbie? What are you talking about, poppet?' Aaron wavered, then split into two before his eyes, which was one hell of a party trick.

'The reindeer, from the telly. Uncle Luke's got a red nose, just like him.' A huge sneeze rocked Luke's frame, drowning out whatever response his brother might have made.

Chapter Eighteen

Daniel swung the axe, splitting another section of log in two. He'd become quite adept at it over the past few days, as the ever-growing stack of firewood in the little shed behind him attested to. It was chop wood, or find someone to shout at, and as it was supposed to be the season of goodwill to all men, the poor log pile was taking the brunt of his frustrations. Nothing was going as they'd planned it. He'd wanted their first Christmas at Butterfly Cove to be perfect, had been so excited at the thought of a real family holiday with everyone they loved around them, and it had lasted all of two days before falling apart.

It didn't help that Mia was sick, and although he knew it was often part and parcel of being pregnant, he felt so bloody useless every time she made a dash for the bathroom. She'd told him having him hovering around her made it worse, so here he was again, making more firewood than they could possibly use even if the cold weather stayed put until next Christmas. A drop of sweat trickled down his brow and into his eye, and he thunked the axe into the log with a curse and swiped the sting away.

'Safe to approach?' Shielding his eyes from the sun, Daniel turned towards Richard, who was standing some six feet away, a steaming mug gripped in each hand.

'Yeah. Sorry, just needed to get out of the house for a bit.' He pulled off the thick, protective gloves he was wearing and tucked them in his coat pocket. The smell of fresh coffee hit his nose and he raised the mug to take a quick sip. Rich, strong and almost too hot to be comfortable – in other words, perfect. He gulped another mouthful and let out a sigh of satisfaction. 'Cheers. I needed this.'

'Thought you might. Madeline and Maggie are already discussing the decorations for New Year's Eve so I decided to escape before they roped me in.'

The party was still three days away, but there would no doubt be a list of things for them both to do as soon as he set foot back inside. Normally, his Mia would have been in the thick of it, clutching her journal full of ideas and pictures she'd clipped from magazines, but this blasted business with Luke and Nee had her camped out on the landing half the bloody time – when she wasn't being sick, that is. 'Mia still upstairs?'

'She came down about ten minutes ago to make a start on lunch. Some kind of curried turkey soup from the looks of it. George is on prep duty, and I saw him chopping fresh chillies.'

Daniel's stomach gave an appreciative rumble. Everything his wife cooked tasted amazing, but her homemade soups were like ambrosia from the gods. 'I should probably go in and lend her a hand.'

Richard sipped his coffee, warm eyes studying him until Daniel wanted to look away. 'If that's what you want, but I'm sure they can manage between them. I thought we might take a walk.' He paused long enough to drain his mug. 'Have a chat, perhaps.'

With a tilt of his head, Daniel finished his own drink. 'Do I look like I need it?'

The older man slung an arm around his shoulder as they began to amble towards the beach. 'Just a bit, son.'

Daniel leaned in to Richard, just a little, grateful all over again for the blessing of this strong, sure man who could read him so well. With the baby on the way, he'd been feeling the loss of his parents as keenly as when they'd first died. And having everyone else's parents around had only cemented the feeling. Their child would never lack for doting grandparents, even if George was the only blood relation who could technically claim the title. And knowing how excited Richard and Madeline were at the prospect of another little one to spoil, it seemed churlish of him to feel so depressed about it. His aggravation with everything and everybody was all tied up in a hot tangle of guilt over having all these wonderful people in his life and still feeling like something was missing.

Digging out the path had been another job Daniel had used to keep himself occupied, so they had no problem navigating their way to the end of the garden. It hadn't snowed since Boxing Day, but the Arctic front had well and truly settled over their part of the country, and even the bright sunshine couldn't get the temperature above freezing. Leaving their mugs on the top step, they made their way down to the beach. The layer of snow was thinning over the sand, and a clear demarcation line showed the high-tide mark.

A dark pebble shone on the sand in front of him, and Daniel chucked it into the sea, startling a hardy gull who'd been bobbing around on the gentle waves. The bird took off with a disgruntled squawk, and he followed the white speck as it crossed the azure blue of the sky. 'I miss Mam and Dad,' he said, more to the departing bird than the man beside him.

'I bet you do. We try so hard to make a show of having a wonderful time, but I always feel the ghosts more closely at this time of year. It's hard not to regret what could have been.' Richard blinked a couple of times, then nudged his shoulder. 'But we're not here to talk about me.'

'We can be if you want.' Damn, he'd been so busy feeling sorry for himself, he hadn't taken note of anyone else's feelings. He should have realised that beneath their obvious joy about the baby, memories of the ones Richard and Madeline had lost in their younger days would be stirring. Turning to face the older man, he held out his arms. 'I'm sorry. I didn't think about how this might affect you too.'

Richard shook his head. 'We couldn't be happier, and that's the honest truth. You know what you and Mia mean to us both.' He stepped forward and the two of them clung to each other. Taking and giving the comfort they both needed, acknowledging both their losses and how very much they had gained through their friendship. The gull squawked overhead, his cry joined by another, and Daniel lifted his head to watch the pair swoop and dive over the waves together.

They walked the length of the curving beach and back, enjoying the bracing sea air, chatting a little when something caught the attention of one or other of them. The peace and quiet, broken only by the hush of waves on the shore, the odd cry of the gulls, did wonders to settle his mood. Reaching the base of the steps, Daniel paused to tap the sand and snow combination from the tread of his boots, casting one final look over his shoulder at the slowly encroaching tide. 'I hope they're not getting too carried away with plans for the party. With the way things are between Luke and Nee, I'm not sure we wouldn't be better calling the whole thing off.'

'Or perhaps it might be the perfect distraction everyone needs. Nee will come out of her room eventually and it might upset her more to discover plans were changed because of her. I know you're a bit disappointed with the way things have turned out this week, but part of family life is embracing the messy bits and helping each other find a way through.' Richard clapped a hand on his shoulder as they climbed back up the steps. 'Besides, Madeline spent a good hour or more sewing a toy parrot on the shoulder of my costume, and quite likes the look of me in an eye patch.'

Daniel laughed at the mental image of Richard as a swash-buckler. 'If you're coming as a pirate, dare I ask what she's chosen for a costume?'

There was a distinct gleam in Richard's eyes as he raised his eyebrows suggestively. 'She's based the costumes on some old romance novel she loves. The cover's falling to bits, where she's read it so often. I'm the base pirate, and she's the lady heroine he kidnaps for ransom and falls in love with. I haven't seen her finished outfit, but there's a lot of petticoats. Have you got your costume sorted?'

'I tried to talk Mia into coming as Catwoman, but she was having none of it, and I think Matty might have already pipped me to the post when it comes to being Batman, so unless I can think of anything more inspired, I'm sticking on a flannel shirt and going as a lumberjack.' He stroked the slightly unkempt beard on his chin. 'It's been the perfect excuse not to trim this for a few days.'

They collected their mugs from where they'd left them earlier and walked the short distance back to the house. With the trees and bushes still covered in snow, it was like something out of a holiday movie set, complete with glittering lights shining on the tree in front of the French windows which led to the dining room. If the weather for New Year's Eve was going to stay fine, he might dig out the external lights they'd strung through the trees for the wedding. He could even fire up the barbecue for a few post-midnight burgers, which would save Mia some of the cooking . . .

Filled with renewed enthusiasm for the party, he ushered Richard through the back door, eager to find out what the ladies had been planning. The sight of his sister-in-law stopped him dead in his tracks. Purple shadows bruised the skin beneath her eyes, and her limp hair had been pushed away from her face with a spotted scarf. The oversized T-shirt she wore was spattered in paint and charcoal smudges, as were the leggings she wore underneath it, and the bare skin on her forearms. Once he looked past the obvious exhaustion in her eyes, he noticed something else – a spark which reminded him so much of his wife. An inner confidence, a substance to her which had been sadly lacking.

He'd never understood the connection between her and Luke before. Brash and forthright, his friend had always seemed a bit too much for the quiet, subdued woman. Luke had personality in bucketloads, and would need a woman who could stand toe to toe with him. Kiki's innate sweetness worked well with Aaron's more gentle nature, but the younger Spenser needed a woman more like his Mia in temperament. She'd told him stories of Nee's antics as a child, and for the first time he could see traces of the girl who'd set her face to the world with plans to conquer it.

'Oh, there you are!' Nee surprised him further by addressing him over the others in the room. 'Do you think I can borrow you for a few minutes?'

'Erm, sure.' He followed her out of the kitchen, exchanging shrugs of bemusement with Mia on his way out.

She led the way to the Harem suite of rooms and paused just outside the door to the sitting room. 'Look,' she said, wringing her hands together in front of her, 'I asked you rather than Mia or any of the others because I didn't want to upset any of them, and what with you being something of an artist yourself, I thought you might understand a bit better.'

Not sure what to expect, he reached past her to nudge open the door. He understood instantly why she might not want Mia to see what lay beyond. Schooling his face not to reflect the tumult of emotions whirling inside him, he took a step inside and tried to absorb the images assailing him.

In the centre of the room stood a large portrait – more a caricature, really – of the grinning man he recognised from the newspaper article that had kicked off all the trouble. Scrawled across the image were the most lurid insults, swear words and terms of abuse in bold red letters. He blinked a couple of times over the imaginative combinations she'd come up with, and mentally added a few new words to his own vocabulary.

The vitriol pouring from the piece told him more than he needed to know about the reason behind Nee's flight from

New York. Pain screamed from every brushstroke, every ugly, scribbled word. It was too potent to look at for long without feeling like a voyeur, so he turned his attention to the other pictures in the room. There was a series of charcoal sketches illustrating the descent of a vibrant, beautiful woman into a slow spiral of self-destruction. The proud jut of her chin, a feature she'd passed down to her daughters, revealed the identity of the woman as Vivian. Each image catalogued the slow ravages caused by a lifetime addiction to alcohol until she was nothing more than a sparrow-thin collection of bones under stretched skin in a hospital bed. Having faced his own demons down, Daniel held a deep sympathy for the woman, but not enough to forgive the indelible scars she'd left on each of her children.

There were other sketches and drawings too, including a still life of a champagne bottle, a wedding band and, he noticed with a wince, a brittle, withered rose. Feeling the weight of the trust Nee must have in him to share these most intimate secrets, he searched for the right words. A response that would assure her he would protect the information and do whatever he could to help her. Not that he had any idea what that might be.

Nee stepped up beside him, tracing the outline of the bottle with one finger. 'I want to burn them.'

Staggered at the suggestion, he opened his mouth to protest at the wanton destruction of such raw, impactful art. Here was life in all its bitter glory, a testament to the savagery of existence hiding behind the smiling façade most people showed to the world.

Easy to see the value when it wasn't one's own damage out on display. He closed his jaw with a snap. Nee was his family and he would do whatever she needed. 'If you're sure that's what you want then we can take them down to the barns. There's a small forge I built for the ironworkers.' Wrestling with his better judgement, he couldn't help adding, 'Or I can crate them up for you. Stick them in storage for now and you can revisit them later.'

She shook her head. 'I know what you're saying, but this isn't for anyone else. I've kept so much bottled up inside me and I needed to purge it. I'm sure I could get an exhibition, sell the lot, because our society is so fascinated by the misery of others, and the old me would have jumped at the chance. I've chased fame before, thought the only thing I needed in my life was acclamation and recognition from the great and the good of the art community.' A bitter smile twisted her mouth. 'But I discovered to my cost that they're not that great, and some are certainly not good. I was so busy running towards what I thought would sate the aching need inside me, I missed the fact I already had it – from Mia and Kiki, and then from Luke.'

Knowing all too well how she was feeling, Daniel hooked an arm around her shoulder and pulled her tight against his side so he could press a kiss to the top of her head. 'The adulation and sparkle blinds you at first, sweetheart.'

She nodded against his neck. 'You've been there.'

He laughed. 'Been there, done that, puked my guts up in your sister's rhododendron bushes.' When she gave him a quizzical look, he told her about his ungainly arrival at Butterfly Cove, adding at the end, 'And for the lucky ones like you and me, rock bottom isn't the worst place to land when you've got the right person to help you up.'

'Like Mia.'

He nodded to the ring dangling from the chain around her neck. 'Like Luke.'

Her fingers raised to close around it and she gripped it like a talisman. 'Yes.' He watched her eyes lose focus and waited quietly until she roused herself from whatever memory she'd drifted off into. 'Right, I'd better give you a hand with these.'

'No, leave them. I can do it.' She'd been running on adrenaline for a couple of days, and he could tell from the way she swayed on her feet that a crash was imminent. 'Why don't you have a nice hot shower and tuck yourself into bed? I'll clear all this away, and you can trust me to do as you've asked. Once I've put them away in the barns, I'll send Mia up with some soup.'

Nee worried at her bottom lip, a nervous trait all three of the sisters shared. 'Is she very mad at me for refusing to see her?'

God, she looked so young, so vulnerable. The nine years between them felt like a generation. 'She's not mad at you; no one is. We were just a bit worried, that's all. A bit of a kip will probably do you the world of good.' He winked at her. 'Besides, once you set foot back downstairs, you're bound to get roped into preparations for the big New Year's bash so you'll need all your strength.'

'Oh. I'd forgotten about that . . .' Her attention drifted away once more.

Taking her gently by the shoulder, he turned her to face the bathroom. 'Shower. Soup. Sleep.' With a little push, he got her at least moving in the right direction.

She paused on the threshold. 'There's one piece on the easel in the corner. Leave that one, please.'

'Of course.'

As soon as the door closed behind her, he set to work. He put the largest picture on the floor and quickly stacked all the others on top of it. Pens, charcoal and pots of paint littered the surfaces, and he was relieved to see she'd torn pages out of a sketchbook to protect the surfaces beneath them. He soon had the supplies gathered up, lids secured and stacked in a neat pile next to the chaise.

Kneeling down, he furled the pictures into a tight roll, which he tucked under his arm before closing the door behind him. With only one set of keys, there would be no chance of anyone nosing around in the barns and stumbling across them, so he would wait until after the New Year to destroy them. Starting up the forge would only invite questions, and he wasn't sure how much of this Nee wanted to share.

With everything gathered up, only the easel in the corner

remained. A cloth covered whatever picture Nee had asked him to leave behind, and the tips of his fingers itched with the need to take a quick peek. He rubbed the pads together to dispel the sensation; Nee had trusted him with so many secrets, he owed it to her to let her keep this one. Checking one last time the bundle under his arm was secure, he backed out of the sitting room and closed the door. The sound of water spattering against tiles reassured him that Nee was following the first of his suggestions, so he left her to it.

Full of delicious soup and freshly baked bread, Daniel dropped his spoon into his empty bowl with a happy sigh. Madeline and Richard had headed home as soon as they'd finished eating. George and Maggie had gone to see them off, and had then volunteered to tidy up in the kitchen. A footstep scuffed on the parquet flooring behind him, and he angled his body towards Mia as she wandered into the dining room. He patted his thigh and she settled on it, leaning against his chest to rest her head under his chin. 'How is she?'

'Better, I think. I wanted to stay and make sure she had enough to eat, but she's sleeping now.'

He curled his arm around her waist to settle her more firmly on his lap. 'Best thing for her. So, what's on the agenda for this afternoon?'

'As little as possible,' she said, hopefully.

He liked the sound of that. Pressing his lips to her ear, he lowered his voice to a husky whisper. 'Fancy a nap?'

'You've no shame,' she said, but there was laughter in her words.

'Absolutely none.' She was definitely considering the idea, so he added an extra bit of persuasion. 'I hid the rest of that chocolate gelato in the back of the freezer.'

Quicker than a flash, she hopped off his lap. 'I'll be waiting upstairs, don't be long!' He decided to pretend at least a smidgen of the lust shining in her eyes was reserved for him.

To his surprise, the kitchen stood empty. The washing-up was only half done and breadcrumbs still littered the chopping board on the counter. With a shrug, he added his bowl and spoon to the soapy water in the sink, and retrieved the luxury ice cream. He was almost to the door when a noise came from the pantry. Ready to dismiss it, his mind well and truly fixed on dessert, he took another step. *There it was again, a funny little gasp.*

Thinking perhaps Mia's dad had gone in there to fetch something and was having trouble breathing, he hurried over to check. The words of concern died on his lips, and he cursed himself for not ignoring the sound. If George was having difficulty catching his breath, it was only because his lips were glued to Maggie's. Closing his eyes, he prayed silently for it to be some wild figment of his imagination before cracking them open again.

Nope. Not his imagination, for even in his wildest dreams (nightmares?) he couldn't have conjured the image of Maggie scrabbling at the back of George's second-best cardigan whilst wearing a pair of leopard-print washing-up gloves. It was enough to put a man off his gelato, for God's sake.

Thankfully, they were too wrapped up in each other to notice him, so he beat a hasty retreat, wondering if there was such a thing as mind-bleach, and just how much he'd need to use to scrub the vision from his poor brain.

Chapter Nineteen

Exhausted after almost no sleep in two days, Nee must have fallen asleep mid-conversation with Mia, for when she awoke, it was pitch dark and she was alone in her room. The muscles in her thighs ached from being locked into one position for too long, and she stretched them gingerly, wincing when her toes hit the cold, empty patch in the bed next to her. Luke's self-imposed exile might have been the catalyst to get her working again, but she'd grown used to sleeping beside him in just those first couple of nights. Stretching her arms and legs out like a starfish, she moved them up and down, to spread a bit of warmth into the bedding outside the little spot she'd been huddled in.

Brain muddled from heavy sleep, her throat dry, she groped for the switch on the bedside lamp. The first thing her eyes focused on was a tall glass of water, and she smiled. Mia just couldn't help herself when it came to looking after others. Propped on one elbow, she drank greedily, relishing the way the cold liquid cleared both her throat and her head. Her stomach rumbled, reminding her she'd slept right through dinner. With the mornings so dark at this time of year, it was impossible to tell what time it was.

Switching her glass for her phone, she frowned at the blank screen and tried to restart it – nothing. The temperature of the air around her told her it was too early for the heating to have kicked in, and she wrestled with the idea of getting out of her cosy bed to hunt for her charger or just turning over and going back to sleep. Curiosity beat comfort and she dived from beneath the covers to rummage in the miniature rucksack she used as a day-to-day handbag. Lucky for her, the plug and cable were curled up in the front pocket where she'd tucked them away, and there was a spare socket behind the bedside cabinet, so she was soon huddled back under the duvet.

It would take a minute or two for the phone to recharge enough to turn on, so she lay back and mulled over everything that had happened in the past week. Trusting Daniel with her paintings and drawings still felt like the right thing, thank goodness. With the worst of the poisonous anger drawn, and her mind rested, she had no regrets at asking him to destroy them. She glanced across at the closed sitting-room door. Knowing she wouldn't have to face them again would make it easier to finish the last piece she'd started once the first frenzy of emotion had wound down.

Venting the worst of her pain wouldn't take away the scars of the experiences, but time would lessen them and she had no desire to keep going over the same ground. For a year, she'd fooled herself into believing she could get over what had happened by simply ignoring it, but it had been with her all the time – like tinnitus, always keeping her slightly off balance and unable to relax.

Embarrassment, shame and hopelessness had kept her silent, a fact she was sure Devin had relied upon, for who would believe her word over his? The answer came instantly in an echo of Luke's words from the beach. *You'll know, and I'll know. And everyone else in your life who's worth anything will know.*

Yes.

Even if nothing came of it, she would send a message to the administrator at the Institute outlining what she remembered of that horrible night. And then she would let it go, because she'd wasted more of her life than a bastard like Devin Rees deserved.

What was it Kiki had said after Mum's funeral? *It's not my shame to bear.* Sure, some people would say they'd brought their own miseries upon themselves – Kiki by staying in an abusive relationship, and Nee for not taking more care with her personal safety – but it was always easy to sit in judgement when you'd never experienced a crushing betrayal from someone you should've been able to trust. *Screw them.*

As for the painting in Devin's forthcoming exhibition? She sighed. That would be harder to let go, and she wasn't sure if she could stand it. It was her work, *her work*, and he would be the one to get the credit for it. Having something she'd created displayed in the national press, lauded by critics and admired by fans, had always been her ultimate goal.

As she'd mentioned to Daniel the previous day, she'd always wanted to be first in the class, top of the pile, acknowledged and applauded. To stand on the mountain and shout at the world, *Here I am. See me!* That need for recognition had burned in her for as long as she could remember. As if her parents would take notice of her if she could just achieve enough plaudits; would love her and praise her, instead of neglecting her and ignoring her.

But Vivian was gone now – and her spirit had left long before her body finally gave out. All those arguments of Nee's youth had been an exercise in futility, for her mother had ceased to be interested in any of her daughters long before her youngest had brought home her first school report full of As. And as for her father . . . he might have spent her formative years obsessed with all things academic, but no one who met him would know it now.

He'd walked away from his career for love of his middle daughter, striking a devil's bargain with her ex-husband so Neil could replace him at the university in return for a quick, quiet divorce. He'd also taken Nee back under his wing and made sure she was okay even whilst facing the painful loss of the woman he'd once loved beyond reason. The man she'd thought she had everything to prove to needed nothing from her but the chance to make up for the mistakes of his past. She could be the artist of her generation, or a woman who lived the rest of her days in quiet obscurity, and George would love her just the same.

Like a weight lifting from her chest, the truth crystallised in her mind and she took what felt like the first full breath in for ever. She had everything she needed to consider herself a success. Art would always be a key part of her life, but she didn't need the world to acknowledge her. The respect and recognition of her family and friends was worth a thousand flash-bulb moments; a million empty plaudits.

When she contacted the administrator, she would lay out the facts of what she remembered of that horrible night and request the return of her portfolio; nothing more. Let Devin Rees keep what he'd stolen and live with the truth of what he was every day for the rest of his pathetic life. And live with the fact that she knew the truth of him and would no longer keep secret his abusive behaviour. No other woman should have to suffer the way she had.

The display light on her phone flashed, indicating the first signs of life. Banishing Devin to the very back of her thoughts, she thumbed the on switch. Daniel had added a booster during the refurbishment of the barns so the internet signal was better than she might have expected given the remoteness of the location. The digital clock on the front screen read 06:20, proving she'd slept even longer than she'd suspected. Pressing the message icon, she couldn't help the twinge of guilt as Luke's name popped up once, twice . . . by the time she counted eight messages from him, the guilt had been replaced by just a hint of smugness. They obviously had different interpretations of the word patience.

Not sure what to expect, she read them in chronological order and her heart began to flutter at the utter sweetness of his words. Not one complaint at her silence, not one request for a response, just little flashes of kindness, and humour, and love. The timestamp of the most recent message was from the previous evening, an observation that it was likely to be the last time she heard from him as he was surely dying of man flu. Clicking on reply, she searched the internet and attached a clip of Olaf, the cute snowman sidekick from *Frozen* sneezing his carroty nose off and added a message: *Such a shame. I'll have to find myself another date for NYE then.*

Teasing him felt like the right way to go; he knew her well enough to read the true meaning behind the message. The cartoon would serve to remind him of that happy afternoon snuggling on the floor with the family around them. The words would tell him she wanted to see him again, and when. Pushing back the covers, she ignored the chilled air and crossed to stand in front of the sitting-room door. Two days would give her enough time to finish the painting. Her stomach rumbled again so she dressed quickly in a thick pair of fleecy leggings, a long-sleeve top and warm cardigan and crept from her room to hunt down some breakfast. Food first; then she'd get back to work.

A thin sliver of light shone under the closed kitchen door, and she could hear the soft murmur of voices through the wood. Apparently, she wasn't the only early riser this morning. She still felt a bit awkward about facing people after shutting herself away, then reminded herself they'd been nothing but welcoming for the few minutes she'd shown her face the previous day. Taking a deep breath, she opened the door and stopped dead at the sight of Luke's parents, still in their dressing gowns, sharing a plate of toast.

'Oh, there you are! Madeline told me you'd been up and about yesterday and we were so sorry to miss you. Come in and shut the door. Can I get you a drink?' Whatever she'd been expecting from Cathy, this effusive greeting wasn't it at all.

A little shell-shocked, Nee did as bidden and slipped into an empty chair at the table. 'Tea, please, if there's some still in the pot.'

Cathy tugged off the knitted cosy and tested the weight of the pot. 'I think there might be a drop left.' She managed to wring about half a cup out, which she pushed across towards Nee before rising to refill the kettle. 'You must be starving. Do you want some toast?' She poked around in the breadbin. 'Or how about some croissants?'

'Anything will be fine, really. I can do it myself, if you like.' Nee half-rose, but Brian urged her back down with a smile.

'Let her fuss, sweetheart. Your mother-in-law is feeling a bit guilty about everything that's happened. I've told her you and Luke are old enough to make a hash of things without any assistance from her.'

His use of the title warmed Nee to the tips of her toes, for surely it meant they still wanted her as part of their family. There was nothing for Cathy to feel guilty about, though. She might have been a touch frosty when they'd first met, but had shown nothing but kindness since then. Confused, she waited until the older woman placed a fresh pot of tea on the table then reached out to touch the back of her wrist. 'What's happened between Luke and me is no one's fault but our own. We've both made mistakes, me far worse than him. Time will tell if we can put them right or not, but I hope we can.'

Cathy's arm flexed beneath her grip. 'I should have minded my own business, though. If I hadn't said anything he wouldn't have gone off and left you.' Worry etched thick lines across her brow and bracketed her mouth.

Nee squeezed her arm, trying to reassure the woman. 'He hasn't left me. He's giving me some space, that's all.'

Not looking entirely convinced, Cathy closed her free hand over Nee's. 'But isn't that what people say when they're breaking up and trying to be friends about it? You're both being so bloody reasonable, it sets my nerves itching.'

Nee laughed. She wasn't sure Luke moving out to Honeysuckle Cottage followed by Nee locking herself away for two days would be anyone's idea of reasonable behaviour, but they were both prone to grand gestures it seemed. 'Perhaps we're finally growing up a bit.'

The idea that had been playing through her mind since Daniel had reminded her about the forthcoming party resurfaced. *Or, perhaps not.* If she could get the others onboard then there was still time for one last grand gesture. The phone in her pocket beeped, and Cathy let her hand go. 'Answer that, dear, and I'll get these croissants warming in the oven.'

Nee read the message from Luke: *I predict a miraculous recovery. Save me a dance on Saturday night x.* If things went as she planned, she'd be saving a dance for him all right. Grinning to herself, she texted her reply: *The first dance x.*

She ran through a mental list of things that would need to be done in the next couple of days whilst waiting for Cathy to resume her seat. The need to finish the painting she'd started pressed down upon her. For everything to be perfect, it would need to be completed. *But how could she fit everything in?*

If she was going to pull it off, she'd need everyone onboard. Starting with the couple sitting in front of her. Taking a deep breath, she extended a hand towards each of them. 'I want to marry Luke.'

It might have been wiser to wait until Brian had finished his tea, as he almost choked on a mouthful. She jumped up to pat his back. 'I thought . . .' He coughed, cleared his throat and tried again. 'I thought you were already married.'

'Well, yes, we are. But to borrow a phrase from you, we made a hash of things. I want to start again. Prove to Luke I'm in this for the long haul and not just going along with what he wants me to do. And this time, it wouldn't be in secret – we'd have all of you with us.'

Cathy beamed. 'Well, I think it's a lovely idea, darling. When were you thinking of doing it? A spring ceremony might be nice, with all the trees in blossom.'

Nee chewed her lip, wondering if she was mad to even give voice to her plan. What the hell. She was Nee Thorpe-Spenser and she could do what she wanted, *when* she wanted. 'Ah, about that. I was hoping we could do at the New Year's Eve party.'

It was her mother-in-law's turn to choke on her tea. '*This* year's party?' She swallowed hard. 'As in the one we're having on Saturday?'

With impeccable timing, her sister wandered into the kitchen, stifling a huge yawn with the back of her hand. 'Excuse me, apparently nine hours' sleep isn't enough for me these days.' She pulled out a chair and helped herself to a cup of tea, half of which she drained before sitting down. 'That's better. Now then, what were you saying about Saturday?'

'Don't do that, you'll want them nice for Saturday.' Madeline tugged the finger Nee had been chewing out of her mouth.

'Shh, you two.' Cathy waved at them to be quiet as she strained to hear what Mia was saying as she paced up and down the kitchen with the phone clamped under one ear. She walked in front of the pantry doorway and Nee noticed for the first time someone had stuck a large sprig of mistletoe above the entrance. Maybe Daniel had pinned it there after catching her and Luke smooching the other day.

She shook her head as she recalled the incident. It was like looking back at a distant memory, or one of those déjà vu moments that sometimes came when watching a film. The woman who'd welcomed those stolen kisses had been so scared of everything, even the hope she'd been feeling, it was like observing a stranger. That Nee had been happy to cling to Luke, to rely on him to lead her along the correct path back to her old life.

Shame burned hot on her cheeks and she raised her hands to cover the heated flush. He deserved so much better than she'd been willing to offer him then – a full partner, someone ready to walk at his side instead of being towed along in his wake. *She* deserved better. Ironic, really, that Devin's ugly betrayal of her trust should be the catalyst which reignited the fire inside her.

The hopes she'd harboured those few short days ago were gossamer-thin, a child's dream. She had no more need of hope, not with certainty burning bright in her heart. Her future with

Luke would be a bright, vibrant celebration – because she would make it so. Starting from Saturday.

'Uh huh . . . Okay . . . That's brilliant.' Nee turned her attention back to Mia as she wound up her conversation. It sounded hopeful and she crossed her fingers like a little girl praying for a wish to come true. 'Lovely, I can't thank you enough, Alison. Give my love to Sue, and we'll see you both on Saturday.' Mia ended the call and returned the phone to its cradle on the wall.

'Well?' Madeline burst out, and Nee couldn't help but laugh. She wasn't the only one desperate for news.

Beaming, Mia turned towards them. 'She said yes!' Her next words were drowned out as they jumped up and shared a group hug.

'Oh, God, Mimi, that's amazing! But, oh, *God*, there's so much to do! Where do we start?' As determined as she was, the sheer scale of what needed to happen sent nerves fizzing through her belly.

Her sister hugged her tight, then drew back to cup her face. 'We start where we always start – with a pot of tea. We're going to sit down and you tell us exactly what you want, and we'll make it happen. Alison has a few suggestions for the ceremony; she emailed them over whilst we were talking. I'll grab the laptop and my notebook and we'll make a start.'

Nee raised her hands to cover Mia's, drawing strength from the utter belief in her sister's dark gaze. If Mia put her mind to something, then it damn well happened. 'I'll put the kettle on.'

'Already done.' They both turned to see Madeline, Maggie and Cathy bustling around: making the tea, setting out mugs and plates, slicing cake.

Mia slung an arm around her shoulders and drew Nee in for a kiss on the cheek. 'See,' she whispered against her ear, 'with three meddling old bags on our side it'll be a doddle.'

Brandishing the knife she was using to cut a Victoria sponge into enormous wedges, Madeline mock-frowned at them. 'As I've told you insolent children before, we prefer the term fairy godmothers.' She put down the knife and clasped her hands together as though praying. 'Although, given the time of year, perhaps Christmas angels would be more appropriate.'

Nee laughed. 'Angels is right, because I'm going to need you all to pull off some miracles between now and Saturday.'

Cathy placed the teapot in the middle of the table. 'I wonder if it's too late to change my costume. I've always fancied being an angel.'

'I'm afraid my halo is more than a little tarnished these days,' Maggie observed, drawing a look from Madeline which said further enquiries would be made about that little aside.

'Oh, not that sort of angel,' Cathy said as she smoothed a hand over her sleek hair. 'I used to have a fabulous Farrah Fawcett flick back in the day.' She positioned her hands into a gun shape and struck a pose straight out of the original 1970s *Charlie's Angels*. By the time Madeline and Maggie had joined in taking up places on either side of her, Nee's sides ached from laughing and it felt so good.

She already had her first miracle right here in front of her.

Chapter Twenty

With the message from Nee buoying his spirits, Luke did what he always did when falling ill and put himself to bed with a Lemsip and a box of tissues. Charlie had decreed Mr Bunny should stay with him, and he had a few blurry memories of Kiki coming in to check on him, but for the most part of the next two days he slept. By the time he surfaced on Saturday morning, he had started to feel vaguely human again. Desperate for a shower, he was halfway to the door before he noticed the dark outline of his suit hanging on the outside of the wardrobe door. In his haste to pack his things, he'd left it hanging in the bedroom back at Butterfly Cove. A large box sat beneath it. Lifting the lid, he grinned to see a fedora, a set of wide dark braces and an inflatable Tommy gun. If he was to be a gangster, maybe he'd get lucky and Nee would be going as his moll and wearing some slinky little dress. The thought sent him towards the shower with a happy whistle on his lips.

Showered, shaved and his belly straining after a huge cooked breakfast, there was little to show he'd been under the weather other than a slight husk to his voice. Making himself useful, he cleared the table and put the pans in the sink to soak. Kiki had followed the children upstairs to help them get dressed. Luke nudged Aaron to lift his coffee cup so he could finish wiping off the table. 'So, what's the plans for today?'

Aaron's eyes skittered away from his, and he buried his nose in his cup, apparently more interested in draining the contents than answering what was a pretty straightforward question. Luke folded the cloth then tossed it in the sink, leaving his hands free to find their way to his hips. His brother had always been terrible at hiding things. 'What's going on?'

'What? Nothing!' Aaron pushed back his chair and brushed past him to put his empty cup in the dishwasher.

Luke took a couple of steps back, putting himself back in his brother's eyeline. 'You're a hopeless liar, Bumble. Why don't you just tell me what you're hiding?'

'Nothing, really.' Aaron scrubbed a hand through his thick hair. 'Look, we weren't expecting you to be up and about this morning, so we've already made plans. Kiki's taking Charlie to a morning matinee at the pictures, and I'm taking Matty down to the cove to try out his new beach cricket set.'

None of which explained his evasive behaviour. Luke brushed it off. A bit of fresh air would be just the ticket to blow away the last of the cobwebs in his head. He clapped his hands together. 'Beach cricket sounds great. I'll go and get changed.'

His brother winced. 'Jeez, I'm sorry, Spud, but with the girls going out, I thought it would be nice if Matty and I spent a couple of hours, just the two of us. You can understand, right?'

Hiding a little pang of rejection, Luke forced a smile. 'Hey, of course. Don't even worry about it. I think it's awesome the way you two have bonded. He'll be chuffed to have your undivided attention.' Much as he adored his big brother, those times growing up when his dad had spent time just with him had been magical.

It hadn't once occurred to him that dumping himself on his brother's family might disrupt their plans. He really had had his head shoved halfway up his arse. 'Go and have a good time, and you guys can tell me all about it later.'

Blotches of colour rose on Aaron's face. 'Thanks, bro. If you're sure you don't mind? You still look a bit pale. With us out of the way you can have the TV to yourself. You can watch whatever you like instead of wall-to-wall Disney films.' Luke didn't say anything. He hadn't minded the films, especially not when he had his niece curled up on his knee, or Nee nestled against his chest. Speaking of which . . . he pulled his phone out of the pocket of his jogging bottoms and checked to see if she'd responded to his latest text.

'Well, as long as you're sure?'

He glanced up briefly to nod at Aaron, who was still hovering on the threshold, a frown of concern etched between his eyebrows. 'Yep, it's fine. A lazy day in front of the telly sounds great. Make sure I'm properly rested for the party later.' His attention was already back on his phone by the time Aaron left the room.

The message from Nee was short, and sweet: *Glad to hear you're feeling better. See you later x.*

Later, at the party, when she might be wearing something short and sexy . . . *Love the accessories for my costume,* he replied. *Any chance of a peek at yours?* He added a winking emoji.

Her wordless response came through a short while later – a photo of a pair of sheer black stockings and a lacy garter laid out on the deep magenta quilt he recognised from the Harem bedroom. Things were looking up, and if those stockings held half the promise he hoped, then a day of rest would be a very good idea.

Squeezed into the backseat of the family's hatchback, with Batman on one side and Elsa on the other, Luke held the now-inflated toy machine gun across his knees. Kiki had offered to sit in the back, but the stiff green-and-red tutu of her elf's costume had proven wider than expected when she put it on. The little silver bell on the end of Aaron's matching cap jingled every time he turned his head whilst steering, and Luke could only be thankful his wife had better taste in matching costumes than her older sister.

His wife. Funny how he'd never stopped thinking of Nee in those terms, even with Aaron's warning about her possibly choosing to move on with her life without him. He'd convinced himself the little text exchanges meant things were okay with them, but that didn't stop his nerves jangling as the car eased its way slowly over the little hill and over the crossroads leading to the cove.

'Look, Uncle Luke.' The nudge from Matty provided a well-timed distraction and he ducked his head to glance out of the passenger window as they drew to a stop close to the barns. Their combined breaths steamed the window, obscuring his view, so Luke swiped his palm over the damp glass. He would never class himself as prone to sentimentality, but that first glimpse of the garden stole his breath.

Like a magical grotto, coloured lights hung from the branches of the trees, sending soft pools of colour reflecting off the snow beneath. The torches which had lined the flowerbeds during the wedding were dotted here and there across the back lawn, casting their own pretty glows onto the crystal-white ground. When his nephew scrambled from his seat, Luke was hard on his heels, unable to tear his eyes away.

He'd taken a couple of steps closer when Kiki called out, 'No, Charlie! Not without your wellies on. Grab her, Luke!' Swooping down, he gathered the little girl up and hooked her over one shoulder, knocking his hat askew in the process. Feet kicking, she squirmed and giggled to be put down, and when he saw the thin ballet slippers she wore, he understood her mother's worry.

He switched his hold to bring Charlie back upright, but kept her perched in the crook of his arm. 'Hang on to this for me.' He handed her the inflatable Tommy gun then plucked off his fedora and set it on her head, almost completely obscuring her face, which set her off laughing again.

A horn tooted behind them, and a grinning Daniel slipped out of the driver's side. A familiar silver-haired figure climbed out of the opposite side and Matty pointed to the car. 'Aunty Pat and

Uncle Bill are here!' he yelled, and zoomed off towards it, cape billowing behind him.

The woman caught the boy in a hug as he charged up to her. 'Steady on there, Batman.' She crouched down to give him a hug. 'Look at how big you've grown. Did you have a nice Christmas? If you ask Uncle Bill, he might have a present or two that Santa left for you at our house.'

Luke grinned at her outfit – a black pinafore, embroidered with flowers worn over a white blouse. Her short hair was brushed into a pageboy style. Mia's in-laws from her first marriage had remained a firm fixture in her life, and Pat and Bill had been only too pleased to welcome Daniel into their fold. He'd been genuinely delighted when he'd told Luke the couple had agreed to come down to the cove to see in the New Year, having spent Christmas with their other children and grandchildren.

Pat waved at Luke over Matty's head. 'Hello, dear. It's good to see you again!'

'You too! Nice costume – Maria, I presume?' She dipped a little curtsey, holding the skirt out to the sides.

Her husband emerged from the rear passenger seat, looking strangely muted in a brown polo-neck and matching dark cords. Matty jumped for him, and Bill hoisted the boy up over his head with a grin. 'Look at you, don't you look splendid?'

'Not dressing up?' Luke asked, as he let a wriggling Charlie down so she could run over to hug Pat.

'Oh, God, don't!' Pat groaned as she hooked the little girl onto her hip then moved past him to exchange kisses with Kiki. 'I'm going to disown him.'

With a laugh, Bill disappeared around the back of the car, Matty in tow. A few moments of rustling later, he emerged wearing what appeared to be a cardboard box. He grinned at Luke and popped another, smaller box on his head. As he turned to give Matty a hand with a huge carrier bag, the box rustled and Luke realised it was wrapped in plain paper, with a thin bow fastened in front.

Still clueless, he shrugged one shoulder. 'You'll have to give me a hint.'

Bill held his arms outstretched. 'I'm a brown-paper package, tied up with string!' Luke groaned at the terrible pun of a costume.

'When I suggested a *Sound of Music* theme, I had high hopes you'd choose to be Captain Von Trapp, or at least a lonely goatherd,' his wife grumbled.

'I haven't got the knees for lederhosen, my love, and no one wants to see my varicose veins.'

Still laughing, Luke glanced behind him to find his brother rooting around in the car boot. 'Do you want everything out now?' Aaron asked Kiki.

She shook her head, sending the little bell on her cap ringing. 'Just the coats and wellies for now. I know Daniel's offered up the barns if we want to stay over, but let's wait and see how things go on, shall we?'

Aaron grasped a large holdall and slung it over one arm as he shut the rear of the car. 'Good idea. I'll drive us home if it comes to it. That alcohol-free beer Daniel gets in is as good as the normal stuff. I can still have a glass of champagne for the toasts.'

'*Aaron!*' Kiki's hiss was accompanied by another jingle from her hat as she whipped around to glare at him.

'Toasts? You're not planning any more surprise speeches, are you?' Luke couldn't resist the opportunity to tease Aaron, who'd sprung a heartfelt surprise proposal on Kiki whilst acting as best man at Daniel and Mia's wedding.

It was hard to tell given the relative darkness of the early-evening sky and the two bright-red circles painted on Aaron's cheeks as part of his elf ensemble, but he could swear his brother blushed as he mumbled something about toasting in the New Year. *Whatever.*

He'd been acting weird all afternoon, refusing to say much about the beach-cricket match when Luke had asked him about it. And after he'd made such a fuss about it earlier too. A chill ran down his back. It was too cold to be standing around pondering the deep inner workings of his brother's brain. He reclaimed his hat, which was still drooping over Charlie's eyes. 'Come on, everyone, let's get inside in the warm.'

The heat and noise rolling out from the kitchen hit him like a welcoming wave. The table, which normally took pride of place in the centre, had been pushed to one side close to the fridge, and the chairs removed. A bright-red cloth covered the table and was in turn laden with plates and bowls filled with snacks and hot hors d'oeuvres. Greetings reached him from every side, and he gathered from a couple of jokes that they were the last to arrive.

Sounds of a scuffle and laughter came from behind him, and he glanced back to see Bill wedged in the back door, the dimensions of his costume too wide for the opening. 'Lift your arms up out of the way,' he heard his brother say from outside, moments before he put those years of rugby playing to use and shoved the older man through the door. The two of them staggered in – Bill's costume resembling a parcel that had suffered the worst deprivations of the postal system, and Aaron's hat hanging askew. Kiki and Pat edged past the pair and moved to the farthest side of the kitchen, making it clear they wanted nothing to do with them.

Still laughing, Luke let his gaze roam around the room, taking in all the costumes as he searched for Nee. Harry Potter and Hermione were helping themselves to the food. It took a moment to place them before he recognised the celebrant from the wedding, together with her wife. He knew they'd become good friends with Mia and Daniel, but it was still a surprise to see them. The couple were talking to a Sixties-style go-go dancer – Maggie, resplendent in knee-high white boots and a psyche-delic mini dress – and Nee's dad, who'd gone all-out with a long white robe and fake curly wig and beard. George gestured with one hand to emphasise whatever point he was making, waving a miniature trident. Poseidon was as good a choice as any for a Professor in ancient Greek studies.

Making his way over, Luke accepted a kiss from Maggie, and a warm handshake from George.

Luke raised his hat to Maggie. 'You're looking splendid, Maggie. Save a twist for me later?' Turning towards the uniform-clad pair, he offered a smile. 'You'll have to forgive me. I know we met at the wedding, but I can't remember your names, ladies.'

The one dressed as Harry Potter smiled a little nervously. 'I'm Alison, and this is Sue. We were at a loose end, so when Mia called to invite us to the party, it saved us from a boring night in front of the telly. I've not been to a fancy-dress party since university; everyone's really pushed the boat out.' The woman drained her glass, which at least served to stop the stream of words.

Sue grabbed her arm. 'Come on, let's stop monopolising Luke and grab a refill. Nice to see you again.' The two women bustled off, leaving him slightly bemused.

With a shrug, he turned back to find George and Maggie had moved away, their heads bent in close conversation. Perhaps he'd overdone the aftershave. Oh well, at least the buffet was clear. He popped a sausage roll in his mouth and surveyed the rest of the room.

From the blonde plaits which almost trailed to the floor, he assumed Mia was supposed to be Rapunzel. The broad shoulders clad in a battered leather jacket over by the door had to belong to his dad, although the brown hat on his head hid his blond-grey hair. The dark coil hanging at his hip made Luke shake his head. Where on earth had his dad got a bullwhip from?

Brian turned at his approach, and all Luke's jokes about his costume died on his lips as the curling tip of an ostrich feather came into view. His eyes followed the waving plume down to a jewelled headband holding back glossy chestnut hair, and down further still to a shimmering silver sheath clinging to a delicate, fine-boned frame. As Nee moved, the beads on the dress caught the light, sending little rainbow flashes dancing over the above-the-knee column. Black gloves covered her arms, and glittering diamante cuffs encircled each wrist. One hand was cocked in a saucy pose, with a long cigarette holder set between her first and middle fingers.

He forgot how to breathe for a moment as their gazes met. Her eyes were all shadows and seduction, ringed in smoky kohl pencil and enhanced with thick curling false lashes. He wanted to drown in them, to draw her close until there was nothing in his vision but those warm, brown pools filled with fire and promise. All those vows he'd made about being patient and giving her time would prove him a liar because there was no way he was letting her out of his sight again. Not tonight; not ever.

Shaping her ruby-red lips into a moue she blew him a kiss. 'You look like you know how to show a dame a good time,' she drawled in a terrible American accent.

Seizing on the chance to mask his visceral reaction to her, Luke raised a finger to tip back the brim of his hat a fraction. 'And you look like just my kinda trouble, doll-face.' He'd meant it as a joke, but it was absolutely true. That inner fire, so long missing, seemed to glow from her every pore. *Incandescent*. He wanted to draw her close and absorb the heat and life of her.

The noise of the party faded behind him as he moved closer, trapping her against the wall with one arm braced over her head. He didn't touch her, wouldn't risk crushing her dress or messing up the make-up she'd so carefully applied. 'I missed you.'

One gloved hand rose to smooth the wide silk tie hanging down his chest. 'I missed you too. I'm sorry I threw sand at you. I want you to know that I understand why you left.'

He risked the softest of kisses against her cheek, taking the utmost care not to smudge her. 'I'm glad one of us does, because from where I'm standing it feels like a monumentally stupid idea.'

A thrill ran through his entire body as her next words confirmed his greatest hope. 'You gave me back my art.'

Much as he wanted to celebrate the news, to punch the air, to spin her around and shout to the rooftops, he had to make one thing crystal-clear. 'No, sweet love. You took it back for yourself. You claimed it – I just gave you the breathing space to do it. Don't give your credit away, not to me, not to anyone. Not ever again.'

The sparkle in her eyes increased and he watched the extravagantly curled lashes flutter furiously as she blinked back the tears. 'I did it.' Her ruby lips stretched into a smile that could only be called triumphant. '*I* did it.' Her spine straightened against the wall so the tip of her ostrich feather tickled his fingers where they curled above her. 'I'm amazing.'

'Incredible,' he agreed, stroking the feather when he'd rather be stroking her skin.

'Sublime!'

'Remarkable!' They were both grinning their heads off now.

'Wondrous!' She giggled. 'You go to my head like the finest champagne. If we carry on like this I'll have more trouble getting my head through the door than poor Bill did with his costume.'

She had no bloody idea. He would make her feel like this each and every day given half the chance. His eyes traced every inch of her face, committing to memory the exact tilt of her head, the angle of her lips as they canted up into an even wider smile. This expression would be the goal he'd aim for, always.

His gaze slid lower, and the bubbles of excitement in his stomach subsided. Her throat was bare. The necklace he'd given her with her wedding ring looped on it was missing. There was no sparkling choker to match the bracelets at her wrists, nothing to offer a reassuring excuse why she'd removed it. He searched over her hands, but there was no bump in the sleek, smooth gloves so she hadn't put it on her finger either.

Her hand rose to cover the naked skin. 'It's not what you think. Luke . . .'

Whatever she'd been about to say was cut off by a shout from across the room. 'Hey, you two! If you want to snog, then take it inside the pantry like everyone else does!'

Blushing, Nee ducked beneath his arm and was swept up into the laughter and conversation around them. He wanted to follow her, but was intercepted by his parents. Brian thrust a cold bottle of beer into his hand, whilst his mother raised a hand to brush a fleck of something from his shoulder.

'You look like you're feeling better, darling.' He'd made it back into Cathy's good books, apparently, which was something to be grateful for at least. If only she hadn't picked this particular moment to demonstrate it. The diaphanous sleeve of her white dress slid down her arm, and he reluctantly abandoned his pursuit of Nee to study the floaty, floor-length gown and the wild dark wig she was wearing. Heavy make-up ringed her eyes, and she'd hidden the tan from a late-season holiday beneath a layer of pale, almost-ghostly foundation.

His dad clinked their bottles together, then raised his own in toast to his wife. 'She makes a smashing Kate Bush, doesn't she?' Ah. He might have guessed, because she was his mum's favourite artist and there was a family story that she'd been named for the heroine from *Wuthering Heights*.

'You look fab, Mum,' he agreed, kissing first her then his dad on the cheek.

Brian circled his free arm about Cathy's waist, and gave her what Luke could only describe as a leer. 'Now if only you'd let me talk you into coming as Babooshka.'

'Jesus, Dad!' Luke sputtered over his beer, trying desperately not to conjure images of his mum in a chain-mail bikini.

'Behave yourself, Brian.' Cathy didn't look remotely displeased, and Luke suppressed another shudder.

Intellectually, he understood his parents shared a happy, healthy relationship. Faced with the reality, though . . . His mind scrambled for anything to distract him from what exactly that might entail. Something really boring, something, anything . . . *The square of the length of the hypotenuse equals the sum of the squares of the lengths of the other two sides.* Yes! Good old Pythagoras. What else, what else? *The three sides of an equilateral triangle are all the same length. Its angles are also equal at 60° each.* He numbed his brain with every mathematical theory he could dredge up until Madeline and Richard joined their little group, thankfully distracting his parents from their flirting.

With an admiring bow at her off-the-shoulder powder-blue gown, he swept up Madeline's hand in his own and placed a kiss on the back. 'My lady, you look ravishing.'

'Hey, I've got my eye on you, young man.' Richard lifted the patch covering his right eye, and they all groaned.

'You should be made to walk the plank for that terrible joke,' Luke's dad said, and he had to agree with him. Their timely arrival assisted him further, for his mum and Madeline were soon in raptures over each other's costumes, giving him a chance to slip away.

He searched the room again, but there was no sign of Nee. He took a couple of steps towards the door leading into the rest of the house, thinking he might track her down and pick up their conversation about her missing ring. The fates were conspiring against him, though, because his brother and Daniel were blocking the doorway and showed absolutely no signs of moving. 'Grab us a refill will you, Spud?' Aaron raised his empty bottle.

'I was just looking for Nee, actually.' He tried to peer around his brother.

Daniel clapped him on the shoulder, but held his position by the door. 'She's fine. Get us a drink and relax, mate. It's supposed to be a party and you've got a face like a smacked arse.'

It was then Luke realised that Kiki and Mia were also missing from the kitchen. Maybe it wasn't just the fates conspiring against him. Folding his arms, he gave them both his best glare, which did nothing but make Aaron grin. Big brothers were arseholes. He tried again. 'What's going on?'

'You'll find out in a bit. Now be a good boy and fetch us those beers.' Daniel's grin was, if anything, bigger than Aaron's. Utterly thwarted, he skulked off towards the fridge.

Yup. Brothers were arseholes. And so were their best mates.

Chapter Twenty-One

Nee froze on the threshold of the sitting room, heart racing a mile a minute. Once she'd confided in Mia about needing to finish the painting, her eldest sister had seized the chance to take control of the arrangements and banished Nee to concentrate on it. They'd wanted to give it the chance to dry as much as possible, so hanging it had been left to the last minute.

A soft hand brushed her arm, and she glanced left towards the woman who'd been mother, sister and friend to her. 'All right?'

She nodded, pressing a hand to the butterflies dancing in her stomach. 'Just a bit of last-minute nerves.' Not about Luke. Those had melted under the intensity of his blue eyes, the fierceness in his tone when he'd told her not to give her credit away to anyone. Ever. She'd never been afraid to show her work to anyone before, but what lay beyond the door was the cornerstone on which she hoped to build her future.

'What can we do to help?' Kiki spoke this time, her tone as sweet and caring as her heart. Whatever life had thrown at Nee, it had gifted her with the best sisters anyone could hope to have in their life.

She reached for their hands. 'You're already doing everything I need just by standing here with me.'

'We're always with you, Nee. Always will be. No matter how far your life might take you from Butterfly Cove, we'll be no more than a thought away.' Mia squeezed her hand. 'Now, come on, show me this bloody picture before we all start blubbing! This hormone cocktail I'm brewing has me all over the place.' She released Nee's hand to press her own to her still-flat middle.

Kiki leaned across to cover Mia's hand. 'Aaron wants to have one of these too,' she said, her voice wistful.

Nerves forgotten in the light of this delicious piece of sisterly gossip, Nee could only gape at her. 'Oh, God, Kiki Dee, what did you say?'

A rosy flush shone beneath the red circles painted on Kiki's cheeks. 'I didn't, not really. We've agreed to take it steady, but the subject is definitely on the table.' She sighed. 'I had all these plans for what I wanted to do with the teashop, but all I can think about is a sweet-faced baby with blond curls and bright-blue eyes.' Raising her hands to cover her face, she moaned softly. 'I blame you, Mimi, for putting the idea in his head in the first place.'

Mia laughed. 'Don't blame me, blame Daniel. He's the one who got me in this condition.'

Holding her hands up, Nee took an exaggerated step backwards. 'Stay away from me, you two. I'm not ready to catch baby fever.'

They both advanced on her, hands held out if front of them like zombies, and she yanked open the sitting-room door, laughing as she ran from them. Mia got halfway into the room before her hands dropped to her sides. 'Oh. Oh, Nee. That's just beautiful.'

Blushing, Nee followed her sister's gaze to the picture on the easel. The echoes of the image Devin had stolen from her had been unconscious at first, but as the piece progressed it had become vital to her to create the perfect antonym. A couple embraced in the centre of the canvas, their dimensions an exact replica of the difference in height between herself and Luke. Instead of black, she'd used soft, pastel shades to fill their anonymous forms in a delicate rainbow. The colours crossed the figures, carrying each stripe in perfect lines over them, a demonstration of the harmony between the two.

Ribbons of brighter colours wrapped around them, bearing the words *family, love, hope, friendship, unity*. All the things she'd risked losing in her desperate scrabble for the false rewards of fame and fortune. If the past week had taught her anything, it was that she was already rich beyond measure, that a life filled with love and laughter should be her goal.

Testing the edge of the painting with one finger, she thought about the message she'd received earlier. This was the first moment she'd had the two of them alone, and she needed to tell someone. 'I had an email this morning, from the Institute.'

Mia's expression turned immediately fierce. 'Whatever they said, forget about it. You don't owe them a damn thing.'

Nee held up her hand. 'No. You don't understand. The head of HR wrote to advise me they would be carrying out a full investigation into Devin's activities. She asked me to keep it under wraps, but the exhibition is being put on hold as well. She wants to talk with me next week with a view to giving a video statement; said there are a number of other past students she'll be reaching out to.' Thinking about it turned her stomach a little, but she'd known sending her original email would be opening Pandora's box.

Kiki rubbed a comforting hand down her arm. 'I'm so proud of you for stepping up, Nee. I'll stay in the room with you when you give your statement.'

'Me too,' Mia added, placing her hand over Kiki's. 'You won't have to do it alone.'

'Thank you, for everything.' Nee blinked hard to dispel the sting in her eyes. 'Right. No more of that bollocks tonight, we've got a wedding to get to.' With trembling fingers, she lifted the precious canvas down, turning it so she could carry it by the thick cord already attached to the rear.

Her sisters ran point, checking the route to the dining room was clear. She tiptoed past the broad backs of Daniel and Aaron

215

blocking the kitchen door then slipped past Mia, who closed the dining-room door behind her. She'd seen the room earlier whilst it had still been daylight, but the sight of it now drew a gasp of wonder. The furniture had been removed – a painstaking task because the antique table had taken several hours of careful dismantling – leaving a wide-open space in the centre of the room.

The huge Christmas tree still claimed pride of place in the corner, but thick ropes of greenery threaded with glistening white lights now lined the edges of the room, casting a gentle glow along the base of the walls. Shimmering curtains of lights covered the side window and the French windows, which were thrown open to reveal the neatly swept patio outside. With a fire crackling in the grate and upright heaters positioned on the patio either side of the open doors, the room was warm enough, without feeling stuffy.

Beyond the doors, the magical wonderland of the garden provided the perfect backdrop with coloured lights sparkling in the trees. Daniel and Luke had spent the morning up and down ladders to hang them, whilst Matty placed torches lit with white LEDs in the snow-covered flowerbeds.

Stepping to the edge of the open windows, a brush of fresh air cooled the heat in her cheeks and carried the soft susurration of waves on the beach to her ears. A round table had been set up just inside the doors, laden with unlit candles. The small box bearing her wedding ring sat there too.

'Do you like it? Is it what you were hoping for?' Mia's anxious questions drew her back into the present.

Turning to her sister, she struggled to speak through the tears clogging her throat. 'It's beautiful. Just perfect, Mimi. Thank you so much.'

With a watery laugh, Mia drew a tissue from her pocket and pressed it gently beneath Nee's eyes. 'No tears! You can't spoil this gorgeous make-up.' They both laughed and Nee sucked in a steadying breath. This wasn't a time for tears, though there would likely be a few later.

'Right, let's get this picture hung and then I think we'll be ready to start.' Mia tossed her long plaits over one shoulder to keep them clear of the fire and, between them, they got the painting attached to the waiting hook above the fireplace.

Kiki stepped back to assess it. 'Down your side just a fraction, Nee. Yes, that's perfect. Gosh, it's so pretty my heart flutters every time I look at it.' She turned a slow circle. 'Everything's ready. Are you?'

Was she? Nee did her own final check, waiting for a reappearance of the nerves she'd been feeling upstairs. Her tummy quivered, but it was excitement, not doubt. Here she was, on the cusp of a new year and a new life bursting with promise. She couldn't wait to get started. 'I'm ready.'

Hand in hand, her sisters left the dining room, and Nee moved to stand beside the table to wait. Hurried footsteps rang on the tiles of the hallway and Luke burst through the door, coming to a sharp stop as the impact of the glowing room hit him. 'Are you all right? Mia said you wanted to talk . . .' He shoved his hat back on his head and whistled. 'God, look at this place. It's incredible. What's the occasion?'

Patience. Patience, Nee. She followed his gaze as it bounced from one thing to another. He glanced at the fire glowing in the grate, over to the sparkling lights at the window, then whipped his head back around so fast, she worried he'd do himself an injury.

'*Nee.*' The rasp from the remains of his cold deepened, sending a thrill of anticipation down her spine. He didn't see her little shiver, though. His eyes were locked on the picture above the fireplace. He took a step closer. 'Is . . . is it . . .?' His voice hitched, and she had to swallow hard before she could respond.

'Yes.'

He said nothing for a few long seconds, just stared up at the image she'd created to symbolise everything she felt for him, everything she wanted from him, for him. For *them*. He backed up, one pace, a second, and her breath faltered. The

217

nerves roared back to life, threatening to choke the excitement. What if she'd misjudged where things stood between them? *No.* Not after the way he'd looked at her in the kitchen, like nothing else existed for him in that moment. She had hope. She believed in them. But she was also ready for him to say something, any time now!

Using the sleeve of his jacket he rubbed his eyes briefly, then turned towards her. 'That's truly how you see us?'

She nodded, and he was across the space between them in an instant. He stood so close, the tips of their shoes touched, and she had to crane her neck to meet his gaze. 'I took the necklace off because I want you to give me my ring again. Properly this time.' Lifting her hand, she pressed a finger to his jaw and turned his head towards the table where the simple band of gold glittered in the open black box.

'Now?' A muscle ticced in his jaw hard enough for her to feel through the silk of her glove, and she stretched her fingers to sooth the tension from his face.

'Yes. Please. I want us to walk into the New Year together, as husband and wife.'

He turned his head to press a kiss to her fingers. 'I love you, Mrs Spenser.'

'Mrs Thorpe-Spenser,' she said, and his eyes widened briefly before he flashed her that beautiful smile, all dimples and hot promises.

A none-too-discreet cough sounded behind them, and she peered around his shoulder to see everyone else had filtered in from the kitchen. 'So, what's the verdict?'

Luke turned at the sound of his brother's voice to find everyone staring at them with expressions of eager expectation. 'You were in on this?' He pointed an accusatory finger at Aaron.

His brother grinned. 'Yep. We all were. The story about playing beach cricket was a cover so Matty and I could help out with the decorating. I felt a bit bad about lying to you, but it was worth it to see the look on your face now.'

Luke could only imagine what his expression must look like, because his brain was still racing to catch up with everything his heart was telling him. Nee was here, *his* Nee, so bright and sparkling and full of life, telling him he hadn't screwed it all up between them. That she wanted them to start again; to *be* again. Placing an arm around her shoulders, he drew her to his side. Now he had her close, he was never letting her slip away from him again. He let his gaze travel over the wonderful, eclectic group he was blessed to call his family and felt his mouth stretch wide in a smile. 'My wife and I are getting married again,' he declared. 'And you're all invited!'

After a quick flurry of activity, during which he kept a firm grip on Nee, even when her sisters came over to help her remove her long gloves, Luke found himself facing a smiling Harry Potter and Hermione. Alison pushed the little round glasses up her nose and adjusted the black robe she wore over a grey school uniform. 'As you can see, I'm not just here for the party. Don't worry, I know you haven't been given any time to prepare, but I'll be doing most of the talking. There will be an opportunity for you to say something when you place the ring on Nee's finger. Will you want to?'

'Yes.' He had no idea what, but he'd worry about that when they got there. Alison carried on explaining things whilst Sue fussed with the candles on the table, but he couldn't focus on what she was saying over the thunderous beating of his heart. What if this was a dream, some fevered conjuring of his cold-addled brain, and he was still buried under the quilt, not standing beside Nee about to renew their vows? He clutched her hand tighter. She felt real enough and there was even a soft squeeze in return, but who knew what a person's mind could do when they wanted something badly enough.

The collar buttoned at his throat grew uncomfortably tight,

and his breathing sounded loud in his ears. Nee tugged his hand, making him glance down at her. 'What's the matter?' she whispered, brown eyes full of concern.

'Nothing.' His shirt began to stick to the clammy skin at the base of his spine. 'I might be having a bit of a panic attack, that's all.'

'Oh, God.' Pushing past Alison, Nee dragged him out on the patio. 'Breathe, Luke. I'm so sorry. I shouldn't have sprung this on you. I just wanted to show you how much I want to be with you. To tell you in front of everyone that matters, that I want to be your wife for ever.'

The cold air delivered a much-needed slap to the face and his constricting lungs eased. Her sweet words of worry further soothed his panicked brain, and he sucked in a deep, calming breath. She cupped his face, drawing his head down until their foreheads rested together, the beads of her headband digging into his skin giving him another sensation to further ground him in reality. 'We can wait until you're ready. I'll give you all the space and time you need.' He could hear the disappointment in her voice as she gave him back his words from the beach, but knew she meant it. That if he wanted her to walk back in there and tell everyone he'd changed his mind, she would do it. *Sod that.*

'I thought this might not be real. That I'd made it all up because it was what I wanted so badly, and it made me panic.'

She laughed, a soft sound of quiet relief. 'I'm very real.' Her fingertips closed over his earlobes and gave them a sharp pinch. 'See.'

The little sting was exactly what he needed, and he straightened his shoulders back. A crowd of curious faces peered at them through the open French windows. 'False alarm,' he said to a ripple of sighs, laughter and a despairing shake of her head from his mum.

The others moved back to give him and Nee room to re-enter the dining room. Alison adjusted the glasses on her nose. 'Right, let's get started, shall we?'

An expectant silence settled over the room as Alison raised her arms in welcome. 'Family, friends, loved ones. We are gathered here on the cusp of a new year to celebrate and witness as Luke and Eirênê reaffirm their life commitment to each other. In the darkest of hours, there is always the promise of the dawn to come. Of new light to guide us even if we falter along our path.' The celebrant reached for their free hands and held them in her own. 'We, your friends and family, are here to remind you that, no matter what obstacles you may face, you never walk that path alone. Help is here, advice is here—'

'Whether you need it or not,' Madeline observed drily and Luke could only laugh.

'Indeed,' Alison continued with a smile of her own. With a nod to Sue, she held out her hand and her wife removed the ring from the box on the table and passed it to her. 'This ring is a symbol of your love for each other. A perfect circle with no beginning and no ending. Eternal.'

She offered the ring to Luke, and he fumbled it with trembling fingers before securing it in his grip. It might have been easier with two hands, but he couldn't unlock the death grip he had on Nee's right hand, and her own fingers were locked tight around his. The slight tremor in her left hand as she raised it eased his own nerves as he slid the band of gold back where it belonged. Lifting their joined hands, he pressed his lips to her ring finger, feeling the metal already warmed by her skin.

Standing tall, he let his eyes roam free over Nee. The Roaring Twenties style of her outfit might be a bit unconventional for a wedding dress, but the beads caught the light from the fire, turning into a million shimmering rainbows, just like the figure in the portrait behind her.

Holding their joined hands out wide, he let all the admiration swelling in his heart burst forth as he spoke. '*Look at you*, you take my breath away. When I think about the first time we met, there's only one word which comes to mind – incandescent. You were

221

so full of fire, I knew I had to have you. To bask in the warmth of your spirit. I wanted you so much; too much, perhaps, before we were really ready for it.'

A tear glistened on her lashes and he released one of her hands to catch it on his thumb. 'But I'm ready now. Ready for anything as long as you promise to stay with me.'

'I'm ready. I promise.' He captured that promise on his lips, careful not to smudge the ruby-red gloss. Later, when he had her all to himself, he'd kiss her the way he'd been longing to all night, until they were both smeared in her lipstick. But that would be just for him. Just for them.

Alison touched his arm, and they turned back to face her. She offered them the wide pillar candle from the centre of the table, wrapping their hands securely around the base before she lit the wick. 'We light this flame as a symbol of the love Nee and Luke share and as a pledge of their commitment to one another. Who will help them keep the light of their love burning bright?'

'I will.' Mia was the first to step forward, accepting a smaller candle from Sue and tilting it to catch the flame from the one he and Nee held.

'I will.' His dad and Aaron spoke together, and Luke couldn't help the hitch in his shoulders as they lit their candles and stepped back.

One by one, the rest of their family pledged their support, lit their candles and moved to join the semicircle forming around them. Even Charlie, helped by her big brother, clutched a little candle in a special holder to protect her fingers. Alison and Sue lit their own candles, standing side by side to close the circle around them. 'If ever doubt, or pain, or conflict threatens to extinguish the light you share, turn to us and we will be there.'

Beyond speech, Luke could only nod as he stared across the flickering flame and into Nee's eyes. 'I love you,' she said, and it was all he needed to know. Then and for ever.

* * *

The candles, still lit, were placed on the table, which had been moved to the corner, away from any breeze which might blow through the door. Luke accepted the hugs and congratulations from everyone, one hand still firmly entwined with Nee's. His mum and dad hung back until the crowd cleared, then stepped up to face them. 'Congratulations!' There was no disguising the pleasure in his mum's voice as she kissed first him, then Nee. 'It's wonderful to finally be able to welcome you to the family properly.'

'We've got you a little something.' Brian held out a sheaf of papers, neatly stapled at one corner.

'What's this?' Nee leaned closer to scan the top sheet, letting out a soft gasp of surprise.

'We made good use of a certain folder full of honeymoon ideas Mia found in your room. We've paid for the cruise, and George is contributing the spending money.'

A lump formed in his throat as he read through the itinerary in disbelief. The two-week Mediterranean cruise would take them to some of Europe's most glittering capitals. 'I don't know what to say . . .'

His mum touched a finger to his cheek. 'Don't say anything, it's our pleasure.' His dad took her hand and they moved away before he could find the right words to express his gratitude.

Luke glanced down at Nee. 'Did you know about this?'

Eyes wide, she shook her head. 'Not a thing. I've been locked away finishing the painting. It's . . . it's too much.'

Folding the papers carefully, he tucked them in an inside pocket of her jacket. 'It's a lot, but they obviously wanted to do something special for us, and it sounds like a group effort if your dad's giving us some spending money too.'

'A cruise,' she whispered. 'Two whole weeks of just you and me on the high seas.'

'With about a thousand other people, though I'll only have eyes for you.' His attempts to draw her close were thwarted by his brother's approach, and Luke bit back a sigh. Those two weeks away from everyone couldn't come soon enough.

Aaron kissed his cheek, then slung an arm around his shoulders as he nodded at their still-joined hands. 'When are you going to let that poor girl go?' he teased.

'Never.'

'Don't blame you. I must admit I had a lump in my throat through most of that. It was beautiful.'

Not one to miss an opportunity, Luke gave his brother a quick dig in the ribs. 'Not too late, Bumble. Why don't you grab Kiki now and get on with it? I'm sure Alison won't mind.'

The arm around his shoulder threatened to slide up into a chokehold. 'Keep that kind of talk to yourself. For one thing, I've already crashed one wedding with my proposal to her so I'm not about to repeat that by horning in on your celebration. And for the other, I'm not getting married dressed as bloody Christmas elf!'

A champagne cork popped behind them, making them both jump and sending Tigger into a paroxysm of excited barking. Glasses were handed round, and Aaron raised an eyebrow at Kiki before taking one. She slipped between Luke and Nee, circling their waists with her arms. She'd abandoned her cap somewhere, leaving her hair to cascade around her shoulders. 'Fill your jingle-belled boots, elf-boy, because I'm not planning on going home any time soon.'

'If you're sure?'

She nodded. 'Grab me a glass too, whilst you're at it. Dad's already decamped his stuff from the garden room to one of the suites in the barns. Mia's changed the bed so we can put the kids up there if it all gets too much for them.' Their eyes all gravitated to where Charlie was dancing with her Nanny-Cat and Grandad Brian. 'Although my money's on them wearing us all out.'

She gave them a quick squeeze before wriggling out to accept a glass of straw-pale champagne. 'Here's to you, my darlings. Second time lucky, eh?' She slid a sideways glance at Aaron. 'For all of us.'

'Cheers!' They shared the toast, and Luke closed his eyes as the sharp bubbles fizzed over his tongue and palate. When he opened them again, his brother and Kiki had moved away to dance together, and he relished the moment of peace.

'Come here, wife.' He released Nee's hand so he could curl his arm around her back and draw her close.

Eyes more effervescent than the bubbles in his glass, she leaned in to his chest and smiled up at him. 'What do you need, husband?'

Tightening his hold, he swayed them gently to the music. 'Just you, love.'

Chapter Twenty-Two

The party spilled out onto the patio and beyond into the snowy garden. Boots, coats and scarves were piled on over costumes and the noise and laughter rose as the burgers from Daniel's impromptu barbecue were washed down with more champagne, or in her case, Mia thought with a smile, sparkling elderflower cordial. Stepping back to take it all in, her eyes rose to study Butterfly House. Lights shone from every window, lighting it up like a beacon against the jet-black sky. She tilted her head further back, admiring the blanket of stars scattered overhead. With no streetlights for miles, the constellations were clearly discernible. Raising a finger, she traced the wonky W of Queen Cassiopeia on her throne, the glittering line of Orion's belt, the little saucepan shape of Ursa Minor.

'Stargazing?' Kiki said as she approached, clutching fresh glasses for them both. 'I should have got Matty to put his telescope in the car.'

'It's the perfect night for it,' she agreed, accepting the glass with a sniff. 'Champagne?'

Her sister shrugged. 'It's nearly midnight and I thought you might want a drop to see in the New Year properly. It's up to you.'

Never that much of a drinker, she'd been scrupulous about

avoiding it since discovering about the baby. A sip wouldn't do any harm, she decided. Leaning to press her shoulder to Kiki's she stared back at the house once again. Her house. Her home. Though, this time last year, she would never have dreamed she'd be standing where she was now.

The dreams she'd had for the rundown place had seemed beyond her grasp when faced with the reality. And yet here they were, a successful guest season under their belts, the studios in the barns tried and tested, and even Kiki's teashop ready for the spring. She would likely have failed, too, had fate in the shape of an interfering old bag not delivered Daniel to her doorstep

Her eyes sought him out, and he was already moving towards her, Aaron, Luke and Nee beside him. His bright, white smile flashed through the dark of the beard she loved so much as he bent to kiss her. 'What are you doing out here in the cold?'

She snuggled into his side. 'Taking stock, admiring the view. Wondering how we've come so far in twelve short months.'

'All of us,' Aaron agreed.

'And this is just the beginning,' Luke added. He stood behind Nee, nuzzling the top of her head as she leaned against his chest. 'I think Maggie might have been on to something,' he said, more to her than the rest of them.

Intrigued, Mia turned to face them. 'About what?'

Her youngest sister smiled, a little shyly. 'Mags thinks our painting would be perfect on a card. Said I should think about doing a series of them. We could leave them blank and people could add whatever message they wanted.' She shrugged. 'I don't know, it's such a private thing, I'm not sure I want to share it.'

Mia could understand that. 'So keep that image for yourself, but why not think about her series idea. Use it as inspiration. We could stock them in the teashop and display them in the rooms here at the house too.'

Luke nodded eagerly. 'I've got a mate at work who's a whizz at graphics. We could talk to him about investing in a decent printer.'

'If you're going to do that, then I'll chip in towards it,' Daniel said. 'I'm thinking about doing a series of limited prints. Some nice black-and-white shots of the cove. It'd be good advertising for the place and add another revenue stream.'

Revenue stream? Where was that washed-up photographer who'd thrown up all over her bushes and turned his back on the art world? It wasn't just the buildings around them that had been transformed. Butterfly Cove had worked its magic on them all, helping them grow and change. She grinned up at him. 'Listen to you, Daniel Fitzwilliams, gentleman entrepreneur.'

'Too right!' He brushed a kiss on the tip of her nose. 'I've given up all those lofty ideals, and I'm strictly in it for the money. I'm even thinking about trialling a couple of residential photography courses at the barns. I've a growing family to support.' His hand slipped around her waist to cover her belly possessively. 'Hey, Nee. We should talk about you teaching some art classes too, if you fancy it?'

'I . . . can I think about it?' The hesitancy in her sister's voice reminded Mia they would need to tread carefully. One successful painting was still a far cry from Nee being comfortable with her art once more.

She didn't need to say anything to Daniel, who'd obviously picked up a similar vibe. 'Sure. There's no rush, I'm just shooting the breeze.'

'If we're investing in a printer, then maybe I could do some recipe cards for the teashop?' Kiki touched Daniel's arm to draw his attention. 'Do you think you could take some photographs for me that we could use to illustrate them?'

'That's a great idea. Maybe you should think about putting together a cookery book. A nice glossy hardback. If we interspersed it with some interior and exterior shots of the house, it'd be perfect as a holiday memento for people to buy.' His eyes gleamed – at the prospect of another revenue stream, no doubt.

Mia let the chatter go on around her, her mind already

picturing a display rack on the wall of the teashop full of pretty cards and mouth-watering recipes. Or a copy of the book, strategically placed in each bedroom for guests to browse through . . . Once people tasted Kiki's cakes they'd snap them up, hoping to recreate a masterpiece of their own to recapture a special memory of a visit to the cove.

The snow around her melted away as her mind's eye filled with images of the trees and shrubs bursting with blossom, couples on the patio enjoying a warm spring afternoon before she served them a delicious meal for dinner.

Images continued to swirl in her imagination. A blazing summer's day giving way to a cooler evening as a welcome breeze blew in from the ocean. A group of artists sprawled in a circle on the grass, enjoying a beer as they discussed their achievements and commiserated with one another about failures, enjoying the rich scents drifting from the barbecue.

Autumn leaves burnishing the garden in golds and bronzes as children ran laughing around the lawn, and a chubby baby with night-dark hair cooed from a blanket up at her.

And through every changing season passing through her mind's eye, the people around her were an integral part of the scene. Nee, with her hands covered in clay, Kiki waving across from the doorway of the teashop, her apron dusted in flour. Aaron and Luke playing football with the kids on the beach, whilst Daniel cuddled the smiling baby and watched from a safe distance. She couldn't wait for it all to unfold.

A warm, tender touch stroked her cheek and she looked up to meet Daniel's moss-green gaze. 'What's put that smile on your face?'

'You. This place. Everything. I'm so happy.'

'Me too, pet. Me too.' She was moistening her lips in anticipation of his kiss when a shout rose behind them.

'Come on, you lot. It's nearly time!' Richard waved at them from the house, and Mia heard the first familiar chimes of the

Westminster bells from the radio they'd put on the patio. They ran back, joining the rest of the group just as the first tolling boom of Big Ben sounded.

'Twelve! Eleven! Ten!' They shouted out the countdown as each bong took them closer to midnight.

Daniel swept her up into his arms. 'Happy New Year, Mia darling!' Her own reply got lost in the heated kiss he pressed to her lips. When he finally set her down, her eyes swept the patio, watching her friends and family hug, embrace, and . . . *oh, God.*

She blinked, rubbed her eyes and blinked again, but it did no good. Over in the shadows by the house, she could definitely make out the outline of a bearded Poseidon kissing a Sixties go-go dancer. She gawped up at Daniel. 'Did you know about *that*?'
He grinned and shrugged. 'That pantry of yours has got a lot to answer for. Looks like everyone's getting a happy ending.'

Turn the page for an exclusive sneak peek at the uplifting first book in the Butterfly Cove series, *Sunrise at Butterfly Cove*!

Prologue

October 2014

'And the winner of the 2014 Martindale Prize for Best New Artist is . . .'

Daniel Fitzwilliams lounged back in his chair and took another sip from the never-emptying glass of champagne. His bow tie hung loose around his neck, and the first two buttons of his wing-collar shirt had been unfastened since just after the main course had been served. The room temperature hovered somewhere around the fifth circle of hell and he wondered how much longer he would have to endure the fake smiles and shoulder pats from strangers passing his table.

The MC made a big performance of rustling the large silver envelope in his hand. 'Get on with it, mate,' Daniel muttered. His agent, Nigel, gave him a smile and gulped at the contents of his own glass. His nomination had been a huge surprise and no-one expected him to win, Daniel least of all.

'Well, well.' The MC adjusted his glasses and peered at the card he'd finally wrestled free. 'I am delighted to announce that the winner of the Martindale Prize is Fitz, for his series "Interactions".'

A roar of noise from the rest of his tablemates covered the choking sounds of Nigel inhaling half a glass of champagne. Daniel's own glass slipped from his limp fingers and rolled harmlessly under the table. 'Bugger me.'

'Go on, mate. Get up there!' His best friend, Aaron, rounded the table and tugged Daniel to his feet. 'I told you, I bloody told you, but you wouldn't believe me.'

Daniel wove his way through the other tables towards the stage, accepting handshakes and kisses from all sides. Will Spector, the bookies' favourite and the art crowd's latest darling, raised a glass in toast and Daniel nodded to acknowledge his gracious gesture. Flashbulbs popped from all sides as he mounted the stairs to shake hands with the MC. He raised the sinuous glass trophy and blinked out at the clapping, cheering crowd of his peers.

The great and the good were out in force. The Martindale attracted a lot of press coverage and the red-carpet winners and losers would be paraded across the inside pages for people to gawk at over their morning cereal. His mum had always loved to see the celebrities in their posh frocks. He just wished she'd survived long enough to see her boy come good. Daniel swallowed around the lump in his throat. *Fuck cancer.* Dad had at least made it to Daniel's first exhibition, before his heart failed and he'd followed his beloved Nancy to the grave.

Daniel adjusted the microphone in front of him and waited for the cheers to subside. The biggest night of his life, and he'd never felt lonelier.

* * *

Mia Sutherland resisted the urge to check her watch and tried to focus on the flickering television screen. The latest episode of *The Watcher* would normally have no trouble in holding her attention – it was her and Jamie's new favourite show. She glanced at the empty space on the sofa beside her. Even with the filthy weather outside, he should have been home before now. Winter had hit earlier than usual and she'd found herself turning the lights on mid-afternoon to try and dispel the gloom caused by the raging storm outside.

The ad break flashed upon the screen and she popped into the kitchen to give the pot of stew a quick stir. She'd given up waiting, and eaten her portion at eight-thirty, but there was plenty left for Jamie. He always said she cooked for an army rather than just the two of them.

A rattle of sleet struck the kitchen window and Mia peered through the Venetian blind covering it; he'd be glad of a hot meal after being stuck in the traffic for so long. A quick tap of the wooden spoon against the side of the pot, and then she slipped the cast-iron lid back on. The pot was part of the *Le Creuset* set Jamie's parents had given them as a wedding gift and the matching pans hung from a wooden rack above the centre of the kitchen worktop. She slid the pot back into the oven and adjusted the temperature down a notch.

Ding-dong.

At last! Mia hurried down the hall to the front door and tugged it open with a laugh. 'Did you forget your keys—' A shiver of fear ran down her back at the sight of the stern-looking policemen standing on the step. Rain dripped from the brims of their caps and darkened the shoulders of their waterproof jackets.

'Mrs Sutherland?'

No, no, no, no. Mia looked away from the sympathetic expressions and into the darkness beyond them for the familiar flash of Jamie's headlights turning onto their small driveway.

'Perhaps we could come in, Mrs Sutherland?' The younger of the pair spoke this time.

Go away. Go away. She'd seen this scene played out enough on the television to know what was coming next. 'Please, come in.' Her voice sounded strange, high-pitched and brittle to her ears. She stepped back to let the two men enter. 'Would you like a cup of tea?'

The younger officer took off his cap and shrugged out of his jacket. 'Why don't you point me in the direction of the kettle and you and Sergeant Stone can make yourselves comfortable in the front room?'

Mia stared at the Sergeant's grim-set features. *What a horrible job he has, poor man.* 'Yes, of course. Come on through.'

She stared at the skin forming on the surface of her now-cold tea. She hadn't dared to lift the cup for fear they would see how badly she was shaking. 'Is there someone you'd like us to call?' PC Taylor asked, startling her. The way he phrased the question made her wonder how many times he'd asked before she'd heard him. *I'd like you to call my husband.*

Mia bit her lip against the pointless words, and ran through a quick inventory in her head. Her parents would be useless; it was too far past cocktail hour for her mother to be coherent and her dad didn't do emotions well at the best of times.

Her middle sister, Kiki, had enough on her hands with the new baby and Matty determined to live up to every horror story ever told about the terrible twos. Had it only been last week she and Jamie had babysat Matty because the baby had been sick? An image of Jamie holding their sleeping nephew in his lap rose unbidden and she shook her head sharply to dispel it. She couldn't think about things like that. Not right then.

The youngest of her siblings, Nee, was neck-deep in her final year at art school in London. Too young and too far away to be shouldering the burden of her eldest sister's grief. The only person she wanted to talk to was Jamie and that would never happen again. Bile burned in her throat and a whooping sob escaped before she could swallow it back.

'S-sorry.' She screwed her eyes tight and stuffed everything down as far as she could. There would be time enough for tears. Opening her stinging eyes, she looked at Sergeant Stone. 'Do Bill and Pat know?'

'Your in-laws? They're next on our list. I'm so very sorry, pet. Would you like us to take you over there?'

Unable to speak past the knot in her throat, Mia nodded.

Chapter One

Daniel rested his head on the dirty train window and stared unseeing at the landscape as it flashed past. He didn't know where he was going. Away. That was the word that rattled around his head. Anywhere, nowhere. Just away from London. Away from the booze, birds and fakery of his so-called celebrity lifestyle. Twenty-nine felt too young to be a has-been.

He'd hit town with a portfolio, a bundle of glowing recommendations and an ill-placed confidence in his own ability to keep his feet on the ground. Within eighteen months, he was *the next big thing* in photography and everyone who was anyone clamoured for an original Fitz image on their wall. Well-received exhibitions had led to private commissions and more money than he knew what to do with. And if it hadn't been for Aaron's investment advice, his bank account would be as drained as his artistic talent.

The parties had been fun at first, and he couldn't put his finger on when the booze had stopped being a buzz and started being a crutch. Girls had come and gone. Pretty, cynical women who liked being seen on his arm in the gossip columns, and didn't seem to mind being in his bed.

Giselle had been one such girl and without any active consent on his part, she'd installed herself as a permanent fixture. The bitter smell of the French cigarettes she lived on in lieu of a decent meal filled his memory, forcing Daniel to swallow convulsively against the bile in his throat. That smell signified everything he hated about his life, about himself. Curls of rank smoke had hung like fog over the sprawled bodies, spilled bottles and overflowing ashtrays littering his flat when he'd woven a path through them that morning.

The cold glass of the train window eased the worst of his thumping hangover, although no amount of water seemed able to ease the parched feeling in his throat. The carriage had filled, emptied and filled again, the ebb and flow of humanity reaching their individual destinations.

Daniel envied their purpose. He swigged again from the large bottle of water he'd paid a small fortune for at Paddington Station as he'd perused the departures board. The taxi driver he'd flagged down near his flat had told him Paddington would take him west, a part of England that he knew very little about, which suited him perfectly.

His first instinct had been to head for King's Cross, but that would have taken him north. Too many memories, too tempting to visit old haunts his Mam and Dad had taken him to. It would be sacrilege to their memory to tread on the pebbled beaches of his youth, knowing how far he'd fallen from being the man his father had dreamed he would become.

He'd settled upon Exeter as a first destination. Bristol and Swindon seemed too industrial, too much like the urban sprawl he wanted to escape. And now he was on a local branch line train to Orcombe Sands. Sands meant the sea. The moment he'd seen the name, he knew it was where he needed to be. Air he could breathe, the wind on his face, nothing on the horizon but whitecaps and seagulls.

The train slowed and drew to a stop as it had done numerous times previously. Daniel didn't stir; the cold window felt too good against his clammy forehead. He was half aware of a small woman rustling an enormous collection of department store carrier bags as she carted her shopping haul past his seat, heading towards the exit. She took a couple of steps past him before she paused and spoke.

'This is the end of the line, you know?' Her voice carried a warm undertone of concern and Daniel roused. The thump in his head increased, making him frown as he regarded the speaker. She was an older lady, around the age his Mam would've been had she still been alive.

Her grey hair was styled in a short, modern crop and she was dressed in that effortlessly casual, yet stylish look some women had. A soft camel jumper over dark indigo jeans with funky bright red trainers on her feet. A padded pea jacket and a large handbag worn cross body, keeping her hands free to manage her shopping bags. She smiled brightly at Daniel and tilted her head towards the carriage doors, which were standing stubbornly open.

'This is Orcombe Sands. Pensioner jail. Do not pass go, do not collect two hundred pounds.' She laughed at her own joke and Daniel finally realised what she was telling him. He had to get off the train; this was his destination. She was still watching him expectantly so he cleared his throat.

'Oh, thanks. Sorry I was miles away.' He rose as he spoke, unfurling his full height as the small woman stepped back to give him room to stand and tug his large duffel bag from the rack above his seat. Seemingly content that Daniel was on the move, the woman gave him a cheery farewell and disappeared off the train.

Adjusting the bag on his shoulder as he looked around, Daniel perused the layout of the station for the first time. The panoramic sweep of his surroundings didn't take long. The tiny waiting room needed a lick of paint, but the platform was clean of the rubbish and detritus that had littered the central London station he'd started his journey at several hours previously. A hand-painted, slightly lopsided *Exit* sign pointed his way and Daniel moved in the only direction available to him, hoping to find some signs of life and a taxi rank.

He stopped short in what he supposed was the main street and regarded the handful of houses and a pub, which was closed up tight on the other side of the road. He looked to his right and regarded a small area of hardstanding with a handful of cars strewn haphazardly around.

The February wind tugged hard at his coat and he flipped the collar up, hunching slightly to keep his ears warm.

Daniel started to regret his spur-of-the-moment decision to leave town. He'd been feeling stale for a while, completely lacking in inspiration. Every image he framed in his mind's eye seemed either trite or derivative. All he'd ever wanted to do was take photographs. From the moment his parents had given him his first disposable camera to capture his holiday snaps, Daniel had wanted to capture the world he saw through his viewfinder.

An engine grumbled to life and the noise turned Daniel's thoughts outwards again as a dirty estate car crawled out of the car park and stopped in front of him. The side window lowered and the woman from the train leant across from the driver's side to speak to him.

'You all right there? Is someone coming to pick you up?' Daniel shuffled his feet slightly under the blatantly interested gaze of the older woman.

His face warmed as he realised he would have to confess his predicament to the woman. He had no idea where he was or what his next move should be. He could tell from the way she was regarding him that she would not leave until she knew he was going to be all right.

'My trip was a bit spur-of-the-moment. Do you happen to know if there is a B&B nearby?' he said, trying to keep his voice light, as though heading off into the middle of nowhere on a freezing winter's day was a completely rational, normal thing to do.

The older woman widened her eyes slightly. 'Not much call for that this time of year. Just about everywhere that offers accommodation is seasonal and won't be open until Easter time.'

Daniel started to feel like an even bigger fool as the older woman continued to ponder his problem, her index finger tapping against her lip. The finger paused as a sly smile curled one corner of her lip and Daniel wondered if he should be afraid of whatever thought had occurred to cause that expression.

He took a backwards step as the woman suddenly released her seat belt and climbed out of the car in a determined manner. He was not intimidated by someone a foot shorter than him. *He wasn't.*

'What's your name?' she asked as she flipped open the boot of the car and started transferring her shopping bags onto the back seat.

'Fitz . . .' He paused. That name belonged in London, along with everything else he wanted to leave behind. 'Daniel. Daniel Fitzwilliams.'

'Pleased to meet you. I'm Madeline although my friends call me Mads and I have a feeling we will be great friends. Stick your bag in the boot, there's a good lad. I know the perfect place. Run by a friend of mine. I'm sure you'll be very happy there.'

Daniel did as bid, his eyes widening in shock as *unbelievable!* Madeline propelled him in the right direction with a slap on the arse and a loud laugh.

'Bounce a coin on those cheeks, Daniel! I do so like a man who takes care of himself.' With another laugh, Madeline disappeared into the front seat of the car and the engine gave a slightly startled whine as she turned the key.

Gritting his teeth, he placed his bag in the boot before moving around to the front of the car and eyeing the grubby interior of the estate, which appeared to be mainly held together with mud and rust. He folded his frame into the seat, which had been hiked forward almost as far as it could. With his knees up around his ears, Daniel fumbled under the front of the seat until he found the adjuster and carefully edged the seat back until he felt less like a sardine.

'Belt up, there's a good boy,' Madeline trilled as she patted his knee and threw the old car into first. They lurched away from the kerb. Deciding that a death grip was the only way to survive, Daniel quickly snapped his seat belt closed, scrabbled for the aptly named *oh shit!* handle above the window and tried to decide whether the journey would be worse with his eyes open or closed.

Madeline barrelled the car blithely around the narrow country lanes, barely glancing at the road as far as Daniel could tell as she sang along to the latest pop tunes pouring from the car radio. He tried not to whimper at the thought of where he was going to end up. What the hell was this place going to be like if it was run by a friend of Madeline's? If there was a woman in a rocking chair at the window, he'd be in deep shit.

The car abruptly swung off to the left and continued along what appeared to be a footpath rather than any kind of road. A huge building loomed to the left and Daniel caught his breath. Rather than the Bates Motel, it was more of a Grand Lady in her declining years. In its heyday, it must have been a magnificent structure. The peeling paint, filthy windows and rotting porch did their best to hide the beauty, together with the overgrown gardens.

His palms itched and for the first time in for ever, Daniel felt excited. He wanted his camera. Head twisting and turning, he tried to take everything in. A group of outbuildings and a large barn lay to the right of where Madeline pulled to a stop on the gravel driveway.

Giving a jaunty toot on the car's horn, she wound down her window to wave and call across the yard to what appeared to be a midget yeti in the most moth-eaten dressing gown Daniel had ever seen. *Not good, not good, oh so not good . . .*

Dear Reader,

We hope you enjoyed reading this book. If you did, we'd be so appreciative if you left a review. It really helps us and the author to bring more books like this to you.

Here at HQ Digital we are dedicated to publishing fiction that will keep you turning the pages into the early hours. Don't want to miss a thing? To find out more about our books, promotions, discover exclusive content and enter competitions you can keep in touch in the following ways:

JOIN OUR COMMUNITY:

Sign up to our new email newsletter: http://hyperurl.co/
hqnewsletter

Read our new blog www.hqstories.co.uk

🐦 : https://twitter.com/HQDigitalUK

f : www.facebook.com/HQStories

BUDDING WRITER?

We're also looking for authors to join the HQ Digital family!
Please submit your manuscript to:
https://www.hqstories.co.uk/want-to-write-for-us/

Thanks for reading, from the HQ Digital team

Keep Reading . . .

If you enjoyed *Christmas at Butterfly Cove*, then why not try another delightfully uplifting festive romance from HQ Digital?